STOCK CAR INFERNO

DAVID L. WINTERS

Shayla,
Hope you enjoy!
David L Winters

Brimstone
Fiction

STOCK CAR INFERNO By David L. Winters

Published by Brimstone Fiction 1440 W. Taylor St., STE #449 Chicago, IL 60607

ISBN: Paperback: 978-1-946758-26-2 Ebook: 978-1-946758-27-9

Copyright © 2019 by David L. Winters

Cover design by JD&D Design, LLC

And Elaina Lee, www.Forthemusedesigns.com

Interior design by Meaghan Burnett—www.meaghanburnett.com

Available in print and ebook from your local bookstore, online, or from the publisher at: www.BrimstoneFiction.com

For more information on this book and the author, visit:
https://www.sabbaticalofthemind.net/

Brought to you by the creative team at Brimstone Fiction: Alexandria Bailey, Meaghan Burnett, Rowena Kuo, & Jessie Andersen

Library of Congress Cataloging-in-Publication Data

Winters, David L.

Stock Car Inferno / David L. Winters 1st ed.

Printed in the United States of America

Dedicated to all the women who push the envelope to succeed.

ENDORSEMENTS FOR STOCK CAR INFERNO

"Winters's writing pulls the reader into his stories. Once you pick up Stock Car Inferno, you won't want to put it down. Bravo, well done!"

- Del Duduit,
Award-winning sports writer and author of *Dugout Devotions*

"Stock Car Inferno takes you into the world of car racing as it continues to show how people are connected and led by their faith in God. It is an enjoyable story that kept me guessing."

- Terrilynn Griffith,
Pastor

"I was excited to read Stock Car Inferno! And what an exciting read! I experienced a roller coaster of emotions. I love it!"

- Deby Allen,
Owner of Zhairfx

"David Winters has done it again! His writing style draws you into the storyline and characters from the very start. I always look forward to anything written by this author!"

- Donna Montgomery,
The High-Heeled Gardener

"The relationships between the characters kept me spellbound. The happiness and heartache they shared kept me turning pages as quickly as I could. It's a very exciting story that definitely left me wanting more!"

- Cheryl Rogers,
Amazon Reviewer

"Edge of your seat story. How far are you willing to go to win? Are you willing to win at all costs?

- Andy Kistler,
ARCA gasman and NASCAR crew member

ACKNOWLEDGMENTS

Thanks so much to the following Hope Flinchbaugh, Dave Fessenden, Rene Holt, Alexandria Bailey and Jessie Andersen for help in editing this book. I also appreciate the support and assistance of test readers Larry and Susan Fouty, Laura Asher, Cheryl Rogers, Donna Montgomery, Deby Allen, Terri Griffith, Kimberlee Cline Greenhill and Kerry Holmes Bremmer.

CHAPTER ONE

A figure cloaked in shadows approached the exterior fence far from his intended target. He slid underneath through a hole he'd dug days earlier. Once inside the security perimeter, he carefully pulled the black satchel in behind him. Then, he waited. Four minutes evaporated in a heartbeat. The overcast skies, essential to his plan, obscured what could have been a three-quarter moon.

Next came the signal he'd been awaiting. A single security guard, having walked the whole perimeter of the acres-long building rounded the corner nearest him. Still at least one hundred yards away, the street light installed next to the giant garage lit the guard up like a spotlight at the opera. No way the security man could see someone crouching in the shadows at this distance. Barely pausing, the guard traversed the side of the building, disappearing around the front.

A creature of habit, the guard made only two rounds per night. The first patrol came at midnight and this one at three a.m. Next, he returned to his guardhouse and would fall sound asleep in minutes, unaware of any danger.

Once the guard had time to settle in, the figure dressed in black crept near the back fence and made his way halfway along the back of the building. Two windows down from the one where he'd painted a small X in black magic marker, the demolitions expert pried open an aging window. With care, he forced it making little sound, certainly nothing audible above the whir of the air conditioning unit in the guard shack.

Climbing in through the window with the satchel proved difficult only because of the difference in grade from outside the building to the inside. The window sill stood only five feet above grade outside. Inside, the drop from the window to the floor must be at least eight feet. Once negotiated, the intruder looked around and identified his target. He took off his gloves and put them in the satchel next to the purpose of his visit.

The car sat splendidly silhouetted by yellow light shining in from the front of the garage. A minute later, the man in black withdrew an oblong object from his bag. He held the device up to the bottom of the car. His small flashlight revealed a perfect fit and exact color match. Months of careful planning and surreptitious reconnaissance paid off to perfection.

An artist of sorts, he painted the underside near the right rear quarter panel with a super adhesive polymer. The motion trigger, which took months of development, must be handled with care. He armed the trigger and pressed the entire device firmly into the epoxy, affixing it to the bottom of the car. It formed a perfect bond and looked indistinguishable from the rest of the underbody.

As he put the top back on the two-part epoxy, a light moved in front of the building. He lay still. The voices of two men indicated they walked with pace past the bay door. Their flashlight bounced in time to their steps. From the jocular tone, he detected no alarm or concern.

Returning to the window where he'd entered, he pushed a heavy toolbox below the sill and locked its wheels. He used the heavy metal cabinet to climb up toward the window. He pulled himself the rest of the way up, climbing out into the dewy night air. Before closing the window, he took a minute to spread epoxy and seal it. Unsure if the men walking in front of the garage might come around back, he paused at the perimeter fence and waited for several minutes. When they never came, he retraced his steps and exited under the fence. He filled in the dirt which he'd stored a few feet away. With any luck, no one would know he'd been there.

* * *

"You are so dead."

"Not so fast, Marc. Take that."

"Trey, dude, look under the solar panel."

Antonio Semones knew nothing about the game, but the electronic sounds in the back seat told him someone lost.

"You got me, freak."

"We both know what this means," Antonio's son Marc said. "I get the first date with Emalyn."

"In your dreams," Trey Williams replied.

"Guys, settle down back there," Sylvia Semones said. "We will be at the hotel in a few minutes. And, Marc, please." His mother turned in her seat to look at him. "I know you're a big fan of Emalyn Martin, but keep it in perspective, okay? We're just going to watch her compete in a stock car race; there's little chance that you're going to even meet her."

"Mom," Marc said as he hunched down in his seat and looked out the window while Trey tried in vain to stop giggling. "We're just kidding around."

"This weather is marvelous," Antonio observed, hoping for Marc's sake to change the subject. He fiddled with the volume on the radio.

"Yes, and these mountains are beautiful," Sylvia said smiling broadly. "I love the Poconos. I am so glad I came along."

"And so am I, babe." Antonio winked with mock lechery. "We are going to have a fabulous time."

"Antonio, not in front of the boys," Sylvia whispered.

As the Audi flew up and down the gentle inclines of the Pocono Mountains, Antonio glanced in the rearview mirror and saw his son's embarrassed eye roll. Antonio smiled at Marc, glad he brought his high school friend along on the trip. Trey seemed like family, as he spent about half of his time at the Semones house. Fortunately, his single mother equally welcomed Marc into their lives.

This kind of driving relaxed Antonio like no other activity: fabulous weather, few other cars on the road, and his family on board for company. Sylvia rolled down her window, just a crack. Antonio loved watching her whiff in the fresh late summer air (already beginning to give a hint of autumn's coming coolness) and drink in the myriad hues of green on the trees and plants. He knew Sylvia's thoughts because she had told him over and over: how wonderful is the weather here in the Northeast! Her native Brazil, at least as she described her hometown area, seemed to have only two seasons: summer hot and midsummer really hot—and very little diversity of foliage. The North American change of seasons fascinated her.

"I am so glad you could get away from the law firm," Sylvia said, checking her bright red lipstick in the mirror on the sun visor. She untied her ponytail and ran a brush through shoulder-length brown hair.

"It's just one work day off—and a Saturday at that—but you are so right. I needed a break; that last case kept me glued to the office for months." He glanced over at Sylvia, his wife of many years. The brilliance of the sunlight bouncing off her shimmering, dark brown hair gave his endorphins a rush. "Hard to believe eight years have gone by since you passed the bar and started practicing with Morgan and Montgomery."

"And to think, you loved me when I was just a struggling ride-share driver."

"And law student," Sylvia smiled proudly at her husband.

"The GPS indicates we should be coming up on the entrance pretty soon."

"There it is ... the Pocono Tiptop Hotel," Sylvia announced. The entrance from the main road sported a seventies-era sign, repainted in teal and pink.

"By the time I called for reservations, not many choices remained, so this place is not gonna be five-star, babe; sorry." Antonio acted nervous as he massaged the steering wheel. "I wanted to get us into someplace like Harrah's, but I found everything booked solid."

"Oh, that's okay." Sylvia laid a hand on his arm. "It would probably have been a little too pricey, and I'm not sure I'd want the boys subjected to the atmosphere of Harrah's, anyway."

"Dude. You have got to be kidding me." Suddenly, Marc's voice got louder and Antonio could see him bouncing around the back seat and pointing dramatically.

"What's going on, son?" Antonio said, trying to concentrate on where to turn into the parking lot.

"That is absolutely Emalyn Martin's bus parked on the side of the hotel. Emalyn Martin is staying at our hotel! This is about the most amazing thing that has ever happened to me!"

"This is so incredible, dude!" Trey shared Marc's enthusiasm about their favorite stock car driver.

"You're right, it is incredible—and a little bit strange." Antonio's forehead wrinkled as he stared at the big tour bus emblazoned with the racecar driver's picture. "I thought most of the drivers just parked at the track and slept in their buses. She's certainly not going to get the VIP treatment at this hotel."

"Maybe she just wants to get away from all the hoopla," Sylvia suggested.

"Dad, pull around there. Let's get a look at her bus." Marc stared with big eyes out the window.

"Hey, who's giving the orders around here? I'm not a ride-share driver anymore, son. First things first—let's go to the front desk. You boys will have plenty of time to snoop around after we get checked into our rooms. I'm sure you'll have many stories to tell your high school basketball team after this weekend."

"Somewhere in this hotel is my future wife," Marc said with a huge grin spread across his face. "I just need my wingman to set her up for me."

"Wing *what?*" Trey responded, puckering his lips. "Not so fast. I am the stud, and you can set her up for me. After all, I am the tall, dark, handsome one. You are the gangly, pale side man."

Marc flashed Trey a dark look then grinned in spite of himself.

Antonio watched this playful exchange in the rearview mirror and chuckled. In their three-bedroom colonial, Marc's bedroom, his private inner sanctuary, held a life-size poster of the toned stock car driver displayed in the center of his wall. Antonio suspected Emalyn's signa-ture black racing uniform and white helmet made her look like a super-hero to his son. Her haunting, hazel eyes sent shivers down the spine of many men and boys. Each curve and dimple on her cute face was probably etched in Marc's brain forever. Now, Emalyn's broad smile and blonde hair lit up the side of her travel bus. That she chose to stay at this same hotel must be his sixteen-year-old's dream come true.

"Well don't embarrass us if we see her," Sylvia said. "You are two mature young men, and I expect you both to act like it. Women deserve your respect."

"Yes, but she is really hot—I mean, attractive, dear," Antonio said, mainly for the benefit of the boys. Marc and Trey whooped as the Audi pulled to a halt near the hotel office.

"What have I gotten myself into, tagging along on this testosterone trek to the races?"

"Mom, a lot of women come to stock car races. The Pocono Grand Prix is one of the top races of the year. You will fit right in."

Antonio doubted that Sylvia would "fit right in" or even enjoy the race, but his gratitude welled up, thankful she valued the time with her family more than her personal convenience. If it cost her sitting in the hot sun and smelling gasoline and burning rubber for a few hours—that price Sylvia would willingly pay. Antonio thought to pack a few essential things including her suntan lotion and wide-brimmed gardening hat.

The four travelers dragged themselves out of the car and ambled to the lobby. Trey and Marc stretched their long arms and legs as they walked. The Audi, while not a small car, could not easily host their six-foot-three-inch tall frames. Of course, the boys found it uncomfortable riding in the backseat of any vehicle for very long. Sylvia sidled to the front desk and took care of business, registering them all and collecting keys for the two bungalows.

Antonio sat and watched the boys amble around the hotel lobby. They first noticed the game room, which showed its age through a scratched plexiglass window. Three tired-looking video games, each at least as old as the boys themselves, rested against the far wall next to some vending machines. Trey used his own money to buy two cans of soda and handed one to Marc. "Hey, there's a pool," Trey said.

"We didn't bring swimming trunks," Marc replied.

"We have shorts. That'll work."

Trey's answer made Antonio smile as he got up from the dusty couch and walked toward Sylvia.

"Dad, look at this tiny workout room," Marc said. "The weight-lifting equipment is really beat and the cardio machines look like they're from the Clinton administration."

"Who needs it? A few miles running up and down these hills will help keep you and Trey on your off-season fitness program. Basketball try-outs are coming up next month, right?" Antonio asked.

"That's right, Mr. S. As returning varsity players we won't get a break. The coach starts over from scratch every fall. We have to earn our place on the team again."

On his way to the front desk to meet Sylvia, Antonio peeked into the hotel restaurant. While the paint looked newer than that in the lobby, the carpet smelled musty and the faded drapes on the windows hinted at happier times. *No, definitely not five-star!* Antonio thought. When he came back out into the lobby, he smiled at the boys taking selfies with a large moose head hanging above the fireplace. He imagined what it would have been like if he carried a camera with him every minute during his own high school years.

"Okay, Sylvia has the room keys. Let's go, boys."

Sylvia led the way on foot to a grouping of three A-Frame buildings that surrounded a private but smaller swimming pool. Having located their area, Antonio pulled the car from the front entrance over to the sidewalk nearest the bungalows. He popped the trunk. The boys each grabbed their own gym bags, and Antonio brought the large roller suit-case he shared with Sylvia.

"Hey, look!" Trey said as he pointed. "There's another pool over here. We have our own pool for just these three units."

"Marc, here are two keys, one for each of you." Sylvia gave him a stern look. "Now don't get too wild in there. If you break something, you'll pay for it. I will make you do chores for months if necessary."

Look around the area, and we'll come and get you in twenty minutes for dinner. Just put your stuff away and get comfortable."

The boys climbed the eight steps to their front door and entered the almost all-wood room. Loud shrieks of laughter poured out into the courtyard.

"That is one interesting bathtub," Marc said.

"Dude, seriously. That is so Instagram worthy," Trey replied.

"Hold up. I don't think the world needs to know that two high school dudes are staying in a room with a heart-shaped bathtub."

Antonio unlocked their door, and Sylvia smiled as she spied their own heart-shaped tub as well.

"Thank goodness I brought my bubble bath," Sylvia said with a glisten in her eye, causing Antonio to blush. As a man of Italian ancestry, he used that as an excuse for his internal motor running hot. Sylvia began hanging up a couple of his shirts and her blouses from the luggage. Antonio tried to get his mind off his wife's still-glorious figure by turning on the television. The double-wide chair felt very comfortable and he soon located the golf coverage, which brought his temperature back down to normal. About fifteen minutes later, Antonio dozed in the chair until he awoke to loud talking outside in the courtyard. Sylvia emerged from the bathroom after freshening up. Antonio threw on his Nikes and bounded to the door. Before he exited, he and Sylvia exchanged curious glances.

"Well, my goodness gracious, you boys sure are taller than August corn in Nebraska! I don't think they grow them your size in Tennessee where I come from. Are you planning to come to my race on Sunday? It is going to be incredible! Isn't this weather the best? We went to Charlotte last week, and I about melted in the heat." Emalyn Martin, quite the rapid talker, held the boys' full attention. Her shoulder-length blonde locks and mirrored sunglasses gave her a chic look, but her voice revealed her East Tennessee roots.

Marc stared at Emalyn Martin, his gaze fixed in awe. Antonio imagined the experience from his son's perspective: his stock car idol posed in front of him. It looked like Marc's brain could not engage. In person, Emalyn seemed shorter than she seemed on television. She wore black skinny jeans and a sleek black leather jacket. Her hands shimmered with a large diamond engagement ring paired with a white gold wedding ring. The other hand also flashed jeweled rings that seemed to mesmerize the boys into a semi-hypnotic state.

"Yes, ma'am," Trey said. "We are super-excited about the race. We're your biggest fans, really."

"Where y'all from?"

"McLean, Virginia." Marc finally regained the use of his mouth. "That's my dad and mom. They bought our tickets."

Immediately Marc's face turned red as Antonio reached the group. He overheard the last sentence and cringed for his son. He and Sylvia extended hands to shake with Emalyn.

"Huge pleasure to meet you, Mrs. Martin. You are an unbelievable driver."

"Thank you so much. I just push my stiletto to the metal and turn left." Emalyn repeated a line she used often, including her signature sweeping hand motion. "This is gonna be one barn-burner of a race. That rascal George Melon-head—"

"You mean George Meloncamp?" Somehow, Marc managed to interrupt the high-speed flow of her words to identify her biggest rival.

"That's what I said, Melon-head. He leads me by just thirty points in the standings. This is my year to win the championship. No one will keep me from taking home that crown. No one! I can't wait to bump Georgie a little. You know what I mean, like into next Tuesday?" Emalyn's infectious smile lit up the courtyard.

"We will be rooting hard for you, that's for sure," Marc said with great sincerity. "Very hard," he added for emphasis. He turned red from head to toe.

A man exited from Bungalow three, Emalyn's room. "Girl, I see you are making more new friends. How is everybody?"

"This is my husband and business manager, Sean Martin." They shook hands all around. Sean stood just an inch or two taller than Emalyn, maybe five-foot-seven. He looked almost forty, ten years older than Emalyn according to her Wikipedia page, which Marc read to his parents just two nights earlier. Trey stared at Sean's black hair sprinkled with gray. Antonio thought Sean's hands showed wear and looked rough, probably from his years as a racecar mechanic.

Antonio backed up, trying to deemphasize the height difference between himself and both Sean and Emalyn. Sean breathed the air at least nine inches below what Antonio and Marc enjoyed.

"We need to meet the sponsors at the restaurant, but first we're going to drop the bus off at the racetrack," Sean explained. "I want my pick-up truck back. The crew boys should have the brakes fixed by now. Hopefully, they got them right this time. Let's get going, girl. Nice to meet you folks."

Antonio remembered reading in a magazine article how Sean took pride in keeping Emalyn on schedule. Her big personality scored well with fans and supported business in general but didn't do much for arriving anywhere on time.

"We've got to keep the sponsors happy," Sean said as he began motioning Emalyn toward the bus. "Next to winning races, it's our main job."

"It has just been such a gigantic pleasure meeting all of you," Emalyn said with natural enthusiasm. Marc and Trey nodded their heads in hearty agreement. "I tell you what," she continued. "Why don't you come down to the pit area before the race on Sunday and meet my whole crew? Would you like that, all of you?"

"Wow! Cool!" Marc said, his eyes bugging out of his face. Sylvia shot him her "calm it down" look.

"Sean can leave passes for all of you at the hotel front desk. Just pick them up before you come out to the raceway on Sunday. Get over to the track at least ninety minutes pre-race to make sure you can get down to us. They're pretty strict about kicking everyone out just before race time. Mom, Dad, is it okay for all of you to come and see me in the pit area?"

"That would be awesome," Antonio said. "We are the Semones family ... Antonio and Sylvia. You met Marc. Trey Brown is our family friend. We are in Bungalows one and two." Antonio gave a bit more information than needed, but his nervousness reflected the preciousness of the opportunity for VIP passes. He didn't want them to miss out.

"Thank you so much," Marc said as he almost shook Emalyn's hand off. Antonio finally put his hand on Marc's and pulled it away from the driver. Sean saw his chance and hustled Emalyn away.

Trey and Marc smiled from ear to ear. Sylvia smiled but shook her head a bit. Antonio, happy the boys got to meet Emalyn, said a small prayer of thanksgiving as they headed to dinner.

The local eatery came highly recommended by the hotel. A neon sign shone a fluorescent light over the stark white exterior of the building. An unexpected slice of vintage Americana lay behind the glass and metal front door. When the four strangers entered, the other diners simultaneously stopped talking, sort of like villagers eyeing foreigners in a vampire movie. The hostess asked how many in their party. This seemed to be a cue for the townspeople to start talking again. Almost in unison, they went back to their conversations. Antonio slid into the booth near the back of the restaurant and Sylvia scooted next to him. Trey and Marc faced them, having a view of the German landscape print on the wall. Faded over time, the now-yellowish patina of the painting gave it a ghost-like ambience unintended by the painter.

As they looked over the menus, an elderly lady wearing heavy make-up shuffled to an organ sitting in the center of the dining room. Her gray locks hung in loose curls around her scalp, as if she removed the curlers but forgot to comb out her thinning hair.

From the first note, she played the ancient organ with great enthusiasm. Sylvia jumped a little as the sound of the organ whirred to life. Suddenly, the decibel level in the restaurant doubled. Townspeople talked twice as loud to be heard over the din. If Antonio's limited music education didn't fail him, it sounded like a polka. He noticed above the bar area a set of boy and girl dolls dressed in lederhosen and covered in about twenty years of dust. Their facial expressions sagged with age, giving them blank looks not unlike some of the townspeople.

"Organ music, now that's different," Sylvia commented, trying to recover. "Polkas and German food. Of course!" Pointing to the menu items, she said, "The picture of the wiener schnitzel looks good to me."

The boys guffawed at the name and decided to split a German-inspired pizza with three kinds of sausage and sauerkraut. Antonio wanted something gooey with lots of cheese. Since he didn't see anything exactly like that on the menu, he went with a cheeseburger, requesting extra American cheese. The food arrived in under ten minutes, and everyone fell quiet as they savored the flavorful fare and German music.

After finishing the large meal while watching a chicken dance and hearing a dizzying number of polkas, the family plus one headed to the parking lot. Antonio smiled, satisfied that the dinner for four at Der Bier Garten totaled less than forty dollars.

Antonio, still frugal after years of penny-pinching, steered his Audi to the Pocono Playhouse. Sylvia had insisted that their trip include one cultural activity. The area's travel website pointed to the Pocono Playhouse for an evening of theater. The marquee announced the play, *Death of a Salesman*.

The theater complex included a quaint grouping of barn-like buildings surrounded by evergreen landscaping and little white lights, illuminating the few deciduous trees.

To the boys' delight, several stock car drivers dotted the audience, using the occasion to parade their wives or girlfriends out in public. As the rest of the group waited for Sylvia to pick up the tickets at Will Call, Antonio looked over the photos of famous faces, once up-and-comers, performing at the playhouse. Due to its relative proximity to New York City, this Pocono hide-away hosted many off-Broadway stars who eventually made it to the big time. Some landed roles on Broadway, others in movies or on television. The wall where the pictures hung hosted a veritable who's who of young, future celebrities dressed as characters from *Mame, Cabaret, Cats, Wicked*, and other shows. Finally, Sylvia returned with their tickets for seats toward the middle of the small theater.

"Isn't that George Meloncamp sitting up front with his wife, and maybe that's Junior in the second row?" Antonio asked Marc and Trey.

"That's George and Junior all right. Look at that blonde on Junior's arm. She has artificial everything." Marc gestured in an exaggerated motion, causing Sylvia to shake her head in disapproval.

"Boys, tone it down" Antonio said, echoing Sylvia's glare. He figured he should straighten up his parenting if he hoped to get anywhere with his wife back at the bungalow. Antonio remembered his own adolescence: the excitement and the confusion. His faith kept him from going completely off the rails, but part of growing up is learning about the opposite sex. *Gender identity is more than a person's own internal dialog*, he thought. It incorporates all the messages, overt and covert, sent by parents, siblings, friends, teachers, and the media. Antonio sometimes wondered who he may have become without the strong male role models in his life. His father could have played any number of quiet movie tough guys but always showed great affection for his children, even when correcting them.

Sylvia turned to Antonio and whispered something romantic in his ear. He responded by doing the same in her ear. She giggled. The boys couldn't have been less interested as they discussed the various drivers and their famous victories, losses, and crashes.

"Sounds like that rivalry between Emalyn and Meloncamp just keeps getting hotter," Marc said.

"I can tell she genuinely dislikes him. If something happens between them on the track, social media trolls will make it sound like it's all her fault. Why didn't I think to get a picture at the hotel?" Trey talked at length about Emalyn's wreck at Daytona that sent Junior hard into the third-turn wall. Although it looked serious, Junior walked away with minor bruises and one broken toe. The media blamed Emalyn, though no fine came her way from the sanctioning body.

"Emalyn isn't afraid to mix it up with the tough boys," Marc said. "But you're right. She gets all the blame. That's why I like her. She's the underdog."

"Her husband looks really old," Trey said. "Older than her, that's for sure. It doesn't help his cause that he has a built-in fur coat. She's married? Who knew? Why can't old men button their shirts more?"

"Arthritis probably," Marc winked as he spoke. Antonio and Trey chuckled, inspiring an older woman seated two rows up to look back at them with a librarian's piercing stare. Trey shrugged his shoulders in response.

The house lights blinked a couple of times, indicating showtime neared. Emalyn and Sean Martin arrived with much fanfare. She greeted and waved to folks who applauded her as she made her way down the main aisle. George Meloncamp grimaced back at her. Finally, he stood up and stared in her direction. The theater became quiet.

"Good evening, Georgy," Emalyn hollered from the seventh row. She blew him a kiss, then offered him a wave like a homecoming queen.

"Look out everyone," George said. "Woman driver coming through."

Boos erupted from the small crowd of three hundred that packed the little theater. Emalyn pantomimed holding a steering wheel as she stepped over the last two people before arriving at her seat. The crowd laughed at her conciliatory gesture. The lights soon went down, putting an end to the altercation, and the show began.

At the end of the first act of the play, Antonio judged from the boys' faces that they enjoyed it as much as he and Sylvia. Antonio loved the story of Willy Loman. Though not normally a fan of Arthur Miller's cynicism, the portrayal of a self-deluded "low man" trying to find the American dream inspired Antonio somehow. By intermission, Antonio's legs burned from the confined seating of the old theater. Eager to stretch his legs, he took drink orders from his family and made his way to the concession stand.

While Antonio waited for his turn at the small stand in the lobby, Emalyn and Sean walked toward the mammoth front doors. Unfortunately, George and his wife headed in the same direction at the same time. When George spotted Emalyn, he couldn't help but throw a bit more kindling on their rivalry fire.

"No hard feelings, Emalyn," he said, offering his hand for her to shake. Antonio watched as she cautiously extended her hand in response to an unexpected token of sportsmanship. Just as Emalyn positioned her arm to shake his hand, George pulled his large palm away with an exaggerated motion and a triumphant grin.

"I should have known better than to trust an old skunk like you," she said, contorting her face into a scowl.

"Excuse me, I forgot for a minute that a cow doesn't have hands, just hooves."

Things went downhill from there. Sean took umbrage at a man speaking to Emalyn that way. He pulled back and punched George right in the nose. George stumbled back several feet and bumped into an old woman using a walker. Emalyn jumped in, pulling off George's wife's wig. For emphasis, Emalyn hurled the big, blonde furball backwards over her head. The nearly bald woman responded by slinging her sequined purse at Emalyn's head, but she missed.

Several patrons and a young usher rushed in to pull the couples apart. In the process, George's wife tore one of the pockets on Emalyn's new leather jacket. Emalyn responded by grabbing an iced coffee drink from a passer-by and flinging it at George, who by that time escaped to several feet away and was headed toward the parking lot.

"I will see you at the track," George hollered over his shoulder as his wife pushed him in the direction of their car and clutched her hair piece.

With furrowed eyebrows, Emalyn shouted from the theater steps. "I am going to kill you out on that track, George Meloncamp. They are going to be picking up little pieces of your sad carcass for weeks."

Antonio shook his head. That was a pretty harsh threat. He hoped it was only that.

CHAPTER TWO

S itting alone in her racecar, Emalyn's face became a picture of laser focus. The bouncy blonde persona evaporated into the ether. She stared straight ahead in a trance of concentration. She envisioned the track the following day: the flag man, the National Anthem, and even the sound of the crowd. For her, motivation didn't come from proving she could do what men do; the whole enchilada meant beating the socks off anyone who would challenge her—male or female. She loved to win.

Saturdays always made Emalyn smile. Qualifying determined her placement within the pack of cars for the start of Sunday's race. In an earlier day, they called this process time trials. The vibe was completely different than race day. Not exactly stress free, but less complicated, less congested with cars and people. While some fans came out to watch the qualifications and practice runs, the crowd was usually much smaller and more laid-back.

Emalyn glanced up at the humongous American flag waving poetically near the top of the grandstand. The richness of the blue sky and the cool air felt intoxicating. The sun shone through the windshield, lighting up Emalyn's dazzling hazel eyes as her senses became one with the car.

The flagman changed his posture. Emalyn's heartbeat quickened. Adrenaline and excitement coursed through her body. Emalyn lived and breathed for these fleeting moments behind the wheel. Stock car racing ran in her blood. Her whole life and all her secrets revolved around the sport. She was living her dream on tracks from Maine to California.

The purr of the car surrounded her. A separate, living being made of fiberglass, plastic, and metal, it melded into her as she waited for the go-ahead. From the helmet headphones came the disembodied voice of Millard Estes, the only professional crew chief she'd ever known, as he led Emalyn through last-minute mental checklists and reminded her to breathe evenly. The familiar voice of the portly, fiftyish man soothed her and brought her adrenaline level back to a manageable zone.

The flagman signaled Emalyn to begin warming up. Her car sprang to attention, and she accelerated into the first turn. Building speed, the engine sounded perfect. The familiar centrifugal force began to pull against her helmet. The car vibrated as it built speed, and the physical challenge of stock car racing began. Sharp focus and a will of iron enabled Emalyn's five-foot-five-inch frame to hold the car on the track and to guide it skillfully through the sweet grooves in the oval surface.

"That's it, Emalyn. Slowly build it. Slowly build it."

Millard must be pleased with the way the car sounds, Emalyn thought. After thirty years in the racing game, a pit boss could sense almost everything about a car just by hearing it roll around the track. Right rear tire a little low, he could hear it. Foil misadjusted for conditions, he could hear it. Driver thinking about anything except the business of driving the car, he could hear that, too, in her voice. Some days, Emalyn could have used a little less of Millard's intuition.

"Do you see that skunk Meloncamp?"

"Emalyn, concentrate," Millard said. "He's sitting where he always sits."

Emalyn imagined the solitary man sitting in section twenty-eight on the far side of the stands. George Meloncamp would be studying every movement of Emalyn's car. His spying included the lines she preferred on the empty track and the handling of the car's rear end. A small amount of drift in the turns provided all he would need to pass

her and move ahead on race day. Though she saw him in her mind's
eye, his gaze didn't worry her one bit. She might even throw in a fake
clue or two, give him something to think about on race day.

She only really knew what the stock car bloggers said about Meloncamp. They never had a civil conversation. Recently, his thoughts lay
splayed for all to read in a no-holds-barred interview with the sport's
most popular blog site. Emalyn remembered each word, having read it
four times. The furrows in his forty-year-old face resulted from many
late nights spent worrying about his two teenage daughters, not
anything to do with racing or Emalyn, he said in the magazine. Meloncamp planned on retiring soon, but the golden handcuffs of the sport
held him in place. His bank account full, even considering his wife's
penchant for remodeling their two large homes, he lacked monetary
incentive to keep going.

According to the blogger, Meloncamp planned to relax in a beach
chair on the Gulf Coast. But before he took his final curtain call, there
remained a little unfinished business. Meloncamp wanted to etch his
name a little deeper into the record book. Winning one more racing
series championship would help. One goal remained for George
Meloncamp—he would not quit "until he drove a certain upstart hill-
billy woman out of racing for good." Emalyn thought about those sick-
ening quotes in the article: "Women, especially ones like Emalyn, have
no place in this man's world of stock car racing." She thought
otherwise.

Qualifying and her practice time informed Emalyn about her car's
power and handling leading up to the next race. The first few minutes
always felt like a getting-reacquainted session with her car before the
inevitable combat erupted in earnest. Emalyn loved to compete,
whether against a clock or against her male counterparts in a race.

After the warm-up laps, the flagman waved Emalyn out for qualifying. Her car screamed around the track at 190 miles per hour in her
first lap. Her face flushed with excitement as the car rocketed from
turn to straightaway and back again. The engine responded to her
demand for more power. The second lap flew by faster and turned out
to be the keeper time, her best of the day. A third lap clocked just
under 189 miles per hour as she unsuccessfully tried a higher line

running through the third turn. As suddenly as it begun, her qualifying attempt ended. She guided the racer toward her pit road slot, listening to Millard through her helmet as she went. She cut power to the engine and slid with ease up and out of the driver's side window.

"Good going, girl. You should be somewhere in the first few rows."

Emalyn nodded her head but didn't take her helmet off. This signaled Millard that she didn't want to talk just yet. Too keyed up for normal conversation, she walked it off. Experience and her stock car hero, the only other prominent woman driver in the sport, taught her that sometimes you keep your helmet on and walk on by. If only she could learn the third part of that advice: keep your mouth shut. Emalyn knew she would always struggle with that one.

As a young child, Emalyn always kept her mouth shut. Her Air Force father moved the family three times while she struggled through elementary school. The only way to survive all those new schools and new people was to keep her mouth shut. At least that's how life progressed until her mama decided she and her two daughters moved for the last time. Sweet Mama risked her marriage by putting her foot down and taking Emalyn and her younger sister, Noelle, back home to Tennessee.

Slowly at first, Emalyn came out of her shell. Regular habits and familiar faces helped Emalyn blossom and bloom. She played in the band at school and made several keeper friends. She began going to church with Mama and her sister. Then, something bad happened, and she never went back.

The boy next door loved cars, which led Emalyn to decide to love them as well. It gave her something to do when her mom and sister headed off to church. In her attempt to get Bobby Benson to notice her, Emalyn learned everything worth knowing about the Chevys of that day. She wanted Bobby to see her as more than just his tomboy neighbor.

Emalyn's mind went back to Tennessee. When her father retired after twenty years of military service, he came home for good at last. She loved spending hours with him on weekends, and he would do anything to make her happy. When she asked to drive midget racers, just like Bobby next door, her father quickly agreed. Little did Emalyn know that beating Bobby sealed her fate. Her win represented the last thing his teenage male ego could handle. Fortunately, her taste for winning overrode her desire for chasing a boy less than excited about her.

* * *

While Emalyn went through her paces at the racetrack, Antonio and Sylvia took the boys to McDonald's for breakfast. After a quick round of breakfast sandwiches, hash browns, coffee, and Cokes, they headed off to the horseback riding trails. Antonio noticed Trey's voice quicken and rise in pitch. The young man also trembled a bit as they neared the riding stables. He loved Trey like his own child.

The large stable was set back from the highway at least a quarter mile. The fences surrounding the grassy fields defined bucolic. From the looks of things, most of their twelve-person riding group oozed inexperience and giddiness. Nervous laughter followed elementary questions about riding. One large man asked their guide about the weight limit to ride the horse/mule hybrids. He looked relieved at the answer: 250 pounds.

"I am so glad we get to ride again this year," Sylvia said behind her oversized sunglasses.

"One of these days, we are going to take a vacation out West to a dude ranch where we can rope and ride for an entire week," Antonio replied. Though an East Coast boy all his life, Antonio longed for the wide-open spaces and adventure, even more since taking a sixty-hour-per-week job as an attorney. Although his rise through the company's ranks felt God-ordained, the whole package of being an up-and-coming Washington lawyer brought a considerable downside to a free-spirit like Antonio. Soon, he would first-chair the next litigation case. But the cost of devoting so much of his life to work gave him pause.

"Very cool," Marc chimed in. His good-natured temperament mirrored his dad's, as did his jet-black hair and lean body.

"If you don't mind getting trampled to death or falling off and breaking your neck," Trey said as he stole a glance at the imposing animals lounging around the corral. Everyone gave Trey encouraging looks as his fear showed through a contorted smile.

"You'll be okay, big man," Marc said.

As the rest of the guests arrived at the barn, the owner's daughter, who would serve as their trail boss, greeted each grouping warmly. When all twelve riders assembled to embark, she provided the required safety orientation with an appropriate old-west intonation. *Perhaps she is from Western New York*, Antonio thought. The succinct safety talk bucked up most of the riders: brief, comforting, and explaining the minimum about what they could expect.

After the orientation, the horse/mule hybrid animals trotted forward one by one, led by one of the stable pokes. Due to the hilly terrain, these extra-sturdy beasts handled the conditions far better than normal saddle horses, but Antonio could appreciate Trey's trepidation as he scanned their large frames.

Sylvia used the mounting stair to get on her tall, gray beast. She settled into the saddle and grasped the reins, showing her authority. Marc and Antonio used their height to easily mount their rides from the stirrups.

"Just stay together, and you'll do fine. The horses know the trail and won't give you much trouble," the guide assured them.

Trey turned pale as he approached the mounting stair, but he kept going, managing to climb onto a big, chestnut brute named Stella. Antonio entertained second thoughts about Trey's involvement in horseback riding when the young man nearly slipped out of the saddle trying to put his foot through the stirrup.

"What if I fall off, break my neck, and end up in lifelong paralysis?" Trey asked.

"Don't worry none, young man," the guide said in her neighborly, western voice. "Stella is a good old gal. She will take care of you."

Trey nodded in reply as he clung white-knuckled to the saddle horn.

Sylvia, Antonio, and Marc played follow the leader uphill and across dale for the next fifty minutes. *The smell of the animals, the gentle bouncing, and the politeness of the beasts made this a nearly ideal memory maker*, Antonio thought, smiling in satisfaction. Almost.

"It's going off the trail!" Trey called out, eyes widening.

Stella, tired of the monotonous journey, decided to take her inexperienced rider off the beaten path and into some low-hanging tree limbs, perhaps intending to knock him off. She neighed in approval as the branches gently scratched her massive hind quarters.

"Calm down!" Marc shouted. "The horse can sense that you're afraid."

With one command from the guide, Stella backed out of the tree limbs and turned in the opposite direction of the rest of the pack. She made her way to the end of the line of horses and riders, obeying the leader's command.

"That is the cutest thing," Sylvia said to Trey as he passed by. "Your horse acted bad, and now both of you have to go to the back of the line. Stella looks so ashamed."

"My people are used to being in the back of the bus," Trey joked, his face indicating he felt a bit embarrassed by his panic moments earlier.

Trey almost never brought up any racial differences between him and the Semones family. Antonio figured he just wanted people to see him as smart and athletic, as a member of the Honor Society and the basketball team. Marc and his family obliged. That's probably one of the reasons Trey remained close.

Just a quarter-mile from the stables, the guide paused.

"We are going to go up and down the trails over there. The animals know the way, just don't get too spaced out from each other. When we head back down, you have the option of galloping the last little way to the corral and barns. Just give the reins a little slack and off you'll go. Hold on tight."

The horses climbed up and down the mountain trail, causing the riders to adjust their posture in the saddle. Once at the bottom of the trail, the group gathered at the clearing. Going first, Antonio urged his horse to a fast trot across the sunny meadow; he pivoted once in the paddock area so he could watch the rest of his crew. Trees obscured part of the meadow, but he could see the riders for the last half of their galloping time.

Sylvia went a little slower, giggling and bouncing the whole way. Antonio could tell she enjoyed her ride. He suspected she would have taken her horse, Penelope, home as a pet—if Fairfax County allowed such things in residential neighborhoods. Marc showed off by standing up in his stirrups but nearly slipped off when his mount lurched forward. Somehow, he managed to stay on and whooped with joy as he entered the paddock.

After Marc arrived, everyone waited anxiously for Trey's turn. Seconds turned to minutes. Antonio began to pray that Trey survived in one piece. Five minutes later, their guide arrived, walking Trey and his horse to the barn. Trey dismounted or fell, depending on the kindness of the description. His rear end wound up on the dusty ground. Thankfully, no one laughed or made fun of him.

In the car, everyone buckled their seatbelts.

"Lord, thank you for keeping us all safe throughout our ride. Bless Trey for tackling his fears. Now, show us how we can be a good witness for you throughout the rest of our trip," Antonio said. Then, he drove away from the horse farm.

By the time the Semones family reached the hotel, lunchtime had passed. The hotel restaurant, still smelling of musty carpeting, fed them well anyway—burgers for the boys and a chicken sandwich for Antonio. Sylvia complimented the variety of ingredients in the chef's salad, though she tired of it about halfway through the mounds of iceberg lettuce, boiled eggs, tomatoes, and blue cheese. She had inadvertently become an arugula lady, notwithstanding her humble beginnings in Brazil.

After their bath and nap, Antonio and Sylvia strolled out to the pool to find the boys resting from their water play in lounge chairs, soaking up the last of the day's sun. To Marc and Trey's obvious delight (as well as Sylvia's motherly concern), Emalyn appeared at the door of her bungalow, dressed in a black, one-piece swimsuit. "Oh, hello boys," Emalyn said shyly. She wore her locks back, collected in a small pony-tail, similar to her race day ritual. Diving right into the pool without waiting for the boys to reply, her rhythmic strokes continued for twenty minutes.

Watching from outside the pool fence, Antonio and Sylvia looked at the door to Emalyn's bungalow expecting Sean to follow her out, but he didn't appear.

"Do you think it's odd that Sean didn't come out to the pool?" Sylvia asked.

"Not really," Antonio said. "Maybe he doesn't swim. Maybe he's just tired."

"I wonder," Sylvia mused.

The sight of Emalyn Martin in their own almost-private pool, swimming laps back and forth, made the weekend seem even more surreal to both high school-aged boys. Looking on, Antonio felt he could not have planned a better three-day vacation for them—but he sensed some tension from Sylvia and was unsure if she would agree. After finishing her laps, Emalyn climbed out near the shallow end, toweled off quickly, and retreated to her room. Antonio suspected the vision of Emalyn etched itself into the boys' minds forever. Their eyes traced her every step to her room.

When the door opened, Sean's sharp voice could be heard even though the pool rested some thirty feet away.

"What were you doing out there?" Sean accused his wife.

"Duh, I went swimming."

"Emalyn, I don't appreciate you parading your body around in front of schoolboys. I'm sure their parents don't like it either." The door slammed shut, but the fight continued, and the couple's muffled voices remained audible at the pool.

CHAPTER THREE

The Semones clan and Trey understood that the trip meant missing their regular church service on Sunday morning, but they would not miss the key part of their lives, worshipping God. Stopping to thank and praise God felt as normal as eating lunch. Their medium-sized, non-denominational church gave the family plenty of fellowship and an abundance of opportunities for service. Ordinary people exchanged extraordinary love as they did life together.

Before breakfast and before the racetrack, Antonio convened the four at one of the picnic tables on the hotel property. Sylvia led them in a well-known worship chorus. Marc read a scripture that Antonio pointed out in the Bible. Trey prayed for their day and for Emalyn. Antonio offered a ten-minute sermonette about true love. He thought the devotions breezed by short and sweet but hoped the mini-church-service took away the lonely feeling that Christians sometimes experience when they travel on Sundays.

Even though they pulled through the gates two hours before the race, the speedway grounds buzzed with activity. Antonio followed the lackluster directions of the parking crew, most of whom looked half asleep. The Audi snaked through the gravel lot in search of the next open parking space. Already half-full, the dusty parking area hosted many SUVs and pick-up trucks surrounded by lawn chairs. Smoke billowed from grills as clouds of pollen and dust permeated the air.

Sylvia donned her white sun hat as the boys scurried out of the back seat. Antonio pinched creamy goop onto his free hand and passed the tube on. Marc and Trey obediently massaged lotion into their faces and arms.

They began the hike toward the main gate. Trey paused, almost overcome with the smell of burgers and barbequed chicken coming from every direction. Walking to the grandstand, they waded through sensory overload. The sun, already bright in the sky, reflected off the dust-filled air. Music, mostly country and pop, blared from vehicles and portable speakers set up in truck beds. Laughter and the smell of beer mixed with the other sights and sounds.

Antonio handed out tickets as each of his tribe members approached the gate. After being haphazardly patted down, the boys proceeded through the turnstiles without incident. Sylvia asked the first responsible-looking usher how to get to pit road. He pointed in the direction of the VIP ramp that passed under the grandstand. The walk around the interior perimeter took them by dozens of merchandise booths of the racers. T-shirts and hats and toy racecars brightened displays at each booth. After the first few booths, unique items began to stand out, such as the George Meloncamp bobble head and the Vic Donovan fringed beach towel.

Eventually, they came to the ramp for pit road and showed the badges that Sean left for them at the hotel desk. The guard called someone on his walkie-talkie, and soon a runner escorted them to Emalyn's pit area.

"One of you must be Antonio. I'm Millard Estes, Emalyn's crew chief."

"I'm Antonio, and this is my wife, Sylvia. The boys are Trey and Marc."

"Well, let me show you what we do here." Millard gave them a complete tour of Team Emalyn's space on pit road. He let the boys hold up two of the signs which guide Emalyn into her slot. Antonio took pictures with his phone in rapid succession. Marc's eyes grew wider with each new revelation of how things really worked down in the pit area. A smile flashed across his face when Millard gave him a headset and allowed him to speak with Emalyn through the radio.

The boys took individual selfies with Emalyn's back-up driver who was also Millard's son, Jesse Estes. Antonio stepped in and took a picture of both boys and Jesse, who looked a bit like an action figure in his tight-fitting, black racing uniform. Due to the height difference between the high school basketball players and the more diminutive racecar driver, Antonio took a step back to get a better angle.

"Where you boys from?" Jesse asked, tilting his head so his brown bangs fell down over one eye.

"Near D.C.," Marc replied.

"Thanks for coming out to meet us," Jesse said, seeming to relish his moment in Emalyn's reflected spotlight.

Trey asked, "What do you have to do to train for driving stock cars?"

"There are several routes. I raced moto-cross as a kid, then midget racers. It also helps if your dad is a crew chief," Jesse said as he whizzed from one side of the pit area to another.

"All I've ever wanted to be is a racecar driver," Jesse said. "I raced on the junior circuit for several years. Now I'm doing my time on the team here working as a mechanic and as the back-up driver for Emalyn. I still race with some friends on the junior circuit when I can."

"Don't let him kid you," Millard said. "It takes a lot of hard work to become a stock car driver and good grades in school."

Antonio grinned at Millard's last words, though he doubted their accuracy. "Do you think Emalyn will take the championship this year?" Antonio asked.

"Well, yeah!" Millard's voice quickened. "There is no reason she can't. The car is running well. The sponsors are behind her all the way. If she can keep her goofy husband from doing anything dumb. Hey, Peyton, lock down that tire there. Do you see it?"

Estes hurried away from Antonio and began working on last-minute details to ensure the pit was ready for racing.

Antonio didn't know what to think of Millard Estes. His close-cropped silver hair and chubby, suntanned face reminded Antonio of his blue-collar uncle from Philadelphia. Estes's short but strong arms protruded from team coveralls, revealing the beginnings of a sleeve of tattoos on his right arm and more ink peeking out in various places. The tattoos seemed unusual for a man of his age. Adding in his comments about the value of education and Sean's behavior, Antonio's calm face belied his confusion.

Suddenly, Emalyn materialized in the pit and stood by her car. She greeted everyone more calmly than she had away from the racetrack. Her vivacious personality of their previous meetings went into hiding. Steely determination was written on her face, and her piercing eyes revealed a very different Emalyn than the boys met at the hotel. They expected warm and bubbly Emalyn in a racing uniform. Instead, they got the polite but cool, no nonsense version. None of that slowed down Trey or Marc as they hung on her every word and movement.

"They look like a pair of golden retrievers," Sylvia whispered in Antonio's ear. "The way Marc and Trey are following Emalyn around the pits, wagging their tails, I expect them to start barking at any moment."

After a too-short, thirty-minute visit, the call came to clear the pits of non-essential personnel. Antonio led his family in a chorus of thanks, good luck wishes, and good-byes before heading off to their seats in the stands.

"Wow! That whole experience blew me away!" Sylvia said, adjusting her hat and sunglasses. Antonio felt glad to see that, even though not a racing fan, his wife appreciated the tour.

"Beyond unbelievable," Trey said. "Can you believe we stood that close to Emalyn *and* her crew chief *and* her car ... on race day?"

"No," Marc replied. "I've seen it on television so many times, but I didn't have a clue. I don't think I am ever going to believe it even with two hundred pictures on my phone. Emalyn brought so much electricity when she walked into the pit. I'm still buzzing from it."

"Your post posing with Jesse Estes and the racecar has a hundred likes on Instagram already," Trey said.

A loud voice boomed through the intercom: "Ladies and Gentlemen, I am Frank Middleton, your announcer for today's race. Please stand, remove your hats, and sing along with new country superstar Harold Wyandot as he sings our national anthem." Everyone stood and

Antonio noticed the remarkable number of people who sang along with the anthem. His heart swelled with pride as the oversized American flag rose majestically into place and billowed in the wind.

After the anthem, a conservative talk-show host gave the call, "Lady and Gentlemen, Start Your Engines!" Like a freight train coming to life, the sound of fifty-two deafening engines engulfed the stadium. Magnetic energy from the crowd rolled around the grandstand in waves. The electricity could have powered a large city for a day. Slowly at first, the racecars followed the pace car around the track, picking up speed as they went. Each car maintained its place in the starting order. When the pace car exited the track and the lead cars returned to the starting line, the buzzing of the crowd increased.

"Look, Emalyn is over there!" Antonio said, pointing to her car as it rounded the track.

The green flag came down and the 550-mile race began. Due to their positions at the start, Emalyn and George didn't drive near each other for the first twenty-five laps or so. Emalyn's white car howled around the track, followed by the eyes of her many fans in the stands and on television. Junior ran first, and Emalyn followed directly behind him for several laps. Cars jockeyed for position, lap after lap. Donovan led for a short time, then dropped back. By the fiftieth lap, Meloncamp passed several cars, and Emalyn dropped back to seventh place. The gap between them shrank to almost nothing.

"Each time the cars round the track and pass our seats, it sounds like high-pitched cats screaming," Sylvia said, covering her ears. "When the cars go to the other side of the oval, I can relax a little."

Antonio smiled at his wife and patted her on the back. "We can get you some earplugs at the merchandise stand."

She responded by shaking her head. "It's all part of the experience, I suppose."

Lap after lap, the tension on the track continued. Marc drank a large lemonade and Trey gobbled popcorn, both nervous as they watched the action unfold.

Antonio eyed the race through his expensive binoculars, a holiday present from the senior partners of his firm last Christmas. While everyone else watched the whole group of racers, Antonio zeroed in on

one driver, then another. Occasionally, his gaze would wander to the
area over the wall in the pits. He stared at Millard Estes and the rest of
Emalyn's team. They waited patiently at their stations until Emalyn
pitted. Then, they sprang to life, fascinating Antonio with how fast
they could work once Emalyn zoomed into the pit area. Tires off. Fresh
tires on. Fuel dumped in the tank. Off she went.

Back in line, she quickly worked her way up through the other drivers. As she rounded the turn near the Semones clan, she swerved and
almost lost it into the wall.

"Emalyn seems to be having some handling problems," Antonio
said.

"She looks loose," Marc added. "The rear of her car is moving
around a lot on the turns."

"I think George Meloncamp is planning to make a move on her,"
Trey said. "This could get ugly."

With the other cars stopping to pit, George and Emalyn found
their way to the front of the pack. The two rivals fought for position.
Emalyn coaxed just a little more speed from her engine when she
managed to hold her line leading into the turns. The rivals battled hard
for first place, but Emalyn managed to stay just in front.

"Her quarter panel got awfully close to Meloncamp's car," Antonio
commented.

The announcer boomed through the public address, "Meloncamp is
coming up on Martin. He is going to the high side. This is what we've
all been waiting to see. Can he squeeze past her on this lap?"

Just about everyone stood up as the feuding racers roared around
the track. For the first two laps of their battle, fans did the wave in
time to Emalyn's revolutions around the racetrack, but eventually
almost everyone just remained standing. Between the sports radio
jocks and Emalyn herself, her rivalry with Meloncamp felt hyped, but
it worked. This duel drove many fans to Pocono: George and Emalyn
battling it out, man to woman.

Antonio strained to get a glimpse as Meloncamp once again tried
to pass Emalyn high as they cleared the third turn, heading in their
direction.

"It looked like Emalyn tried to run Meloncamp into the wall," Antonio yelled.

"Oh, I'm sure it wasn't on purpose," Sylvia said.

"Here they come!" Trey shouted.

A flash of light enveloped the whole scene below them, followed by a wall of shrill screeches. A huge explosion echoed around the track, and everything seemed to lapse into slow motion. Blasting heat rose up from the track, and Antonio backed up a step. A cacophonous symphony rattled around in his brain disorienting him. Defensively, he closed his eyes and put a hand out toward the direction of the wreck.

Pieces of car debris, mostly very small pieces, flew in every direction, raining around the spectators, including Antonio, Marc, Trey, and Sylvia. One piece of shrapnel penetrated Sylvia's left arm as she instinctively tried to cover her face. She shrieked in pain. Suddenly, the horrific flash and terrifying wave of sound waned. Everything returned to real time. The last of the shrapnel landed with tiny pops on the concrete around the Semones family. The crowd of people froze for a moment. Marc's face reflected red from the fireball, then Antonio noticed the buzz of the crowd grew louder and louder as everyone morphed from stunned silence to panic and checked on their loved ones.

Emalyn's car rattled to a stop in the grassy infield. A third car, dragging something metallic on the track, left a trail of sparks before coming to a halt. Other drivers executed a variety of maneuvers, trying to avoid the debris field as best they could. Antonio believed at least two cars sustained tire damage from the pieces of wreckage.

There remained little to see of Meloncamp's car except for the rear bumper sitting askew on a single, visible tire. Several feet away sat an unrecognizable clump of metal. Simultaneously, sirens began to echo around the track as fire control and other emergency vehicles entered the track to search for the injured.

Still trying to process what happened, Marc and Trey could only stare at each other. Antonio turned to them both. Trey shuddered, visibly shaken. Marc reached out and grabbed Trey's arms to stop him from trembling. Antonio asked if everyone felt alright. He patted Trey on the shoulder, offering comfort.

Sylvia showed Antonio her arm,

"Oh, goodness," Antonio said.

Trey almost passed out from the sight of Sylvia's blood. He sat down to steady himself.

With haste, Antonio took hold of Sylvia's arm and determined the metal was too deeply embedded to pull out by hand. "Sylvia, if I try to pull the metal out, it might cause more bleeding. Hang tight a second."

Antonio ripped off his dark blue shirt and tied it loosely around his wife's arm. Despite the pain, Sylvia smiled a bit when she saw the paleness of Antonio's well-toned upper body. "Guys, I'm thinking that maybe a beach trip would have been better than this racing getaway."

Antonio smiled back, knowing Sylvia used humor to calm her men.

Someone behind them asked, "Where's George's car? It disappeared!"

"I think it blew to bits," Marc responded.

Trey winced at the words and the imagery. Without warning, Trey fell over onto Marc.

As more emergency vehicles rolled onto the track, some of the fans in the stands instinctively turned to leave. Antonio noticed a lady in front of him crying out in pain and tugging at her companion's sleeve. When the woman pivoted toward her husband, Antonio could see a shard of shrapnel sticking out of her face, just below her eye. Gathering his group, he pointed to the jammed stairs. They would have to make their way through the crowd to get medical treatment for Sylvia.

"Trey and Marc, we need to take Mom to the hospital right away to get her arm looked at. Stay with us." By this time, several people in their row began to file toward the concrete stairs. Others stood at their seats, hypnotized by the flurry of activity on the track. Due to the indecision and sheer number of people trying to leave at the same time, Antonio knew they faced a slow walk back up to the concourse level.

The speakers around the grandstand came to life with the voice of the track announcer. "Everyone, please remain calm. If you are exiting the grandstand, please move slowly and courteously. There is no immediate physical danger. Please remain calm. If you or someone you know needs medical attention and can walk, come to either Gate fourteen on the north side of the grandstand or Gate twenty-eight on the south side of the grandstand. Triage stations are ready to serve injured patrons. Paramedics will evaluate injuries. Ambulances are available near those exits, and paramedics will be on hand until everyone is seen. If anyone is badly hurt near you, please signal an usher in your area of the grandstand. They will assist you and find the right help as soon as possible."

"I think the closest triage station is by Gate twenty-eight," Antonio said.

As they climbed the stairs behind the other patrons, Marc glanced back often at his mother and at the infield where Emalyn's car came to rest. Antonio did the same, watching an ambulance roll up the track to the place where George Meloncamp's car exploded. The ambulance attendants got out but looked confused as they walked around, searching for Meloncamp's car or any sign of his body.

On the infield, a lone firefighter used a fire extinguisher on Emalyn's car. "There doesn't seem to be much fire," Marc said. "Those guys are spritzing off Emalyn's car, but it isn't even smoking. Trey, are you okay?"

Antonio put one hand up to steady Trey as they inched their way up the steps. "It's going to be fine. Don't worry, Trey."

In another moment, Antonio looked back at the track one last time to see Emalyn climb out of her car head first. She looked dazed, wobbling a bit, but she didn't fall. An emergency medical technician took her arm and led her toward the waiting ambulance. Antonio noticed her unsteadiness increase, but at that point he felt more concerned about Sylvia's arm and keeping Trey from passing out. They made their way in a tight pack to Gate twenty-eight. The scene was chaotic as several people with minor injuries sought the attention of one of several paramedics. An older man in street clothes announced himself as a doctor and unwrapped the shirt from Sylvia's arm. Opening the first aid kit someone handed him, he sprayed disinfectant around the shrapnel and packed the area with gauze. Then, he taped it all up and led her towards one of the waiting ambulances.

Antonio and the boys hurried to their car, already fully packed for their trip home after the race. They managed to get ahead of much of

the speedway traffic. Antonio found Sylvia already in a bay at the emergency room when they arrived. After settling the boys in the waiting
room, Antonio headed back through the mechanical doors to the ER,
planning to sit with Sylvia.

"What are they giving you?" Antonio asked, looking up at the IV
drip.

"An antibiotic and saline," she replied. "Where are the boys?"

"Waiting room. The traffic out of the racetrack proved much worse
than this morning. Sorry it took so long."

Sylvia patted his hand in response. Her wound, dressed at the
triage station, remained secure with no leaking, but her face showed
wear from the ordeal. Antonio brushed her cheek with his hand and
silently offered a little prayer of thanksgiving to God. They sat word-
less for several minutes before the silence evaporated.

From the adjoining bay, Sylvia and Antonio heard a familiar drawl.
"Well, I told you I am all right. Just let me get back to the track so I
can continue the race."

"Mrs. Martin, we need to thoroughly check you out before we can
release you. You may have a concussion or another serious injury. You
need a thorough evaluation."

"Well then let's get a doctor in here and get 'er done," Emalyn
protested.

In less than a minute, the curtains in Emalyn's bay whooshed open
as the assigned doctor and nurse entered. They spoke in quiet tones as
they examined Emalyn. Minutes later, they exited with the same
whooshing sound.

Sylvia gave Antonio a look that told him go check on their new
friend. Obediently, Antonio peeked around the drawn curtain and saw
Emalyn wearing a hospital gown, a blanket, and a nasty shiner. "How
are you, Mrs. Martin?"

"Call me Emalyn. I am anxious to get back to the track, that's how
I am. Wait. I remember you from this morning and from the hotel.
You are Dad to those real tall boys, aren't you?"

"Yes. What a nasty crash. I'm not disturbing you, am I?"

"I am glad someone is here for me. Afraid my noggin took a bit of a hit. My doggone husband got lost in the crowd and hasn't shown up here yet."

"The traffic getting out of the racetrack is bad. It took us until just a few minutes ago. Are you going to be all right?"

Uncharacteristically, the lady not afraid to hurl around the track at close to 200 miles per hour looked bewildered. Her lower lip quivered a little, but otherwise her expression grew blank.

"My goodness." Antonio moved closer to Emalyn. "What is the matter?"

"I am just so frustrated. That George Meloncamp got in my way on purpose and now we are both wrecked out of the race. It's Fortuna, my bad luck. Wait until next time. I will race him into the ground if necessary. Our sponsors just complained about cost control, and I go and wreck our best car, the one that has been running so well. I'm just a mess!" Emalyn couldn't hold back tears. They rolled like raindrops down her cheeks.

Antonio offered her some tissues, and then his hand to hold. "Can I pray for you?"

"I haven't prayed in years." Her face told Antonio deep waters flowed beneath that answer. She grasped Antonio's long, manly hand, as if urging him to begin the prayer.

"Our Dear Father, you know why everything happens. You know how hard Ms. Martin—"

"Call me Emalyn."

"Emalyn has worked to become a racecar driver. Please heal her body. Bring her husband here to comfort her. Help us to see Your presence in this whole thing. Show her that you want back into her life. Let Emalyn feel Your love today and in the coming weeks ahead. Amen." Antonio squeezed her hand and smiled as she opened her eyes.

"That calmed me down so much," Emalyn said. "Thank you."

Antonio heard the doctor and nurse whoosh into his wife's bay next door. "Emalyn, I have to go. My wife took a piece of shrapnel, and they are probably going to take it out now. Here is my business card. It has my cell phone there. If you need anything, just give me a call. I'm not sure how long we will be around here, but we certainly wish you the best."

"Please tell your wife I am so sorry she got hit, even though it is totally George Meloncamp's fault. I will be wishing good thoughts for her too." Emalyn's face beamed sincerity.

Antonio smiled and reversed his steps into Sylvia's bay.

The doctor, of Indian descent, spoke in a deep and soft voice. He looked at Sylvia with kind eyes as he spoke. "Okay, so this is pretty straight-forward. A surgeon will be down in a few minutes to remove the piece of metal from your arm. It is small enough that we can prep the area and remove it right here. The main risk is infection. Follow the post-op instructions. We will get you fixed up, and you should be on your way in a couple of hours." With that, the doctor exited, and the nurse began gathering the necessary pads and sterile wipes from drawers in the examining bay. Antonio then heard a loud hoot in the next bay.

"Oh baby, you made it!" Emalyn's voice reverberated throughout the halls of the emergency room.

"Sorry it took so long. The police talked to our crew chief and quite a few other people. I decided to hang around and hear what they said. Then, of course, the traffic over here would make a groundhog hide for six more weeks. Always is horrendous at Pocono Speedway, even on a good day."

"Police? Did they restart the race?"

"No baby, they called it off." Sean paused for a moment. "I don't know how to tell you this. George lost his life. His car blew into a million pieces."

"What? Oh no!" Emalyn's voice trailed off ...

Antonio imagined her brain could not process the information. There is something about professional drivers and their internal wiring. On some level, they must understand that racing is dangerous, but they shove the most severe consequences into a closed room within their minds.

After a few moments, Emalyn spoke. "How? Why?"

"They really don't have a clue right now. It is going to take a lot of investigating, and they can't let cars back on the track until the police and race officials have some time to figure it out. Jesse and I watched the replays on TV while waiting for his turn to be interviewed by law enforcement. It didn't look like any car explosion I've ever seen. You bumped George and his car went into the wall. Next thing, his car lit up like a fireworks display. There is practically nothing left of it."

The next voice sounded unfamiliar. "Initial tests and x-rays are negative, Emalyn. The doctor and nurse want you to do several things to avoid complications. Take the full course of your antibiotics and change the dressing on your foot as instructed. The nurse will go over everything before you are released. Get the antibiotic prescription filled tonight so that you can begin taking it immediately. Other than that, check back with your family doctor in a week to make sure your foot is healing correctly. We will get you going soon."

Antonio heard no more before the surgeon arrived to remove Sylvia's shrapnel. The doctor used a local anesthetic, but Sylvia's fingernails left significant impressions in Antonio's hand.

Antonio wiped a sweaty palm over his hairy arm. "Dear, uh, that kind of hurts,"

"Ye-ow!" Sylvia's scream went on for several seconds before she regained her composure.

An hour later, Sylvia left the ER. Antonio collected the boys and pulled the car around. Marc helped his mother out of the wheelchair, though she didn't feel like she needed any help. Everyone remained exceptionally quiet as the Audi whirred over the Pennsylvania hills, through Maryland, and back to their Virginia home.

CHAPTER FOUR

Rocco and Marta Semones held hands while they waited for the single-cup coffee maker to fill her travel mug. His massive digits encompassed her hand, emanating his protection and love. Fragrance wafted up from a bouquet of flowers, reminding Marta of the previous night. Once again, Rocco swept her off her feet—almost a weekly occurrence. He knocked at their condo door like an expectant beau and cordially asked the favor of her company for a date. Marta wondered if this ritual equaled another round of amends for their first date that went awry, eight years earlier. On what would have amounted to their first real date, Russian mobsters came to her door before Rocco showed up. They drugged Marta, rolled her up in an oriental rug, and kidnapped her. Fortunately, she survived that ordeal thanks to Rocco and his brother, Antonio. The ordeal made Marta stronger and more resilient.

Last evening, Rocco stood there looking handsome as ever, his outstretched and beefy hand holding a bouquet. He smiled at Marta, and his dancing eyes made her heart flutter. Her cream-colored silk blouse and mid-length navy skirt captivated his attention until he stared into her brown eyes. She couldn't refuse his boyish invitation to dine at a little French restaurant in the District's northwest quadrant, offering mood lighting, violin music, and just the right amount of shelter from an early summer shower. The floor-to-ceiling windows sat open and the sheer drapes danced lazily as the breeze moved through the restaurant. Marta loved the occasional aroma of mist and fresh-ness, uncommon in the usually sultry city at this time of year.

The food tasted and looked exquisite; the service, impeccable. Her mind remembered every sensual moment at the eatery, thinking about the big news she dropped on her husband and the handsome cut of his jaw as it quivered. The night couldn't have been more perfect. After dinner, they went home to spend the remainder of the evening snug-gled on the couch, watching a 1980's disaster movie. They loved any kind of disaster movie, as long as it included police, firemen, and shameless overacting.

"I am going to miss you today," Rocco said.

The warmth in his loving, brown, cow eyes held Marta spellbound. "I'll miss you more," Marta gave her usual reply.

"Did you enjoy Towering Inferno last night?" Rocco asked.

"You or the movie?" she said, smiling demurely.

Rocco stared at his wife. She grew more stunning each year, though she would deny it. He focused on her frizzy, brown hair, and cool, light brown skin, still infatuated. She often wore business suits to her job near the Capitol but never without a silky, feminine blouse in some pastel color. She didn't disappoint on this gorgeous morning.

"What is it about Tuesdays that make me not want to go to work?"

"We lived it up during a great weekend and the fun just kept coming last night, but all that fun has a price tag, sir. Fancy dinners and home decor don't pay for themselves," Marta said, glancing at the over-sized clock on the living room wall. They'd only moved in last month, and she loved shopping for their new condo, their first big purchase together after living in Marta's small place for the first seven years of their marriage.

"Amen," Rocco said. "Same is true about new condos at Ballston. I better get a move on. I can't disappointment my brother. But first, I need one more kiss from my marvelous Brazilian bride."

After kissing her lips and gently patting his wife's hair, Rocco put on his extra-large, extra-tall sport coat. He stretched out his arms to make sure his shirt cuffs stuck out just a quarter inch beyond the sleeve of his jacket. Since going to work with Antonio at the law firm, expectations required him to dress well, or at least better than his M.O. as a police detective.

After a short Metro ride, Rocco walked to the stone and steel, twelve-story structure that towered over their block of K Street, at least to the twelve stories that District of Columbia zoning regulations allowed. The ornate corbels and significant upper floor windows added gravitas to the historic building. Morgan and Montgomery occupied the top three floors and employed one hundred sixty people. Partners and key support personnel enjoyed luxurious offices beyond the well-appointed reception areas on the twelfth floor, which also housed a paneled boardroom and a second large conference room with video-teleconferencing capabilities.

Antonio's recent promotion brought him from the bullpen and cubicle farms of the tenth floor up to the modest but comfortable offices on the eleventh floor. The royal blue carpeting, large windows, and glass office dividers gave the eleventh floor an ethereal, open feel.

In the tenth-floor kitchenette, Rocco grabbed a ceramic mug from the cupboard and placed it below the single-cup coffee maker. He looked at his reflection from the metal and plastic coffee machine, checking his hair and looking to see if his crow's feet expanded since the last time he checked. Detecting no changes, he smiled approvingly. *Not bad for a 40-year-old.*

He stopped and grabbed his notepad from his tiny office. As one of the firm's two investigators, he rated a small office so he could lock up confidential information. He felt no complaints about the size of his quarters. His paycheck nearly doubled since he retired after twenty years as a police detective. Even better, his new salary was in addition to collecting his police pension.

Rocco slipped past the elevator door as another passenger departed and pressed eleven. As he gathered his thoughts, he tried not to be distracted by the opulence of the law firm's elevators in comparison to the dingy elevators at police headquarters.

"Look at my little brother in his big office," Rocco said, arriving at Antonio's doorway.

"Happy Tuesday, Roc. What's going on?"

"I am certainly loving civilian life. No one shooting at me. Thanks for telling me about this job. Imagine what Mom would think about us working together at the same firm. Starbucks coffee in the break room. Somebody wake me, I'm dreaming."

"How is Marta?"

"The bride is quite well. Seven years to the date since our wedding, and we now have a bun in the oven."

Startled, Antonio bounded from behind his desk and tackled his brother with a hug. "No way! That is the best news I've heard in forever. What is it? When is she due?"

"Sylvia probably knows all about it already. She and Marta are tight, but I got enlightened last night in a most unique way."

"How's that?"

"I thought I surprised her with dinner at the French restaurant, but when we got there, Marta asked for a table for three. So, I'm like, who is the third? I keep looking at my watch. Finally, I ask Marta who is joining us, and is he or she still coming, or can we go ahead and order. For Pete's sake, I got hungry. She just said, 'Oh, we are all here.' So, I tell her that I only see two people. She says, 'Give it time. You will see three.' The words made my brain melt. Then, I got kind of choked up and couldn't talk until I drank a bunch of ice water."

"I'll bet the two of you are on cloud nine."

"I have never been happier. Never."

"I hope this doesn't make Sylvia want another one," Antonio said. "She and Marta like to do everything together."

The phone rang and Antonio noticed the label: twelfth-floor reception. "I have to take this," he said.

"Your 9:30 appointment is waiting in the conference room for you," Jenna said.

After telling the receptionist he would be right up and offering a wave as Rocco exited, Antonio checked his e-mail and calendar. He found no listing for a 9:30 appointment on his calendar. He scooped up his notepad portfolio, silver pen, and jacket. If a partner said he had a 9:30, he had a 9:30, but why couldn't they give him a little chance to prepare?

The conference room could easily seat sixteen people around the large glass and metal table. When Antonio peered in through the glass door, he saw just two people in the room. Only the partner's face looked in his direction; the guest's back was to the door. Richard Montgomery signaled for Antonio to enter and sit next to him, opposite their guest. As he circled the blonde woman, he recognized their visitor—Emalyn Martin. A month had passed since the Pocono Grand Prix. Antonio hadn't thought much about the wreck or Emalyn for several weeks.

"Good to see you, Mrs. Martin."

"You too, Antonio. Please, call me Emalyn."

After shaking Emalyn's outstretched hand, Antonio sat next to his boss.

Montgomery cleared his throat. "Antonio, I brought you in on this specifically at the request of Mrs. Martin. She tells me she knows you, that you in fact witnessed the Pocono racing accident last month."

"Well, yes, but—"

"Let me bring you up to speed," Montgomery continued, cutting Antonio off. "You'll probably hear about this on the news tonight, but Emalyn has been indicted in Federal District Court for the death of George Meloncamp. The FBI believes someone planted a bomb on or in Meloncamp's car after officials certified it for the race. The only persons with any possible access to his car seem to be other race teams and security personnel."

"It looks like I am in a lot of trouble, Antonio. I just can't stop running my big, fat mouth. Apparently, all those threats I made against George pointed a big arrow of suspicion straight at me. He's dead, and I'm suspect number one."

"When did the indictment come down?" Antonio asked.

"Last Friday, right after the pole qualifying for Talladega. So far, the stock car racing union hasn't suspended me, but I expect they will soon enough. The faster we can get suspicion off me and onto the real killer, the better. We could lose hundreds of thousands of dollars if I get suspended for the rest of the year."

"Antonio is one of our best lawyers," Montgomery said. "Normally, only a partner would serve as first chair on such a high-profile case, but since you already have a connection to Antonio, we can make an exception. Antonio, I have every confidence that you can handle this case; my only concern is with Mrs. Martin's notoriety. Can you deal with the media attention this may bring?"

"I believe so, sir," Antonio replied, hoping he sounded more confident than he felt.

"Good," Montgomery replied, obviously expecting no other response. "You are in good hands with Antonio, Mrs. Martin. Fortunately, we also have his brother on staff—a former police detective and an excellent investigator—who will look into this matter and work closely with Antonio."

"That sounds good to me," Emalyn said in a soft voice. "I knew when I met you in the Poconos that I could trust you, Antonio. Something about you screams noble to me. When I got the legal papers, your card still graced my desk at home. I called and made an appointment right away."

"Our firm has offices in Pennsylvania, and we will expend whatever effort is necessary to clear your name," Montgomery promised. "You are being charged in federal court, and Antonio will lead your defense."

Antonio spoke up. "Emalyn, what else do you know so far? Is there anything that you've found out or heard through the grapevine that might help us get started with the investigation? Why do the police suspect you?" Antonio observed Emalyn as she prepared to answer.

"Obviously, the ongoing feud with Meloncamp and my regrettable statements about him led them to my door. The profile of explosive residue used to blow up his car is similar to some explosive that my husband, Sean, used in Afghanistan, back in his Army days. The cops may have other evidence too, but that's referenced in this document. That and a bunch of other stuff I don't understand completely. The actual charge is conspiracy. I guess that's because neither one of us can be traced directly to Meloncamp's car during the period when the bomb must have been planted."

"Who do you think might be responsible?" Antonio asked.

"That is awfully hard to say," Emalyn began. "Since he epitomized a lying sack of ... succotash, it could have been anyone. Any one of the top ten or twenty drivers would benefit from his death. I have trouble picturing another driver being responsible, but the business people behind some of the teams ..." Her voice trailed off for a moment. "Drivers live for the competition and the chance to race each other into an early grave." Emalyn paused and chuckled sarcastically. "Just plain killing another driver would take all the sport out of it."

Antonio replied that perhaps other drivers drove more ruthlessly than her, but Emalyn shook her head in opposition. The head motion sent her dangly earrings swinging.

"No, no—don't you see? Any argument for suspecting another driver is just as strong an argument for suspecting me, and I swear, none of them are valid. We all have too much to lose. Why would anyone throw away their racing career? It is so hard to get to be a driver and to get a car. Once you're in, the only thing you care about is staying behind the wheel."

Antonio pushed further. "Are you sure there's nothing else you can tell us?"

"Some racing teams, successful or not, are always having money troubles. George drove for one of those teams. I suppose it is possible that his owner may have stood to gain a bunch of insurance money in the event he died in a race. Mine is written that way, double pay-off if I buy it on the track."

"Okay, we will check into that. Our retainer is going to be $50,000 to start. It could go up three or four times that if we go to trial. Then, we will bill you monthly," Antonio explained. "At first, most of the costs will cover our investigator turning up as many facts and other plausible suspects as possible. We will keep an eye on the D.A.'s office and file any pre-trial motions that are appropriate as we go along. Do you want us to proceed?"

Emalyn gulped and, if anything, looked all the more worried when she heard the fee for the retainer; but she didn't question it. Instead, she said, "Thank you so much, Antonio—and Richard. I have a really good feeling about having you as my lawyers. Let's get going clearing my name."

"We can handle it," Antonio assured her. "I will be in touch later this week."

* * *

The next day, Rocco drove his Pathfinder to the Poconos and checked in at the same hotel where Antonio and Emalyn first met. After checking into the bungalow where Emalyn stayed, he talked to most of the hotel staff about Emalyn and her husband, Sean. He also retraced their steps to the Gilbert Supper Club, where she and Sean met with her team sponsors and owner. There he met an aging and overly made-up waitress named Delores, who gave Rocco the low-down on Emalyn and her party.

"Yeah, she sat right over there with a big group. They monopolized table five for at least two hours. I'm not complaining though. I served them, and they left a very hefty tip on top of the eighteen percent surcharge. Race weekends are always great for us servers and the busboys, what with all the fancy out-of-towners."

Delores's gravelly voice, damaged from years of cigarettes and hard living, would have distracted a detective with less experience, but Rocco focused on her words. He wrote everything down even if the words seemed inconsequential.

"Did you pick up much of their conversation about the upcoming race?"

"Of course not. I mind my own business." Delores curled her lip on one side and looked at Rocco expectantly. Not immediately making her intentions clear, she scratched her scalp through layers of sprayed hair. Rocco pulled out a twenty-dollar bill and handed it to Delores. She tucked it into her blouse pocket with bony fingers.

"I may have picked up a morsel or two. Not that I pried or hovered or anything. Just that same courteous service I give all my customers."

As his custom dictated so many times with informants, Rocco looked through Delores, his expression telling her to move the story along. She got the hint.

"It seemed that Emalyn's sponsors wanted her to tone down some of her comments about other drivers. They felt it was bad for business. A little rivalry is a good thing, but they wanted her likable enough to sell her merchandise. Who wants to buy T-shirts and decals and things from a sourpuss?"

"Emalyn in particular?" Rocco asked.

"Yes. And others too. You see, her sponsors are always trying to portray her as this sexy Dolly Parton type, but she's more of a sassy, blonde Shania Twain if you ask me. Anyway, she sounded all agreeable and everything. Truth is, her promises aren't sincere at all. She mouthed off to George Meloncamp the very next night right at our theater just down the road. They wrote it all up in the paper on that Sunday. Then, that very same day, she kills George in that race. I just think she can't control her mouth or her actions. She gets around some people she doesn't like and wham! She kicks them right in the caboose."

"We don't know for sure that she bore any responsibility for Meloncamp's car exploding, do we?"

"She knocked him into that wall like Kyle Schwarber knocks home-runs. She sent Meloncamp into Forever Land."

Across the room, a thin, balding man wiped down the bar with a stained, whitish towel. "Aw, Delores, you don't know what yer talking about."

The waitress stuck her nose in the air and strutted off with Rocco's twenty. He could tell that Delores had spilled her last secret for the day. Realizing his first source of information took off to catch a smoke break, he decided to ask the bartender what he meant. The man with the rag snickered. "She couldn't tell the difference between a routine quarter panel bumping incident in a stock car race and a car being blown to bits by a bomb. If I was you, buddy, I'd check out the RaceRX Racing Team. If Emalyn didn't kill George directly, someone at RaceRX done it. They wanted both Emalyn and Meloncamp out of the way so their golden boy could drive off with this year's championship."

"Okay, I will follow up that lead. Did any of the other drivers say or do anything pertinent to the death of George Meloncamp?"

"Not really. Most of them just keep to themselves. The Marshall kid sat at the bar a while on Saturday night."

"The driver for Foyt Racing?" Rocco asked.

"Yeah, that's the one. You don't see too many stock car drivers drinking to excess in the middle of the season. They get blood tests.

Anyway, Marshall seemed in a talkative mood. Per him, Meloncamp planned to take Emalyn out before the end of the season. Apparently, Meloncamp felt it his duty to stock car racing to take care of Emalyn before he retired."

"Any idea how he planned to get rid of her?"

"No. That's all he said."

"Thanks again. I will follow up."

Next, Rocco drove out to the Pocono track and caught up with Tom Bailey, the lead inspector for the stock car union. As he approached the man, he tried not to notice the significant acne scarring Bailey's cheeks. Notwithstanding the pock marks, a bright smile welcomed Rocco.

"Hi, I'm Rocco Semones. I work with Emalyn Martin's defense team."

"Oh yes, you called ahead," said Tom Bailey, repositioning his ball cap. "You showed a lot more consideration than the FBI did. They just swooped in unannounced and confiscated most of the wreckage. So, if you're looking for evidence, you're too late, sorry."

"Oh, that's no problem. As a non-expert on car racing, I'm just trying to understand what happened at the track that day and why George Meloncamp died. Emalyn is in some legal trouble related to the accident. This is just background information for the lawyers that make up Emalyn's defense team."

"Finding out what happened is why we're all here," Bailey said. "Stock cars do not routinely blow up like that. Everything about the design and most of the materials used in the car specifically guard against fire and explosions. From the video, it's clear to me that explosives did the damage. The FBI is supposed to be here again today, but they already found a few bits of residue and went off half-cocked in my estimation."

"Do you think Emalyn is responsible for George Meloncamp's death?"

"Yes and no. Her car ran loose that day. That just means that her steering underperformed, not working exactly right. When she banked in the turns, her car went sideways. She compensated or overcompensated, some would say, and fishtailed toward other drivers. In Meloncamp's case, he tried to pass, even though his team probably told him to be cautious around her. When she saw him coming up behind her on the outside, she may or may not have let the car slide into him a bit, with no love lost between those two. But she couldn't have been looking for a wreck. She is too close to the top of the point standings to risk not finishing that race."

Rocco pushed for more. "Tell me more about the bad blood between her and Meloncamp."

Tom Bailey went on to explain the long history between Emalyn and George. It started with comments George made about the sexy new female driver trying to invade their man's world. "A lot of the good ol' boys liked that kind of talk. George sounded like a dinosaur—never politically correct or even polite for that matter. The words turned into aggressive behavior on the track, and eventually, Emalyn began jostling his car back when she could. Emalyn forced Meloncamp out of races twice while managing to finish the race herself. He didn't like a girl, or woman, getting the best of him."

"So, you agree with the FBI that someone planted a bomb aboard Meloncamp's car?"

"One has to start with that supposition. The replays show the explosion emanating from the right rear quarter panel. As I said, these cars don't just explode on their own. The FBI found what is likely residue from a bomb. But the clincher is the size of the explosion. There is nothing on the car—not even the fuel tank—that could explode that big."

"When are cars inspected prior to the race, and who has access to them after the inspection?"

Bailey pondered the question before giving a multi-part answer. "There are specific times the car is checked. Race officials look for certain things before the qualifying on Saturday and before the actual race on Sunday." He paused. "What you're asking is, when could someone plant a bomb on the car? That is a tough one. Cars are locked down after the Saturday afternoon inspection and no one can get to them again until Sunday morning. Teams get their cars back at about the same time on Sunday, so there is no long period when the cars are left unattended and not locked up. I don't see how someone could gain access once the cars are locked up. Frankly, that is where I've spent a lot of my time. If there is a security weakness at our tracks, I want to diagnose it and close the gap for good."

Rocco suggested the two men walk around the facility so Bailey could explain the process each time the car is stored and moved. They spent about an hour going through the unloading deck, the garage areas, and the short distance from the garages to the track. They examined the bay where Meloncamp's car may have been fatally fitted with an explosive device. Later, they walked almost the length of the facility to the stall Emalyn's car occupied. The two garages sat positioned hundreds of feet apart.

"If someone tampered with his car in the garage area, it would more likely be someone from one of the teams near George's assigned garage," Bailey said. "An outsider would stick out like a sore thumb. Mechanics from the other teams possibly."

"Who occupied the bays on either side of Meloncamp?"

Motioning with his hands, Bailey said, "Foyt Racing occupied the east side, and RaceRX had the other side."

"Do you suspect either of those teams?"

"No reason to suspect them yet," Bailey replied.

"I am not alleging it, just asking your opinion."

"My opinion is anyone in front of or behind George Meloncamp in the points standings owned a motive. Or it could be terrorism, or it could be an ex-girlfriend. It could be the owners of his car got into financial trouble and wanted to cash in on his insurance policy. Who knows at this point?"

"Well, thank you for your time. Here's my card in case you think of something more." Rocco shook Bailey's hand then turned and began the walk up and out of the racetrack infield.

Next, Rocco left the Poconos and aimed his car in the direction of the suburbs of Philadelphia, pondering the unpleasant task ahead of him: talking to George Meloncamp's people to find out what, if anything, they knew. On his way he made two calls, first to Antonio to bring him up to date on his meeting at Pocono and tell him about the Philadelphia excursion. Antonio warned Rocco that the conversation probably would not be pleasant, but they needed whatever information

Rocco could get out of George Meloncamp's racing team. After he finished with his brother, Rocco talked to Marta for a few minutes—mainly about their plans for when he returned. Then, he selected a Patricia Cornwell audio book from his laptop and played it via Bluetooth through the car's speakers.

The miles between Pocono Raceway and the Philly suburbs flew by fast with the whodunit unwinding on his audio system. Rocco's rental car soon wove through posh neighborhoods, and he admired the well-groomed lawns. He would later report to Marta how much he dreaded talking to those associated with George Meloncamp's team following such a devastating loss only a few weeks earlier. Like many tasks in detective work, they stink while you're doing them, but the pay-off comes when the mystery is solved. How Rocco loved giving everyone closure. This side of Rocco delighted Antonio. His brother could dig into and complete an arduous task while others would still be complaining about the size or smell of the job.

Rocco kept very detailed notes about this meeting and all of his casework. The meeting with Frank Winston was no different.

The modern colonial home sat on two-thirds of an acre. The front yard looked small, but towering trees in the back hinted at the views from inside the house. A well-dressed redhead answered the door and showed Rocco into a paneled office to the left of the front entryway. Two large windows with colonial grids framed a glass table, probably used as a writing desk. Rocco snapped two quick pictures of the office on his phone. Later, Antonio would remark to Rocco about the two golf trophies on the credenza. The large silver and brass trophies represented wins, including the U.S. Amateur many years earlier.

Rocco noticed only two things sitting on the desk: a three-by-two-foot calendar and a laptop, closed and sitting atop the calendar. The cord from the laptop trailed over the side of the table, eventually leading to the floor outlet under the table. One wall of the office featured color photos of racecars in victory lanes. Most of them included George Meloncamp, often with flowers around his neck or some local beauty queen kissing his cheek. Rocco's camera clicked as he took more pictures. Footsteps on the hardwood floors indicated someone approaching the room.

"Frank Winston, glad to meet you." The owner of Rally Farms Racing extended his hand to Rocco.

"Likewise, and thank you for seeing me so soon after the accident," Rocco said. "I'm sorry for your loss."

Winston took his place in a large leather chair behind the glass desk, while Rocco sat in a reproduction Windsor chair. A grandfather clock ticked from one corner of the room, emphasizing the passage of time with every tick-tock. The team owner sported a deep tan, his face weathered from many days at the racetrack or the golf course ... or both. Winston's white hair and glasses reminded Rocco of the Fairfax County, Virginia elite with whom he sometimes came into contact in his days as a police detective. They always seemed to be the victims of crimes and never the accused.

"It shocked all of us, obviously. We're still recovering."

"Yes. It must be very hard. You know why I am here. Emalyn retained our law firm to investigate and defend her. While she feels terrible about what happened to George, she needs us to understand completely what happened out on the track and beyond."

"Let me stop you there for a minute. In my opinion, Emalyn Martin is trash and the epitome of everything that is going wrong in this sport. She is aggressive, can't drive well, and uses the track to compensate for other problems in her life. While I doubt that her antics on the track at Pocono solely resulted in George's death, I also believe that he would be alive if she hadn't lost control of her car and pushed him into that wall."

Rocco remained silent for a moment, as much to let Winston simmer down as to collect his own thoughts. The interview started off on the wrong foot, and he wanted to redirect it before Winston threw him out on his ear.

"Do you know of anyone, besides Emalyn, who may have wanted George Meloncamp dead?"

"George drove professionally for many years. Over the course of a career, I'm sure he rubbed some people the wrong way. But any of them could have latched onto a hundred chances to get even with him. I've asked myself, what is different lately? Who is new in George's life, or who is mad at him now? The only answer is Emalyn. She screamed at him at a theater the same weekend as the race. Their feud fed the appetites of people inside and outside of our sport." Winston pressed his lips together.

"Obviously it has been all over the media that explosives are suspected to be the reason the car blew up. Do you agree that is likely?"

Winston leaned back in his chair and thought for a moment. "I've never seen a car explode like that before," he admitted. "If the investigators eventually come to that conclusion, I can accept it."

"Can you see any way that someone, apart from those on your race team, could have gotten access to the car to plant an explosive device?"

"If someone used a bomb, I can guarantee you no one on our team played any part in it. The guys loved George. Their livelihood depended on him. Most of them have been working with George for fifteen years or more. No one from our team would have benefitted from his going down, particularly since he ranked so high in the point standings. This seemed likely to be his last championship season. I'm positive he would have retired if he won the crown. Everyone on the team would get bonuses if he won. Why would they kill him?"

"I understand," Rocco said. "Is it possible that someone not involved with racing wanted to hurt George or even you for that matter? As team owner, his death couldn't have been good for you."

"True," Winston said, scratching his forehead. "While George's death is a monetary hit for me, larger in total dollars than you would imagine, I have all the money I need. Several years ago, I sold most of my stock in the company I founded. Racing is a hobby for me. The money is just peanuts. I love action, but I'm not expecting to make a lot of dough out of it. If someone wanted to get at me, this made a pretty dumb way to go about it. No, I'm pretty sure George drew someone's ire and the rationale seems transparent."

"Would it be okay if I talked to the people on your race team? I just want to get a better handle on what happened to George."

"No! I'm not going to allow you to do a fishing expedition on my team. You are looking for someone else to pin the murder on. If you have specific questions, submit them through my lawyer's office. Here is his business card."

Winston handed the pricey-looking parchment card to Rocco. The interview went nowhere. Rocco cut the conversation shorter than he would have liked and returned to his car. He listened to more of his audiobook and thought about everything he'd heard so far. He raced down Interstate 95, hurrying home to Marta and their unborn baby.

CHAPTER FIVE

Sylvia packed sandwiches and snacks in the blue mini-cooler: turkey and gouda with pickle relish and mustard for Antonio. Marc preferred turkey and swiss with lettuce, tomato, and mayo. She arranged a mix of carrot sticks, celery, and pieces of cucumber in two plastic lunch bags. Small containers of ranch dressing rounded out the snacks.

"Wow. That looks good, hon," Antonio remarked.

"Remind Marc to wash his face with the medicine stuff at night and in the morning. If he forgets and you guys eat a bunch of greasy stuff, he will have an acne outbreak right before basketball practice starts up for fall."

"Yes, dear." Antonio tried to sound nagged, though his wife's care for their son just made him appreciate her more. If they could have five more children, he would be on board. The emotional strain of several miscarriages over their seventeen years of marriage left them reluctant to try for another pregnancy.

"Marta and I are going to try out that new Thai restaurant at Ballston," Sylvia said. "Bev and her sister are meeting us there, and you know how loud we get. If you need me, text me, because I won't be able to hear the phone in the restaurant."

"We won't need you. It's only two hours down there, traffic permitting. Emalyn is meeting Rocco and me for an early supper to strategize for the hearing next week."

"Marc is going to a business meeting with you and Rocco?"

"No, Emalyn and Sean are meeting Rocco and me. One of Marc's former basketball coaches is running a clinic down there this afternoon," Antonio said. "Lots of college scouts are supposed to be there. If everything works out right, I will drop him off. They will run him silly up and down the basketball court while I go to my meeting. Hopefully, he will get noticed and receive a scholarship offer. Later, I will pick him up, check into the hotel, and we will both get some sleep. The race is tomorrow."

"If only life worked out so conveniently on the scholarship offer. Besides, what would we do with his college fund money?"

"I'm picturing us on a five-month sabbatical in Australia with the college fund money."

"That sounds nice, Antonio. I take it Emalyn still isn't suspended?"

"No. Since the matter seems up in the air to the stock car sanctioning body, they are letting her race. I wish the prosecutor would give her as much benefit of the doubt. I guess he doesn't get any extra money when she races, like the sport does. She is one massive draw."

Marc sauntered into the kitchen wearing basketball shorts and a practice jersey over a T-shirt. Antonio hoped the duffle bag he carried contained at least one change of shirts and underwear.

"Do you have everything you need to wear tomorrow?" Sylvia asked.

"Yes, Mom. No, Mom. Love you, Mom," Marc answered playfully. He bent down and kissed his petite mother on the cheek. He placed his bag on the cooler, grabbed the handles, and headed out to the car.

Having grown up taller than average, Antonio knew what it felt like to tower over his mom. Although the physical size made it hard for Marc to accept discipline from his mother, she could still run circles around him psychologically. Her teaching credentials and experience made her a master at understanding and shaping young minds.

Sylvia kissed Antonio, letting her eyes linger on his handsome face. Antonio could see the ambivalence in her eyes. He knew his wife didn't want him to go, but he saw a huge stack of ungraded papers sitting on the coffee table. The night alone would give her peace and quiet to complete her backlog.

The trip to Richmond went mercifully fast after Antonio got past the Fredericksburg exit. Marc studied the plays he needed to know for the basketball clinic that afternoon. As unpredictable as Saturday traffic can be, Antonio thanked God that it moved along at a steady pace.

When he looked up from the mini-playbook, Marc asked Antonio a surprising question. "How did you actually start believing in God? For yourself, I mean? I know the story of how you accepted Christ. You told me like thirty times, but how did you actually come to believe there even is a God and that he cares about you as a unique human being?"

Antonio gripped the steering wheel a little harder, and a flush came to his cheeks. How would he answer the question? What motivated Marc to ask? He prayed a quick prayer, not wanting to mess up what could be an amazing God moment with his son.

"Well, Marc, it all happened kind of fast. During an altar call at church, I heard a voice telling me to go down front. I asked the voice, "Are you God?"

"'Yes, I am,' He said. Then the voice encouraged me to believe what they were telling me and to go down front. The whole experience overwhelmed me at first, to know that God exists. Since then, I've rode spiritual ups and downs, but you learn more about Jesus and God as you go along in your relationship. Remember that Jesus only asked his disciples to follow him, not believe the whole kit and caboodle right off the bat. That's why I study the Bible and go to church. God keeps teaching me something new about himself, and what I already know sinks in deeper."

"I don't know if I've ever heard that voice. Do you think I'm a Christian?"

"God doesn't do exactly the same thing with every person. Maybe he is using some other way to tell you he is real, something specific for your personality. How does it feel when you go to church with your mom and me?"

"It feels good, actually. Sometimes during the sermon, I get bored, probably since you don't let me take my phone to church. But I feel warm and good inside. It's like a special warmth that makes me know church is the right way to spend Sunday morning."

"I believe the Holy Spirit witnesses when we hear God's Word, letting us know we are in the right place. It is a feeling you will have your whole life. It is meant to guide you home to God and to keep you seeking him. I think of it as a light when I feel a little lost. Psalm 119:105 puts it this way: "Thy Word is a Lamp unto my feet, and a light unto my path.""

"Do you believe God will talk to me like he talked to you?"

"He wants to communicate with each of his creations. People block him out with all kinds of things: television shows, hobbies, anything. It really is all about serving self or serving God. I know he wants to communicate with you, but it is more than feelings or voices. It is about faith. Can I pray for you now?"

"Sure." Marc bowed his head and Antonio placed his large hand on his son's shoulder. Marc looked up for a second to make sure his Dad kept his eyes open. The car continued down the highway at the speed limit.

"God, Marc wants to hear you for himself and know you for himself. Sometime in the next few days, please speak to Marc and let him know for sure it is you. Whether it is during the day or at night, speak to Marc and give him assurance that you are there and that he is your son."

Antonio paused to think for a moment before ending the prayer.

"Dad! Dad!" Marc yelled.

"Did you hear from God already?"

"No, Dad—there is a yellow jacket on your forehead!"

Startled, Antonio waved his phone excitedly at the bee. Back and forth he swatted at the yellow-and-black critter buzzing in his face.

"Roll down your window, son. Let's shoo him out. Get out of here!" Antonio commanded with one big sweeping motion of his right hand. Unfortunately, his grip on his phone was too loose, causing it to slip out of his hand and conk his son in his left eye.

"Ow!" The phone bounced off Marc's eye and onto the floor. "You whacked me!"

Out of the corner of his eye, Antonio could see that the phone hit Marc in just the right spot; that was going to leave one doozy of a shiner. "Well, you wanted a sign, and I guess you got one," Antonio said, trying not to laugh. Marc put his hand over the injured eye and leaned forward in his seat. He planned to milk this for its full value; probably going to cost a new iPad, Antonio suspected.

"And you did this at a key moment in my spiritual development," Marc said. "I'm pretty sure that's a mortal sin."

"We are not Catholic son, so we don't believe in mortal sins. Let's take the next exit and try to find you some ice to keep the swelling down."

Instead of Antonio's favorite XM channel, Chill 53, they listened to hip hop with only moderately offensive lyrics for the rest of the trip to Richmond. Antonio felt he owed it to Marc, who held the improvised ice pack gingerly under his eye. Antonio tried not to grin at the silly situation he got them into by holding his phone with no intention of using it. Eventually, Antonio found the correct exit just north of Richmond and delivered Marc to the high school for the basketball camp.

"This is Marc Semones," Antonio said to the ladies at the registration desk. They checked the list and marked his name.

"Marc, you can put your gear in the locker room. Just follow the signs," said a middle-aged woman whose nametag read ROSEMARIE. "Use a padlock. We are not responsible for lost or stolen items. Then, go to the gym and start warming up."

"Excuse me, do you know what time the clinic will end? I am picking Marc up afterwards." Antonio flashed his best sheepish look.

"Somewhere between four and five p.m." Rosemarie replied without looking up.

Antonio gave Marc the call me signal with his index and pinky fingers. Marc pantomimed back that he would text him and trotted off toward the locker room. Antonio stared at his son as he walked down the stark, tiled hallway. He thought about how much he loved Marc and how soon their family would change. Marc would head off to college, probably meet some young filly. Antonio and Sylvia would be empty nesters at a very young age, too young.

Just a bit farther down I-95, Rocco waited for his brother at an almost empty Applebee's Restaurant. Antonio arrived just after one p.m. Soon thereafter, he got a text that Emalyn got held up at the track and would be thirty minutes late. The brothers passed the time catching up and going over Rocco's detailed investigative notes. Antonio grinned in admiration as he scanned Rocco's hasty but detailed scrawl. The guy really possessed a gift for extremely vivid descriptions. "Based on your interviews so far, who do you think killed George Meloncamp?"

"That's hard to say," Rocco responded. "No single suspect stands out."

"Did anyone give you any substantive leads?"

"Frankly, none of the people I've talked to know who did it. Apparently, there is a great deal of skepticism that someone within the racing community would kill another driver. There is too much to lose. The drivers have worked their way up over many years. They aren't going to just throw it away by plotting to kill another driver. If the FBI's assumption proves correct that explosives caused George's death—and I'm sure they are the cause—it would take someone with real demolition expertise. So far, the only person in the picture who fits that description is Emalyn's husband, Sean."

Just as Rocco's words began to sink in, another voice commanded their attention.

"Well, sweetie, you are a sight for sore eyes!" Emalyn announced as she entered the restaurant and spied Antonio. Sean trailed at her side.

"Emalyn, Sean. Come sit down and let's talk. I don't believe you've met Rocco, the investigator from our firm."

"Well, it is great to see you again, Antonio," Sean said. "Rocco is also your brother?"

"Yes," Antonio affirmed.

Emalyn hugged Antonio and stuck out her hand to Rocco, who quickly clasped it. "Well, you favor each other. Sorry I'm late; my quali-fication time ran later than we thought because of the rain this morning. Everything got pushed back. The good news is I'm in the third-row tomorrow, just where I like to be."

"That's just where she likes to be when she's not in the pole position," Sean said, sounding like the straight man in a comedy act.

Antonio and Rocco smiled at each other. For just a split second, time stopped, and Antonio completely saw his brother. His face, his hair, his broad shoulders—Antonio sensed God's presence in a strange way. It felt like trying to decode a message without possessing the key. He looked at Rocco throughout their lives as brothers do, but this felt like the first time he totally focused on his brother's face and really saw him. Looking into his eyes, he tried to memorize them.

"Do you want to order food?" Antonio tried to keep the impatience out of his voice, but the extra wait for Emalyn to finish up at the race-track made Antonio a little nervous about finishing on time to pick up Marc. He hoped to speed up the meal and the meeting. A funny feeling crept into Antonio's brain about leaving his son at a strange school in a town where they didn't know anyone.

The waitress breezed over to their table and took drink orders for the two new guests. At Antonio's urging, she also recorded everyone's food order. Emalyn opted for a tuna sandwich with fruit on the side. She planned to share her meal with Sean, but he would have none of it. To her disdain, he ordered his own cheeseburger and fries. "You are going to die of a heart attack just like Lorrie Morgan's third husband ... or fourth ... can't remember which."

Antonio wanted to order something lawyerly but debated between the smothered nachos and the turkey Reuben.

"Not Lorrie Morgan. You're thinking of that other blonde country singer," Sean said, as if only two such animals existed.

"Boys, let's focus." Emalyn feigned a pained expression. Antonio guessed she felt hungry and wanted to get the order in so she would see food before she passed out from low blood sugar.

"Smothered nachos for me," Antonio said, deciding that his legal persona could survive a departure from convention. When the waitress walked away, he looked at Emalyn and Sean. "The reason I wanted to see you in person is because I think the prosecutor is going to increase the charges to murder at the hearing next week. There is something going on, but so far, they are trying to keep it from us."

"Oh, my Lord, no!" Emalyn said. "Is it possible I am going to prison next week?"

"Based on what?" Sean asked.

"They haven't shared any new evidence, but I expect to receive another paper dump tomorrow night. If they do use that strategy, they're hoping we won't have time to read it all before the hearing on Tuesday," Antonio explained. "We have to be prepared for anything. They may try to hold you without bond, Emalyn. It is possible you won't get to come home immediately from the courthouse after the hearing."

For once, Emalyn felt speechless. She sat staring across the table at Antonio. A gentle quivering of her right cheek accompanied the bewilderment in her face. The confidence of the tough-as-nails diva driver began to crack like a mirror, the fault lines small at first, ever growing. That wasn't the picture Antonio wanted to see.

"It is only a possibility, but I want you to be mentally prepared for the worst. Of course, I will argue against it and do everything I can to keep you out of confinement."

"Prison ... you mean I am going to prison. I, I didn't do anything." Emalyn's face continued to twitch.

"And you haven't been found guilty," Antonio said. "The law says you are innocent until proven guilty. They will only keep you without bail if they can convince the judge you are a flight risk or a danger to others. I will argue that you are so well-known that you are not a flight risk."

Antonio moved on to discuss various facets of George Meloncamp's death and the legal strategy involved in proving definitively that Emalyn entertained no real motive, and even less opportunity, to tamper with his car. "Obviously, in a jury trial, if it comes to that, such an approach would be desirable. The prosecution maintains the responsibility to prove your guilt. We don't have to prove you are innocent, but just plant enough reasonable doubt that you can't be convicted."

Antonio explained how he would work to get sympathetic ears in the jury box and how jurors tended to be easier on celebrities. "Your image is everything should we go to trial. We want the entire jury pool to believe there is no way you could have committed any crime, particularly murder."

Rocco then asked a series of background questions about stock car racing, Emalyn's race team, and the car inspection process. Antonio could see Rocco's police radar going off while questioning Sean. Rocco's eyes darted back and forth, more penetrating than before. He leaned closer to Sean as his voice quickened.

"Sean, exactly when and how do the race officials examine the cars before race time?"

"Well, er, they inspect it more than just one time ..." Sean wiggled in his seat and wiped his forehead with a napkin.

"Well, goodness, Sean," Emalyn said. "You know this process like the back of your hand. Just spit it out."

Antonio didn't think Sean meant to lie, necessarily. Rocco's expression spoke volumes, obviously distrustful. Sean knew something relevant and important to his wife's defense but wasn't saying it. Antonio could feel it.

Soon the food arrived, and everyone ate what felt like a last meal, as if food could comfort and soothe everyone's body and soul for more than a moment. At the end of their meal, Antonio declared the mission accomplished. "Thanks everyone. I think we are all on the same page at least for Emalyn's hearing. It should be perfunctory anyway. Look at the time. I have to pick up Marc from his basketball camp. We'll see everyone at the track tomorrow morning for the race."

* * *

On Sunday morning, Antonio and Marc arrived at the Richmond Raceway just before starting time. "Hi, Rocco. What did you find out?"

"Hey there, Marc, Antonio." Rocco looked alert, though casual, in his polo shirt and khakis, Antonio thought.

"I spent the morning watching the procedures, including unlocking the gate to the garages. While the gate and fencing provide a level of security, it would be easy enough for someone to breach the perimeter of the garage areas overnight. Tom Bailey, the same inspector who met me at Pocono, took me on a tour. We looked at some of the other team garages. One thing I am sure about is that once all the teams got back into their garage areas, it would be very difficult for anyone to tamper with another team's racecar. Too many people are around and strangers would stick out and be noticed."

Rocco told Antonio about him and Bailey interacting with Team RaceRX. "One of the mechanics looked mildly familiar to me, but I couldn't place him; the dark hair and average, Caucasian features did little to make the man stand out. It bugs me though. As a former cop, too often the familiar faces represent unsavory characters from old cases. Perhaps the man could have been just a witness or a family member of a crime victim. I just can't be sure where I knew him from."

"Can I help you with something?" a man asked. The name Gene embroidered on his RaceRX coveralls, a towering giant walked toward Rocco.

"I'm Rocco Semones, with Emalyn's legal team." Rocco extended his hand, but the man showed Rocco two greasy mitts.

"Gene Chisolm, RaceRX mechanical team. We're kind of busy. Can I help you?"

"Just wondering if you saw anything unusual at Pocono just before George Meloncamp's crash."

"Not really. The pre-race and race routine seemed the same until Emalyn bumped George and his car exploded. Talk about different. You don't see racecars explode like that much."

"Any idea how a car could blow up like that?"

"I suppose anything is possible, but to me ... it looked like explosives must have been wired to George's car. In twenty-five years in and around racing, I've never seen anything explode like that or so thoroughly demolish a car."

"Any theories about who or why?"

As he formulated his answer, a voice called Gene's name.

"Be right there," the mechanic said over his shoulder. "Look I have to go, but honestly, I don't have any idea why George's car blew up or why he lost his life. Emalyn possessed the most visible bad blood feud with George, but racecar drivers get into beefs with each other all the time. It comes with the territory. Hard to believe anyone would intentionally kill another driver."

The familiar refrain: that recurring denial of a motive for killing another driver. Rocco didn't know what to think of it. "Thanks for your time. Here is my card if you think of anything else."

Rocco and Bailey traced the route from the garage to pit road, eventually coming to the stall where Emalyn's car would pit during the race. Her team went about their pre-race rituals. Antonio joined them down in the pits. Rocco talked with Millard Estes again and shared the little information he gathered in his recent visit to Pocono. Antonio thought Millard seemed more on edge than he had at Pocono. Rocco's police instincts told him to press in, but Estes became occupied with something about the rear end on Emalyn's car. He asked Rocco to call him the following week to continue their discussion.

Antonio introduced Rocco to Millard's son and hovered nearby as they talked.

"Jesse Estes, I'm Millard's son."

"Rocco Semones. I'm looking into George Meloncamp's death for Emalyn's defense team."

"Yeah, that explosion freaked everyone out," Jesse said.

"Any theories about how someone could get a bomb planted on one of the cars?"

"If a person gets determined enough, he can do about anything. The garage areas are locked up after final inspections, but these racetracks aren't exactly Fort Knox. I'm sure anyone on the circuit could figure a way back in, say if they forgot something."

"And how would they do that?" Rocco asked.

"Just talk to the guard or sneak through the fence," Jesse said.

"Have you ever needed to get back in?"

"Not personally, but some of these teams manage to make small adjustments to their cars Saturday night. It's called cheating, but how else could a car that barely qualified run several miles-per-hour faster on Sunday? You tell me."

"I don't know," Rocco answered.

Just then, the all-clear signal blared loudly. Antonio, Rocco, and

Bailey left the pit area, just missing Emalyn, who ran late coming from her travel trailer to the pit area. The three men went up to their seats, meeting Marc who apparently stayed busy eating nachos and drinking sodas while Antonio and Rocco met with Bailey. A hotdog wrapper and an empty box with cheese dripped on it sat where Antonio would put his feet.

"Go dump this in the trash, buddy," Antonio said.

When he returned, the three settled in to watch the race and laugh about some of Rocco's famous police stories from when he was on the force.

About halfway through the race, Rocco stood up. "I need to head back to Washington. I'm flying out to Ohio in the morning if the office ever calls with my flight information."

"Okay, Roc," Antonio said. "Keep in touch."

Rocco fluffed up Marc's hair. "See you, kid. Let's head to the gym when I get back for some more hoops."

"You bet, Uncle Rocco," Marc said.

The race itself unfolded in typical hard-fought fashion. The lead changed hands many times and Emalyn stayed in the thick of it. Junior led for more than twenty laps near the end of the race, until the eighth to last lap. Antonio and Marc cheered as Emalyn pulled in front of the Toyota Sinclair car, putting her in the lead. The crowd erupted, a cacophonous mix of cheers and boos. Whereas Emalyn almost uniformly drew cheers at Pocono, other emotions now spewed out of some in the racing crowds since the death of George Meloncamp. Hero or villain, Emalyn produced the same effect. She sold a lot of tickets for her sport.

"Some of these people don't care for Emalyn now," Marc said, dejected.

"That's how life is, son. One day we sit on top of the heap, and another day the crowd finds a new darling. The important thing is to hold onto your integrity. If you know you've tried to do the right thing, it doesn't matter so much what others say or write about you."

Emalyn's car soared around the track and held off Junior at the back turn. Just one more lap to go, and everyone jumped to their feet again. Emalyn expended everything her car could give, racing all out for the checkered flag. Junior finished two car lengths back as Emalyn won at Richmond. Marc jumped up and down, waving Emalyn's team towel that Millard Estes gave him.

According to custom, she celebrated her win with donuts in the infield, spinning her tires and tearing up grass as she went. Emalyn eventually burned rubber in Victory Lane and threw off her helmet as soon as she parked. Antonio and Marc watched through binoculars as she drank the sponsor's soft drink and spiked the empty bottle down on the pavement. The win put her squarely in first place in the point standings and on the front page of the sports sections in many cities.

For good or bad, the win pulled the spotlight in Emalyn's direction. The next day, several sports columnists would debate the wisdom of her continuing to race while being suspected of murdering another racer. Everyone would have an opinion, but for these few moments in the winner's circle, Emalyn and Sean could not have cared less. They seemed happy again, with racing and with each other. Winning resolves a multitude of problems. Sean stood with his arm around Emalyn, so proud of her. Cameras took hundreds of pictures. And everything felt right in their made-up world.

After a quick post-race meal at a Mexican restaurant, Antonio and Marc hit the road back to Washington. Antonio's stomach felt so full, he imagined that he waddled as he made his way to the car. Marc even groaned a little as he folded himself into the passenger's seat. Just a few miles after they began their trip north on I-95, strange feelings invaded Antonio's thoughts. A car seemed to track with their lane changes. *Were he and Marc being followed?*

Antonio sensed a dark presence, something felt before. From back during his ride-share driving days when he ferried people around to pay for law school and living expenses, this sensation haunted him like a doppelganger from the past. In the rearview mirror, he watched a Mustang, dark blue or maybe black, tailing him lane change after lane change. Thinking perhaps the mustang's moves reflected a mere coincidence, Antonio slowed down to sixty-five miles per hour. Still, the Mustang stayed two or three car lengths back. Antonio could feel sweat in his armpits.

He sped up to eighty miles per hour. Again, the Mustang followed, changing lanes with Antonio's Audi as they passed other cars and semis.

With Marc in the car, Antonio felt differently about danger. Not just his own life and health, he also had to protect his son. "God don't let Marc get hurt in all this," Antonio prayed silently.

At one point, the Mustang drifted back a few car lengths. For a few seconds, lights from a large highway interchange illuminated the interior of the Mustang. Antonio got only a glimpse. He saw the driver of the Mustang, a white man with dark hair, but few distinguishing features stuck out in a momentary glance at night.

Eventually, Antonio saw a road sign, reading STATE POLICE NEXT EXIT. He decided to get off I-95 and see if the Mustang followed. If he did, Antonio would drive to the police station. If the Mustang didn't follow, Antonio would chalk it up to early mid-life paranoia. He didn't tell Marc the reason for his exit. Marc remained so engrossed in his tablet video game that he failed to notice the drama unfolding behind them.

The Mustang followed Antonio closely down the exit ramp and pulled up right behind the Audi at the stop sign. Because he glanced back often in his rearview mirror, Antonio failed to see the sign indicating which direction to turn for the state police post. He guessed wrong; the Mustang followed close behind. Antonio decided to turn into a busy gas station and figure out once and for all the intentions of the Mustang's driver. The nefarious pursuer also turned into the gas station. Cars blocked Antonio's view of the Mustang. *What to do?*

Antonio pulled through the rows of pumps but didn't stop. He accelerated, throwing up gravel as he exited the service station. In a split-second decision, he turned away from I-95 and headed toward the countryside where he felt confident the police post must be very near.

Antonio looked around anxiously for any sign of the police outpost. He thought their station house must be up ahead in the next mile or two, but he guessed wrong again. Then, just as he sped up, he heard a single gunshot from the trailing car.

"Dad, what ... what's going on?" Marc's voice grew louder, punctuated with the staccato cadence of fear. "Is that car following us?"

Although the bullet missed their car, the near panic in Marc's voice sliced right through Antonio. "Dad, he's shooting at us!?"

Glancing over at Marc and seeing the fear written on his face, Antonio tried to comfort him. "Don't worry, son. God is taking care of us."

"Dad, look out!" Marc yelled as the Mustang tried to pull alongside, eventually bumping the Audi's rear fender.

Holding the car on the road, Antonio continued to accelerate, taking them farther and farther from the main highway—and the state police. A second bullet flew through the back windshield, blowing a big chunk out of the center and raining pebbles of glass down on Marc and Antonio.

The distraction of the breaking glass caused Antonio to look back just as he entered a sharp curve. *Too much speed.* The expensive tires tried desperately to grip the road but to no avail. The Audi ran over the embankment and slid down the steep but mercifully short hill. The car slid sideways and continued down the hill.

Marc's urgent voice cried out: "Dad, help me!"

Antonio tried to put his hand between Marc and the windshield. Almost at the bottom of the hill, the air bags deployed as the Audi rolled over. Antonio's hand roughly connected with Marc's face, breaking Antonio's middle finger and Marc's nose. The headlights remained on as the car landed on its roof. The dust began to settle, along with a deathly quiet. Nature paused to digest what happened. Crickets ceased their chirping, and a hoot owl waited as it processed the interruption. Antonio felt his consciousness slipping away.

CHAPTER SIX

On the shuttle from long-term parking to the airport terminal, Rocco spotted a well-known country singer clutching her guitar case, lost in her thoughts. Rocco wanted to say something to her about how much he enjoyed her latest release. He tried to think of something clever or charming, but the look on her face told him, "Go away. Not now." When she noticed Rocco continued staring, she gave him a straight-forward look as if to say, "Yes, it's really me. So, what?"

Rocco lost his nerve. The shuttle ride ended, and he hustled into the terminal. After going through security, he found a comfortable spot and dialed his wife.

"Marta, my love, I'm at the airport."

"I thought you would come home tonight."

"Change of plans. Sharon from the office couldn't get me a reasonably-priced flight for tomorrow morning. So instead, I'm heading out to Ohio tonight. Circumstances dictated that I drive straight to Reagan National from Richmond. I miss you, my love. Your long, wild hair. Your smooth, light-brown skin. Your deep, dark eyes."

"I miss you more. Thanks for inventorying my good points. If I'm ever on the market again, I'll remember to include them in my personal ad. I'm here reading Nora Roberts' latest, curled up on the couch. The baby kept asking about Daddy today."

Rocco smiled as he considered the image of Marta on the couch and his unborn baby talking to each other. "Now tell me this. How is it possible, since Baby X hasn't been born yet?" Rocco asked.

"One kick means: 'change positions.' Two kicks mean: 'no more spicy food.' Three kicks mean: 'I want Daddy.'" Marta laughed at her own joke. "How did the race with Marc and Antonio go?"

"Just great, but I left early. Listened to the end on the radio while heading north. Emalyn won, which may not be a good thing. It is bound to put pressure on the racing association to suspend her. Oh, and something strange happened. I saw this guy who looked very familiar, but I couldn't place him. He is a mechanic for another race team. Do we know anyone in stock car racing other than Emalyn?"

"No one to my knowledge. We hardly even know Emalyn, for that matter! Could it be someone you saw on television? You watch the races occasionally, don't you?"

Rocco thought for just a moment. "Maybe, but I don't watch a lot of stock car racing. That's more Antonio's thing with Marc."

A voice boomed over the loudspeaker, forcing them to stop talking until the message ended.

"Did I hear a boarding call for Columbus in the background?" Marta asked.

"Yep. I'd better go, Sweetie."

"You be careful out there in Ohio."

"I will," Rocco said, his voice cracking. After a pause, "I should only be gone a day or two, home by Tuesday night at the latest. I love you, Baby."

"Love you more."

Rocco lifted his athletic frame and walked to the check-in desk. He handed his boarding pass to the agent and rolled his single bag behind him onto the jetway, bending down a bit to get from the jetway onto the plane without hitting his head.

* * *

Ninety minutes south of the airport, Antonio gradually regained consciousness. His first perceptions signaled pain in several parts of his body. In addition to his broken finger, his jaw felt majorly tweaked and his ribs and breastbone felt bruised from the airbag. He wondered if he would be able to walk on his right foot. It didn't feel right. *Wait, where's Marc?*

"Marc, are you all right?" No response. Panic crept over Antonio. His mangled body felt trapped, frozen in the car. His son could be in the clutches of a killer. *Where's Marc? Why didn't he answer?* Hanging upside down, Antonio struggled, harder than he ever had in his life, to pivot his head around. While Antonio lay bleeding, Marc went missing. Antonio's body quivered, bringing his numb hands to life.

The dashboard cast a blue pall inside the car, while the headlights shone against a clump of bushes. Other than one illuminated clump of dark green, everything beyond the vehicle swam in indistinguishable shades of black. Antonio took a few minutes to get his bearings and unfasten his seatbelt. He willed himself free to find his son. Marc needed him.

The upside-down posture of the car created problems for Antonio. He felt dizzy and couldn't think straight. With some difficulty, he got loose from his seatbelt, easing his head and neck down onto the ceiling of the car. He pushed outward on the driver's side door but found it was wedged into the hillside. Exasperated, he paused for a few seconds. Then, Antonio fought through his nausea and crawled on his back, lobster style, out the open door on Marc's side.

"Thank God you are alive, Dad," Marc whispered loudly as he ran over to the car. "Who's chasing us?"

Antonio's whole body filled with euphoria at seeing his son alive and not badly injured. He threw his arms around Marc and stroked the back of his head with his good arm.

"I don't know, son. Thank God, you're alive. Let me look at you." Antonio checked Marc up and down. "It looks like your nose might be broken. Can you walk okay? Did you see anyone after you got out of the car?" The adrenaline of searching for Marc subsiding, Antonio began feeling pain from his own injuries. His head throbbed and his right foot ached.

"Not really. I hid in the bushes over there," Marc said pointing to a clump of underbrush. "Someone stopped and looked over the embankment. I think he got back in his car and might have driven off, but I'm not sure. Dad, I'm pretty sure he had a gun. I tried to keep my head down."

Looking up at the moon, Antonio asked in a hushed voice, "How long did I stay passed out?"

"Several minutes. I tried to call 9-1-1 from the bushes, but there's no signal out here."

Antonio thought for a minute. "Do you see the tree line over there?"

Marc nodded, and the two began walking carefully—each step painful for Antonio—and a bit fearfully. They followed the bottom of the embankment for a quarter mile, retracing the curve that scuttled the Audi. Antonio assumed nothing about whether their pursuer remained in the area, but his mind stayed focused on escape. Twice the father and son stopped and listened for sounds from the road above. The second time, they heard loud footsteps. Antonio signaled and they both dropped to the ground, nestled in tall grass.

The sound of gravel being displaced echoed in the night air, but it remained difficult to tell the distance from whoever or whatever made the sound. As they crouched together in the tall weeds, a set of deer antlers appeared over the top of a small hill, followed by large brown eyes. The deer, illuminated in the moonlight, walked unconcerned along the road they drove on minutes before. Antonio motioned for Marc to continue walking to a clump of trees just ahead of them. Staying low, they made it to a small stand of poplars and soon realized that the trees lined a gravel and dirt road just beyond. The makeshift road served as a driveway leading to a farmhouse, barely visible from the main road. A few lights beamed out from the house, a bright, white one on the porch and a fainter, yellow light inside. They began walking in that direction.

"Dad?"

"Yes, Marc?"

"I heard the voice, you know ... from God ... when I waited to see if you would come out of the car alive. God spoke to me."

"What did He say?"

"The voice said Jesus is real and that I can trust him. I made Jesus Lord of my life while I waited for you to wake up."

A few tears flowed down Antonio's face as he stopped walking and just hugged his son. If it took an accident for Marc to find God, then all the aches and pains were worth it. He thanked God for the wreck, for Marc's decision, and, in advance, for a way out of their current distress.

By the time they reached the farmhouse, Marc's nose continued turning various shades of black and blue, and Antonio's face sported dry streaks of blood. Their clothes were soiled from crawling away from the car and damp from hiding in the grass. The wooden porch creaked as they climbed four steps. A raccoon scurried out from beneath the pine flooring and disappeared into the moonlight.

Marc knocked on the screen door, but no one answered. An uneasy feeling crept up Antonio's back. Marc peered in through the elongated glass panel next to the door, then knocked again. Finally, a single table lamp came on in the entryway, casting yellow light on darkly-stained hardwood floors. An ancient woman wearing a cotton nightgown and pastel robe came toward the door, pausing at the glass panel.

"Who are you men, and what do you want?" she grumbled through the glass.

The sound of her voice moved Marc backward, and Antonio stepped up to converse with her. "We had in an accident on the road," Antonio replied. "There's no cell phone service. Can you call 9-1-1 for us?"

The woman peered toward Antonio for a moment. Then, she turned and walked away from the door, saying nothing. Her reluctance to help them made no sense to Antonio. If they had asked to come in the house, he could understand her suspicion. Then, Antonio and Marc heard a twig crack at the side of the porch, followed by the unmistakable sound of a shotgun being cocked. Antonio instinctively shielded his son with his body.

"We don't get many strangers out in the country." A man, appearing to be in his seventies or eighties, stood glaring at Marc and Antonio. His eyes glowed dark and piercing. The skin on his neck wobbled as he spoke. His slanted eyebrows and beard stubble made him appear extra angry.

"Sorry to alarm you," Antonio said. "We're injured. Our car went down an embankment just up the way, and we need help. Can you just please call the police for us? Someone ran us off the road."

The man eyed them up and down, apparently sizing up their motives. Finally, he nodded and returned the way he came from the side of the house. A storm door slammed shut in the distance.

Soon, the woman turned the deadbolt and opened the front door. She carried a tray and brought them each a glass of ice water. Antonio and Marc sat on the lone bench on the front porch. They noticed that the ice water tasted bad and assumed it was from the ice cube trays sitting in the freezer for months, if not years; the couple did not seem to get many visitors. Even so, they felt grateful for something to drink.

The woman's gray hair lay pressed against her head, probably from sleeping. "No offense," she said. "We have to be very cautious living out here. Most of our friends have been robbed or burgled at one time or another. The mister has been a gun man all his life. His father taught him to hunt, and he stayed at it. Brought me home a deer last fall, does almost every hunting season."

When the older man reappeared through the front door, Antonio and Marc noticed that he left his shotgun in the house. After ten minutes, the police came blaring up the driveway, lights flashing and sirens blasting. An ambulance came a few minutes later.

* * *

The next morning, Rocco received a text message from Antonio, warning him that some unknown predator stalked himself and Marc after the race. Whoever ran them off the road could not have been happy with the law firm nosing around the Meloncamp murder. Rocco promised to be careful and to stay in touch. He left his motel near the Columbus airport and made his way to Gahanna, Ohio, home of the RaceRX racing team. Upon arrival at the RaceRX facility, Rocco pulled up to the front of the mixed-use building. It lacked ornamentation, landscaping, or much aesthetic value. Modern enough, the large glass windows at either side of the front door showcased an early version of their iconic racecar. The plastic transfer on the windows allowed light to shine through in both directions.

Upon entering, Rocco walked by a large trophy case and approached the front desk. "Rocco Semones, here to see Owen Vetter."

The attractive secretary walked Rocco to the office of race team owner, Owen Vetter, located in the back of the building.

"Mr. Vetter, thank you for taking time to see me," Rocco said, extending his massive hand.

"My pleasure," Vetter said. "When they go after one of our own, I got to try to help."

The rear wall of Vetter's office held a bank of windows, looking down on the giant auto shop area. Although Rocco entered from the first floor in the front, the building was erected into a hill, allowing for two stories in the back. Rocco drifted over to the windows and peered down at the goings on in the auto shop below. In addition to five bays for cars, the walls on each end housed specialized areas. On the far end, the body fabrication area fascinated Rocco. Racks of inventory climbed the wall with larger parts like fenders and bumpers attached to the wall with large hooks. On the other end of the cavernous garage, racing tires lined the wall from the floor to about six feet high. Movable stairs could be wheeled along the racks to get the tires on the upper shelves.

Rocco continued to take in the ambiance and activity in the garage. Large American and Ohio flags hung down from the ceiling. Racecars occupied three of the five bays, two of them hoisted up on lifts. About five men buzzed around the cars, some holding tools as they worked. Sparks flew from one corner as the welder joined sections of a chassis. Nearby, a body fabricator sanded a fender.

Vetter led Rocco away from the picture window and invited him to sit at a round, glass table. Rocco sat balanced on one of the brewer-style chairs. He possessed a severe personal phobia of brewer chairs, going back to his high school football days. Such a chair had horribly embarrassed Rocco. When he plopped his two hundred-pound body in the brewer chair one day, something didn't feel right. The flimsy metal gave way, and Rocco rode the chair all the way to the floor, accompanied by his teammates' hysterical screams and laughter. Even his best friend said he'd looked like a captain going down with his ship.

Vetter poured coffee for Rocco and himself. Rocco sat on the edge of the chair. When they settled down, Rocco began the interview.

"On the phone you sounded pretty certain the incident between Emalyn and George looked like just an accident."

"I've known Emalyn since she started racing and her father since before that. When he got out of the service, he helped Emalyn get started in racing. Our kids raced midgets together for a while. Little do people know the hours parents spend driving to and from the races, waiting around and learning the ropes so their kids can race. The two of us hit it off. Anyway, it's extremely hard for a woman to get the job as stock car driver. The only reason Emalyn got her current ride is that her dad bought in as part owner of her team before he passed away. He came along with cash at just the right time."

Vetter stopped to sip his coffee and Rocco did the same. Then he asked, "Does Emalyn deserve to be a driver, with her current skill level?"

"Once Emalyn got behind the wheel, she proved she deserves it. She's only been in the big leagues for about four years, but she is a competitive racer."

"Do you think Emalyn caused George's death?"

"It seems unlikely she would risk her chance at being a driver." Vetter scratched his moustache and refused to make eye contact. "Besides, I don't think she would intentionally hurt a fly, not outside the rules of racing. She sounds tough with the trash-talk, but she is a country girl at heart."

"It looks like there may have been some tampering with Meloncamp's car. Any idea who might want him out of the race ... or worse?" Rocco took a healthy swallow of coffee.

Vetter stared at Rocco for an uncomfortable few seconds. His body language troubled Rocco, but he couldn't quite figure out why.

"The idea of it just plain creeps me out. I am surprised to hear about the tampering. We are a pretty tight-knit community. We have squabbles, and boys will be boys, but we all know how dangerous it is out there. I can't imagine another driver or team purposefully sabotaging a competitor's car to make it wreck."

"Please don't take offense at this. I'm just exhausting every possibility to gather information. At the Pocono race, your team occupied one of the bays next to Meloncamp. Did your people see anything out of the ordinary? Any strangers lurking around, or just anything that deserves a second look? I'm being paid to investigate, and I don't feel like I would have done my job without asking."

"I understand. Let me have a meeting and ask everyone on my team. I'll do it today, before I go out of town, and get back to you. Obviously with something this big, the crew chief and I have already talked about it. There is no harm in my asking the others point blank as well. Is there a number where I can reach you?"

Rocco left his card on the table next to his empty coffee cup. After asking several more questions, none of which provided any usable information, he stood up to leave. Looking down once more at the shop floor, someone caught Rocco's eye. The familiar face he noticed in Richmond chatted with another mechanic on the floor below. If only Rocco could remember the man's name or where he knew him before. Somehow, he perceived it to be important, but he could not make his mind remember—at least not from this distance.

"Mr. Vetter, can you tell me the name of that guy down there? The one by the middle bay with the sleeve of tattoos on his right arm."

"That's Sandy Macon. He has been with us for several years. Pretty straight arrow, foreign guy. He immigrated to the U.S. ten years ago or so. He has a legit green card. Is there something wrong?"

"No, he ... uh ... he just looks like someone I should know from way back. The name doesn't ring a bell though. Thanks for your time."

Rocco's bad feeling persisted about the guy in the shop. He still couldn't place him, but he knew for sure he saw that face before, in person, not just a photo on a wall. The name Sandy Macon wasn't familiar. A criminal from Washington? Maybe years earlier Rocco scanned him on a BOLO bulletin? Like most cops, Rocco possessed a deep memory, particularly when it came to bad guys. He sat in his car for a few minutes, deciding on his next move.

As Rocco finished typing his notes into his laptop, his stomach told

him lunchtime neared. He turned the key to start his car when he saw
Sandy pulling around the building in his dark blue sports car. Rocco
decided to follow him. To his surprise, Sandy drove to a very unlikely
place.

"Hi, Baby." Rocco crooned into his phone.

"It is good to hear your sexy voice," Marta replied. "Where are
you?"

"I'm in the parking lot of Six Flags Over Jesus."

"Where?"

"Some mega-church here in Columbus, Ohio. I've been following a
guy who works for RaceRX. He came here at lunchtime. I thought I
recognized him, but now I'm not so sure."

"I miss you, Honey."

"I miss you more. It looks like I'm coming to a dead-end here. I
should be back tomorrow, but I need to go to the office before I come
home. With any luck, you should see my smiling face for dinner
tomorrow evening."

"Can't wait for that. I might make pot roast with little carrots and
potatoes."

"Oh, Baby, the guy came out of the church already. Got to go. Love
you."

"Love you too." While Rocco liked these quick check-in calls, he
knew Marta preferred a longer, more satisfying talk. His natural aver-
sion to talking sometimes caused confusion in the early days of their
relationship. Rocco adored Marta, but saying goodbye to her on the
phone felt like trying to escape from his lonely grandmother at the
retirement home. It brought on bouts of guilt and relationship claustrophobia. Marta would just have to wait until her detective husband
caught his bad guy and came home to her.

Sandy walked to his car and climbed in, his tall, lanky frame a bit
large for a sports car. Rocco waited to follow the car onto the main
road, staying at a distance and hoping not to be noticed. While Sandy
remained in the church, Rocco had managed to plant a tracking device
under his car. The blips showed up on his GPS app, allowing him to
follow from a distance without being seen.

Soon it became clear from the direction he headed that the

mechanic intended to return to RaceRX. Rocco decided not to follow him but instead chose to check on a couple of other leads. He would go to Sandy's house after he got off work.

Next, Rocco drove to a cemetery several miles away. He parked his rental car near the office and headed inside.

"Hi I'm—" Rocco stopped mid-sentence, motioned to be quiet by an older gentleman wearing a blue and grey flannel shirt. Standing behind the desk, the man pointed toward a well-worn green couch. As the worker turned to face Rocco, it became clear that he held a phone to his ear.

"No, ma'am. I'm telling you there is no one named Arnold Ziffel buried in this cemetery. I'm sorry to hear that he treated you like a pig. Thank you for calling." The man set the phone down hard on the counter. This motion caused the ripples of skin on his neck to quiver in time to the movements of his mouth. No more words came out, but it seemed like his mouth kept moving several seconds after the conversation ended, as if he had words that wouldn't quite come out. *Maybe that's what self-control looks like.*

"Darn kids got nothing better to do than torment an old grave digger. Samuel is my name. How can I help you?"

"Rocco Semones. I'm looking for a friend's grave. Do you have a computer where I can look it up?"

"No computers here. All the information sits right here in this book. What year did your friend die?" Sitting on the counter, a large three-ring binder held the locations of the remains of everyone unfortunate enough to find their way to Heavenly Gardens Memorial Park.

"2014, I believe. Morris Grismer."

Samuel opened the large book and paged through until he made it to 2014. After several minutes he turned the book around so that it faced Rocco. With smug satisfaction on his face and fingers disfigured by arthritis, Samuel slid his large index finger down near the bottom of the entries. "That's it right there. See it?"

Rocco squinted in the dim lighting of the office. The name appeared to contain an "M" as the first letter of a first name, but the cursive scrolled ornately to the edges of legibility. "Uh huh," Rocco said. "A little hard to read, but okay. Where is that one?"

"Don't fault my wife's writing," Samuel barked. "The woman came down with cancer. Her chemo caused her to write like that; worked up until the end almost. Back in her heyday no one wrote better than my Isabel."

"No offense intended. The lighting seems a bit dim in here. If you can just point me to the right area, I will be on my way."

Samuel pulled out a map that showed distortion from many generations of photocopying. Rocco reached toward the map, but Samuel jerked it away. "Map won't help you if I don't mark the grave on it. That's the problem with young people, always in such a big doggone hurry, going off half-cocked without knowing where you're going. Every one of you will end up in a cemetery like this anyway. What's the hurry?"

Rocco decided to say nothing more until the map landed safely in his hands. Samuel used a nearly-dry yellow highlighter to indicate the whereabouts of grave 753. "Look for the big headstone with the cross on it, near the entrance to the lower garden area." Samuel tapped the highlighter on the map, apparently showing the relationship between that marker and grave 753.

As Rocco got behind the wheel of his rental car, he felt creeped out by his interaction with Samuel. The elderly gent's piercing eyes and angry tone reminded Rocco of his family's annoying neighbor growing up. Rocco lost a lot of baseballs and Frisbees to that old coot.

The little road back to the lower garden felt tiny, and Rocco rejoiced that no other cars clogged his way through the sprawling cemetery on this particular day. He passed a tent, set up over an open grave. Mourners would soon arrive and it would be someone else's turn to be sad and wonder about life's larger questions and eat too much at the wake.

Little signs directed Rocco through numerous forks in the narrow road. Names like Baby Land, Saint Mary's, and Peaceful Oak went off in diverse directions. He parked his car next to the entryway that read *Lower Gardens*. A gate and three steps down led to the secluded lower gardens section. Out of the car only a few moments, Rocco began perspiring as the August sun beat down. Locusts buzzed in the maple trees that lined the steps and continued along the main walkway. The large stone marker with a cross forged into the design lay just ahead.

Rocco prayed as he walked. Several gravestones in this section looked on menacingly as Rocco tried to orient himself using the map and the gravestone with the cross. If his calculations proved correct, his friend's headstone would be found six headstones west of the cross. But which way is West? *Sun, where did you go?* Rocco felt turned around and a little dizzy from the heat and the locust sounds. The massive shade trees blocked his view of the horizon. "Lord, help me find this marker," Rocco prayed aloud.

There! Rocco approached the cold-looking grey stone. Before even closely examining it, he reached in his pocket. He placed a set of dog tags and a chain on the top of the medium-sized headstone. The inscription read: "I know that he will rise again in the resurrection at the last day – John 11:24." The moment he read the scripture verse, Rocco's head cleared and he felt much better. He stared at the names of Morris Grismer and Denise Grismer, etched artfully into the bottom of the stone. The dates under Morris read "1967–2014." A single date and a dash indicated Denise remained alive: 1964–. Something didn't add up. Morris may indeed have been Emalyn's father's name, but wasn't her mother supposed to be dead?

Rocco snapped two pictures of the gravesite. One clearly showed the names and dates on the stone; the other one, shot from back a few feet, featured the dog tags and the entire tombstone. He emailed the photos to Emalyn and to Antonio. Maybe Antonio knew the story of Denise Grismer and her relationship to Emalyn.

CHAPTER SEVEN

The modern interior of the courthouse seemed stark and unfriendly to Antonio. The sleek, black marble floor amplified every footstep, and the brownish-gray wood reaching to the high ceiling did little to absorb the harsh, reverberating sounds. The all-glass entrance kept the lobby well-lit and uncomfortably warm. The wood benches along the windows, the only organic element in the interior design, seemed added as an afterthought.

He watched as his client appeared through the massive revolving doors and approached the metal detector. When her large red, white and blue necklace and American flag pendant caused the metal detector to beep, Antonio noticed the nervous reaction on her face. Instead of allowing Emalyn to simply take off the jewelry, the athletic female guard patted down Emalyn and used a wand to isolate the metal necklace. The experience did nothing to calm the racecar driver's nervous energy.

Sean looked to have just as must angst, trying to make eye contact with his wife but to no avail. Antonio wondered if Sean's love for Emalyn bubbled up in times of stress.

Antonio met them on the other side of security and escorted them to the appropriate floor where the hearing would take place. He suggested they wait in a small seating area in the cavernous hallway. The clerks, or sometimes the bailiffs, emerged from one of the large courtrooms and called out each case in this hallway. For a pre-trial hearing, no jurors lurked about, and Antonio felt more relaxed than during a trial. The prosecutor and her staff clustered around a few chairs on the other side of the large lobby. He recognized them from earlier proceedings when he used to second chair with more senior members of his firm.

"Antonio, I am so nervous," Emalyn blurted out.

"Don't worry. We can handle anything that comes up."

"Honey, just trust your attorneys. This is probably just one hearing, one step in a long journey to clear your name." Sean's eyes darted back and forth as he spoke, glancing at Antonio for confirmation. In this situation, decorum insisted on no alcohol in which Sean could find refuge and no speeding car cocoon for Emalyn. Antonio wondered what God might be up to in leading this couple through so much adversity.

Antonio prayed silently for his client and her husband. In his spirit, he trusted the Ultimate Judge to use Emalyn's circumstances for every-one's good. Just a feeling he got in his personal devotional time that morning, Antonio believed that Emalyn's case would stretch on well beyond today—and maybe well beyond this year. His spirit, troubled by several aspects of the case, tried to discern a clear motive for anyone to kill George Meloncamp—except maybe Emalyn. Antonio knew intuitively that his client stood innocent, but he could admit to a certain plausibility to the prosecution's case.

Antonio believed Emalyn was unprepared for the trouble coming into her life and perhaps unable to control her tongue. Lack of self-control would spell major trouble on the witness stand. Antonio also worried about Sean. Maybe it stemmed from his drinking, but Sean looked like a wild card. Perhaps some unknown evil beat beneath his hairy chest, but Antonio couldn't picture Sean as a murderer. He kept the couple busy with chitchat, asking about Sean's childhood.

"I'm from North Carolina. Why? Does that have something to do with the hearing?"

Antonio laughed and shook his head. "No, no, just curious."

Sean grinned and nodded his head as if to say, "Okay, I see where you're going with this." He leaned back, relaxed. "My parents were decent folks, Methodists—or at least Mom seemed like a saint. Both worked in furniture factories. I came along the youngest of three. My siblings were older, so they raised me like an only child."

"How did you get into racing?"

"Oh, racing ruled where we lived. A lot of people went out to the local track on Saturday nights in the summer. I worked as a mechanic here and there, eventually getting a job with one of the junior circuit racing teams. They're smaller and pay a lot less, but that's where I met this sweet lady. One look at her smile hooked me."

Antonio watched Emalyn's face as Sean spoke. He expected her to smile more, but the uneasy look on her face discounted Sean's flowery recollections. She bit at her lips and tapped her fingernail on the coffee table. She stared a hole through Sean, perhaps wishing he'd stop talking.

A nine-foot-tall wooden door opened ominously with an extended creaking sound. A male clerk announced in a monotone voice, "A hearing regarding The People vs. Emalyn Martin will begin in fifteen minutes in Courtroom 3001. Will all relevant parties please assemble in the courtroom?"

Emalyn's face said she suddenly longed to go to the powder room in the worst way. Guessing this could happen with his first-time defendant and her husband, Antonio ushered everyone to the restrooms on the other side of the large hallway. After a few minutes, the threesome reunited in the hall then Sean and Emalyn followed Antonio to the courtroom. He escorted Emalyn to the defense table and pointed Sean to the sturdy wooden chairs just behind them.

The prosecutor intentionally did not look over at Antonio, so he got up and walked to the prosecution's table. He extended his hand and stated his name, though he had previously met all three members of the district attorney's staff. Antonio's inaugural flight in the captain's chair of a murder case filled them with confidence. Once at trial, he would have plenty of help from his assigned partner, but this hearing became part of his test to see if he stood ready for his new responsibilities. The members of the prosecution team shook his hand and introduced themselves.

Walking back to their table, Antonio noticed someone from his firm enter quietly and sit in the back row of the courtroom. His colleague lurking thirty feet away must have come to monitor his performance and report back to the mothership. Antonio's nerves jangled just a bit, but in his mind he quoted his favorite scripture from 2 Timothy: "God hath not given us the spirit of fear, but of power, and of love and of a sound mind."

After formalities, Judge Tonya Norris went over the ground rules for the hearing, and the prosecution began filing perfunctory motions about discovery. The first big issue of the day turned out to be a request that Emalyn put up a million-dollar cash bond.

"Your honor, Ms. Martin poses a flight risk," said Prosecutor Barron. "She has substantial means and a passport. What keeps her from flying off to Canada and then onto Europe or somewhere, and never returning to the United States?"

"Their only evidence is a renewal of Emalyn's passport." Antonio explained Emalyn needed the passport for an upcoming race in Toronto some thirty days out. "Ms. Martin is a world-famous racecar driver. Where is she going to hide?"

After some back-and-forth between counsel, the judge decided to split the baby. Emalyn could either surrender her passport or provide a cash bond in the amount of $500,000. Antonio requested and received a short recess to discuss the options with his client.

"Antonio, I haven't got $500,000 in cash," Emalyn said the moment she sat down in the conference room.

"Despite her earnings, we don't have hundreds of thousands in the bank," Sean said.

"There are taxes, and Sean just bought us a big house in Malibu," Emalyn said.

Antonio didn't see the Malibu beach house coming, but he tried to roll with the punches. "Okay, no problem. You can just surrender your passport and forego the Toronto race."

"That could be a problem," Emalyn said.

"You see, if she doesn't drive in Toronto, the stock car union could find it easier to suspend her."

"Let's not try to find things to worry about. Emalyn can surrender her passport and stay out of jail. That seems like a fair trade." Antonio got that look on his face that shut down any argument.

The threesome returned to the courtroom, and Antonio told the judge Emalyn's choice. The chief prosecutor stood.

"Your honor, we have a video that has just come to our attention late yesterday, and we would like to bring it to the court's attention," Prosecutor Barron announced, proud of himself.

"Here it comes," Antonio said to himself. Then, he said out loud, "Objection, your honor. Why couldn't they provide this to me yesterday if they received it then?"

"Your honor, we needed time to review it and understand the implications of the evidence to determine its relevance."

"I will allow it, but you are on thin ice, counselor."

Antonio grew angry. *Why is it always 'thin ice,' but allowed anyway? When will a judge finally say, "You skated on thin ice, but you broke through the ice, flailed about, and drowned in that argument. Case dismissed"?* Just once in his life, Antonio wanted to hear those words.

Placing a DVD in the player and fooling with the remote control for a moment, one of Barron's underlings got the video to play. It showed a short man, mid-forties, with his back to the camera walking from Emalyn's garage bay at the Pocono Motor Speedway. The stout man ambled down to the bay of RaceRX, right next to George Meloncamp's team in the garage area. Flags for the various teams hung prominently in front of their assigned garages, making it easy to discern team locations.

It seemed to Antonio like a substantial walk between the various bays, and it took a few minutes on the video. The longer the video continued, the more Emalyn tensed up and the tighter she gripped the arm on her wooden chair. Her hand turned white, and it started to look painful. Antonio reached over and tapped her on the wrist. She released her death grip. Antonio finally recognized the man in the video and understood Emalyn's reaction.

As other race teams departed and officials finished with certifying cars for the race the next day, the area became nearly deserted. The man in the video acknowledged two members of one departing race team. Then he stopped to talk with someone at RaceRX. The man took an envelope from his sport jacket and handed it to the RaceRX mechanic. At this point, the man who delivered the envelope turned and walked back from where he'd come. As he moved toward the first mounted surveillance camera, anyone in the courtroom could identify Emalyn's husband.

"Sean." Emalyn spoke under her breath in such a forlorn tone that, without thinking, Antonio whipped his head around.

"Your honor, the prosecution would like to call Sean Martin."

"Objection, your honor," Antonio exclaimed, though he held no real grounds in mind for the objection. He stood up slowly trying to think of something, but could only say, "Relevance. And—and a witness should not be forced to testify against his spouse."

"I will allow it," the judge said.

"May I have a moment to confer with my client's husband?" Antonio asked.

"No. I think we want to hear what he has to say," the judge said. "Come up to the witness stand, Mr. Martin. You are going to be under oath. Realize that anything you say can and will be used against you. If you feel an answer to any question might incriminate you, you may refuse to answer on those grounds. Do you understand?"

"I understand." Sean's heart began racing faster than Emalyn's car on a straightaway. His face turned cinnamon red as he walked the fifteen feet from his seat to the front. He climbed into the witness box and swore his oath. As the video played a second time, Antonio did not like the look on Sean's face. *This is not good.*

"Is that you in the video?" Prosecutor Tamara Barron began her questioning.

His weak voice replied in the affirmative. She asked several questions about the time of day and the procedures about certifying cars as approved for racing the next day. Next, she asked him the $10,000 question: "Tell me about the contents of the envelope. What did it hold?"

"I refuse to answer on the grounds it will incriminate me," Sean said. Antonio winced. *It may incriminate you.*

"Why did you give him the envelope?"

"I refuse to answer on the grounds it might incriminate me."

"Did it represent payment to plant a bomb in George Meloncamp's car so that it would explode, killing him and eliminating Emalyn's chief rival for the stock car crown this year?"

"Absolutely not!" Sean shouted.

"Didn't you intend for him to plant—"

"Objection, your honor," Antonio said. "Mr. Martin has answered the question. Prosecutor Barron is badgering him."

"Sustained," Judge Norris said.

"Your honor, permission to treat Mr. Martin as a hostile witness."

"Ms. Barron, need I remind you this is not a trial? I've given you considerable leeway so far; aren't you pushing it just a bit?" The judge stifled a chuckle. "The only hostility I've seen has been on your part, counselor. Do you have any more questions for Mr. Martin?"

"No, your honor." The prosecutor turned and flashed Antonio a triumphant smile. "Your witness."

Antonio stood. "Sean, did Emalyn have knowledge of the envelope or your contact with the man in the video?"

"No," Sean replied.

"Did you pay the man to tamper with George Meloncamp's car in any way?"

"No," Sean declared.

Antonio felt helpless as he watched what happened next.

"Does prosecution plan to bring formal charges of conspiracy to commit murder against Mr. Martin?" the judge asked.

"Absolutely, your honor," Barron said with authority.

Sean looked sick, and his heartbeat appeared on the sides of his neck, or at least it seemed so to Antonio. Sean bent his head forward and looked down at his shoes, the pair Emalyn picked out for him on this important day. He put one hand to his right temple, as if his head felt about to explode.

Antonio saw this sort of thing before. Most people could not imagine in their wildest dreams a future that includes prison. Some people end up in jail, but Sean probably never expected he would be one of them.

Caught off guard, Antonio didn't know exactly what to say. Since Emalyn retained him, not Sean, and he knew no real grounds to protest Sean's arrest, what could he do? However badly it reflected on Emalyn, this surprise fell at Sean's doorstep. Antonio felt compelled by the situation to say something. "Your honor," he said, "we don't have any evidence about what the envelope contained, nor have we heard testimony from the man who received the envelope."

"You're right, Mr. Semones," Judge Norris said. "But those are issues for another day. Mr. Martin is remanded to immediate custody on the charge of conspiracy to commit murder. A hearing regarding his bail is set for three days hence." With that and a quick bang of the gavel, the proceeding ended. Antonio tried to object again but with no success. The hearing ended and the bail hearing wouldn't come up until Friday.

Antonio and Emalyn left the courthouse, while Sean faced spending the next three nights in the federal lock-up. Antonio accompanied Emalyn to Sean's pick-up truck. She looked a bit lost as she climbed behind the wheel. She planned to return with Sean to their hotel in Richmond for the night. With his incarceration, everything changed.

"Do you mind dropping me at my office? It's a few blocks away." Antonio asked. He could have taken the subway but thought Emalyn could use a few more blocks of company.

"Oh, no problem," Emalyn said.

Antonio went to the passenger side, getting in just in time to see Emalyn adjust the rearview mirror. "I better call the executive director of our race team, Milos Norman," Emalyn said. She used the truck's Bluetooth system to dial Milos.

"Milos, I'm glad I caught you. This is Emalyn."

"Oh, hi, Emalyn. How did things go in Washington?" Milos asked.

"That's why I am calling. They didn't keep me, but surprisingly, they arrested Sean. They think he got involved in some sort of conspiracy related to the bomb in George's car."

"Oh, Emalyn, that's ridiculous! Do you have good counsel?" Milos always showed a fatherly concern for her. Emalyn smiled in Antonio's direction.

"Yes. The prosecution pulled this video out of a hat at the last minute. It appeared to show Sean giving an envelope to a member of the RaceRX team, the very team parked in the bay next to George at Pocono."

"That doesn't sound good. Do you think Sean became involved somehow, in murder?"

"Milos, I've known the man for most of my adult life. I sure don't think he could kill anyone, but we need to talk about the implications. The next race is in Kentucky. I know you can't come for all the races. Can you make a point of coming to the next one?"

"I don't know if we can wait that long, Emalyn. Where do you plan to be for the next few days?"

"I'm getting a hotel here in Washington to be near Sean. He will be scared no doubt. If I can help him, I want to be here."

"Okay, I will fly out there tomorrow. Let's meet at your lawyer's office. He should be in the meeting with us so I can ask him questions. Does that sound okay to you?

"Yes. Thanks. That will be good. I will text you his info."

After hanging up, Emalyn pulled over at Antonio's direction. "My office is just over there," Antonio said. "To get to Virginia, just keep going straight until you see the sign for I-66." Emalyn politely said goodbye to Antonio and texted Milos the address of Antonio's law office and his phone number. She then set out to find a suitable hotel across the river in Virginia. She needed pampering ... maybe a spa workout, massage, and good room service.

* * *

Antonio felt exhausted as he pulled into the driveway of their handsome colonial. He still ached all over from his car being run off the road. The lawn appeared manicured, which he attributed to Marc and Sylvia. His son acted like a machine when it came to heavy work around the house. Even in the August heat, he powered through outdoor tasks barely perspiring. *Oh, to be that young again!* Sylvia came behind Marc with her cute gardening hat and gloves. She rounded the corner of the house carrying a large handful of weeds and small twigs. She looked phenomenal even drenched in sweat.

"Honey, the yard looks stunning."

Wiping her brow with her sleeve, she smiled at Antonio. "Marc mowed the lawn before going off to shoot baskets with Trey. I can't wait to get in the shower."

Antonio grimaced as he exited the car, his shoulder still particularly sore from the crash. "It all looks amazing, very professional."

Sylvia disappeared into the shadows of the garage to deposit the yard waste in the appropriate recycling bin. Antonio heard her delicate footsteps in the garage and then the family room door open and close.

After retrieving his briefcase from the trunk, Antonio followed Sylvia into the house through the garage. Their familiar family room embraced him like an old friend. A few of Marc's basketball trophies beamed from the fireplace mantel, and the super-comfortable sofa grouping called out to his aching body. How many great evenings had he spent with his family on those couches?

Rounding the corner toward the stairs, he noticed Sylvia's gardening clothes sitting on top of the washer and heard the water running. Her post-gardening habit included showering in the down-stairs guest bath before wrapping herself in a luxurious, white towel and dashing for their bedroom two floors above. Boy, she looked cute when she did that dash. He wanted to add his work clothes to the pile and join her in the shower, but his body remained too beat up, and there was no telling when Marc might return.

Up on the main floor, something smelled exquisite in the crockpot. A spinach salad adorned the bar top with white plates and bowls sitting next to it. This kind of casual meal alone with his wife formed the perfect antidote to a long day at the office. Antonio trudged up to the bedroom he shared with Sylvia and shed his now-overripe suit, done-in by the hot weather and environmentally-friendly temperature at the law office.

After a quick shower, Antonio dressed and headed downstairs. Sylvia looked anxious as she concluded a phone conversation.

"Marta. She is getting concerned about Rocco. He didn't call her all day, so she expected to meet him at home tonight for sure. It is unusual for him not to call or at least text her. He called early last evening, but she hasn't heard from him since. She tried Rocco's cell phone several times but received no answer. She then called me to ask if you heard from him. Did he come into the office today?"

"No, I haven't talked to Roc today. Emalyn's hearing took up most of the day. They charged her husband at the hearing and locked him up for a few days. Emalyn remains out on bail."

Antonio called Rocco's cell phone number. Getting no answer, he looked up the home number for Sharon, their office manager. Antonio paced as he talked to Sharon then said goodbye to her after just a few minutes. Sylvia dipped the boeuf bourguignon into the bowls for herself and Antonio, balancing slices of scrumptious, thick whole grain bread atop the rims of each bowl.

"Sharon hasn't heard from him, but she'll check the firm's travel system to see if Rocco has charged anything on his company travel card. She can log in remotely from home. It will take her just a few minutes to boot up and connect from her home computer. Let's dig into this masterpiece you cooked while we wait."

Each bite of the delicious concoction soothed Antonio. He gently stroked Sylvia's hair between bites. With the stew mostly gone, Antonio called another colleague who was in the office. She hadn't seen Rocco all day and doubted he returned from travel. She absent-mindedly suggested Antonio try Rocco's home number. Antonio felt like saying something harsh but kept his tongue in check. Of course, he would have tried his brother's cell number before calling a complete stranger at work. Antonio launched into the spinach salad next and it proved the perfect follow-up to the bourguignon.

A few minutes later, Sharon called back. She explained that Rocco didn't check out of his hotel in Columbus, so he must have still been in Ohio. Also, he hadn't used his office charge card all day. Sharon promised to get the firm's IT manager to check Rocco's email account and Blackberry.

"When we finish, I have to go over to Marta's. She needs me," Sylvia said. The bond between Sylvia and Marta went well beyond their common Brazilian roots. Years of faith and friendship, struggling to make their way in a new country, brought them closer and closer.

"Let's both go," Antonio said. "We should all pray together."

After rinsing the dinnerware and setting it in the dishwasher, Antonio grabbed his wallet and keys. Sylvia said a quick word of explanation to Marc by cell phone as they drove to the Ballston neighborhood in Arlington. First, they hugged and reassured Marta. Next, they prayed for several minutes. Although still visibly concerned, Marta calmed down considerably. She decided to wait through the night to see if Rocco called by morning. If not, she would fly to Columbus and file a missing person's report with the police there.

The three of them sat on the couch with the television droning in the background. Antonio watched the football game but didn't care about either team. Sylvia sat with her arm around Marta, much as she'd done when they first met as schoolgirls in Brazil. They both lived in the same working-class neighborhood and attended a church-run grade school. Some aggressive boys had once chased the girls around the schoolyard during recess time. As Marta fled a particularly fearsome boy named Poncho, she squealed before falling down and skinning her knee. Sylvia helped Marta to her feet and walked her over to the teacher supposedly responsible for keeping order on the playground.

After the school nurse dutifully cleaned and dressed Marta's knee, she started to cry again as the principal decided to send her home for the rest of the day. Sylvia sat by her side with her right arm tucked around Marta's neck. Minutes passed before Marta's mother came to take her home. The next day, Marta sought out Sylvia and they became fast friends.

Sylvia departed Brazil first to attend a small teacher's college in Virginia. Marta later wished she'd followed her friend, having had difficult times at her home city's largest university. Their divergent paths separated them for six years before Marta decided to get her own fresh start in Washington, D.C. She called Sylvia and instantly found a roommate in her new land. Sylvia couldn't believe her best friend actually made the jump from Brazil to Washington. To her it seemed like it was so many years ago.

After Sylvia and Antonio went home, Marta walked onto her

balcony and peered up to the sky. The moon shone down, illuminating the area around her building. "Where in the world could Rocco be?" she whispered. Marta knew her man remained out there somewhere, and she intended to find him, no matter what.

* * *

Emalyn rounded the track at Charlotte Motor Speedway, running fourth.

"Okay, Emalyn. Let it out in the backstretch," Millard said.

She politely obliged, pushing the car to the limit of its capacity. By the turn, she moved up to third place, just behind the RaceRX car. "Handling much better," Emalyn said through her Bluetooth mic.

The crowd roared as Junior took over first place from Tex Silverman. Emalyn stayed on the tail of the RaceRX car for two more laps.

"See if you can get by RaceRX before the next pit," Millard said. "The next pit is five laps away."

Emalyn knew Tim Johnson, the RaceRX driver. He actually treated her like a human being from the first time they met. His lanky frame and dark brown hair reminded her of Antonio, except for Tim's mustache. Antonio, clean-shaven, also dressed a lot better than the RaceRX driver. She tried to pass underneath on the far turn, but Tim's car responded and he held her off for another lap.

With three laps to go before the pit, Emalyn slipped by Tim as they passed the flagman. "It felt like I scraped him. Does anyone see debris?" Emalyn's voice sounded more upset than normal. Under the circumstances of her indictment and various negative stories in the media, she wanted to run a clean race if possible.

"He is leaking liquid," Millard said. "Whoa! That's not good."

As Emalyn rounded the track, she spotted the RaceRX car in the infield in flames. A fireball spewed out of the driver's side just as Tim pulled himself out of the window and fell to the ground. Flames and smoke poured from his car as the safety crew rushed to him. The first Hazmat corpsman raced to where Johnson lay and doused the fire with his extinguisher. On Emalyn's second time around the track, under caution, she saw Tim roll over on his own.

"What happened?" Emalyn shouted into her mic.

"Pit, Emalyn." That's all Millard could say. She pulled her car around the track and followed several other drivers into pit row. Her hands shook as she released them from the wheel. Gasoline and fresh tires later, she pulled back out onto the track. Her mind wandered as she drove the remaining laps under caution. Eventually, the race restarted, and Emalyn gathered her focus for the last forty-five laps. She went out of her way to avoid trouble for the rest of the day. Her mediocre efforts earned her a seventh-place finish.

Following the race, she sat in her hotel room talking with Millard and Jesse.

"What in the world is going on?" she asked.

"This has been such an insane year," Jesse said.

"Thank goodness Tim Johnson doesn't appear to be badly hurt," Millard said, opening an iced tea purchased from the vending machine on their way to Emalyn's room.

"We brought you a gyro," Jesse said. "Not too many things open on Sunday night."

"Thanks." Emalyn opened the bag and took out the foil-covered sandwich. "Millard, do you think someone has declared open season on drivers?"

"There has got to be something going on."

Jesse looked up from his iPhone and said, "Tim's out of the hospital. They say just a couple of minor burns on his hands." He showed the picture to Emalyn.

"Thank goodness," Emalyn said. Scrolling down the picture on Jesse's phone, she raised an eyebrow. "Those bandages look pretty big. I hope his burns aren't severe."

"You know, there is a chance that Tim's accident is just a coincidence," Jesse said. "There is a difference between a car blowing to smithereens and a possible fuel leak causing a fire."

Millard thought for several moments. "That's true. We shall see."

CHAPTER EIGHT

A tall man parked in the bank lot and hurried inside just after it
opened. His steely glare caused the usually chatty teller to cut
short her greeting. She looked down at the note. In careless handwrit-
ing, it read: CHECKING ACCOUNT $1,500.

"Oh, I see. You want to withdraw $1,500. I will just need your
photo I.D. and your ATM card."

The man looked at her with a blank stare as he reached to withdraw his wallet from his jeans pocket. He handed her his driver's
license.

"Thank you, sir. Do you have your ATM card?"

At first, the man paused as if he didn't completely understand her.
Then, he pulled out the requested card and slid it into the tray. The
teller collected it from her side of the glass and looked up the account
on her terminal.

"Do you want any special denominations for the money?" she
asked, trying to sound cheerful.

"No hundreds!" Sergei Andropov grunted in a thick Russian accent.
His irritation permeated out and melted his blank expression.

The teller excused herself and went to the back to get enough
fifties and twenties. Having just opened, her drawer didn't have enough

of the desired denominations. Sergei tapped his oil-stained fingers on the counter and shook his head. Eventually, she returned and counted out his money.

"You have a nice day, there," she called after him as he snatched up the money and exited, like he had just robbed the bank.

* * *

"Depravity is not a condition that arrives in a moment. It is a way of life that begins in the mind and leads to a single, small moral failure." Alex's words rolled around in Sergei's head, back and forth like a perpetual-motion art piece. Whether working on a racecar at his job or doing laundry at home, Sergei mulled over the latest gems spoken by his longtime best friend. "The sins of the fathers and mothers lead to character defects in the parents, which spawn more sins and more consequences for their children. The trouble you and I suffered in the orphanage came as a result of our parents' poor choices and moral failures, but we can break the cycle. Jesus can help us."

Sergei heard what Alex said, but he just didn't view life the same way. Since renting the farmhouse in Ohio, Sergei cherished his freedom and even, to some extent, his adopted country; but he also looked back at their old life in Russia with nostalgia. Nostalgia led Sergei to decorate his living room with a large Russian Federation flag, extending across almost an entire wall.

Sergei's girlfriend, Caroline, loved the flag and said she felt a spiritual connection to it. Strange for a suburbs girl who grew up in Ohio. Caroline thought the flag grounded her and reminded her of what Occupy Wall Street represented. Sergei thought his former country's political system was a complete failure, but he said nothing to Caroline. He didn't care about her politics, and he liked having a steady girlfriend for the first time in his thirty-six years.

Sergei recalled Alex's words from a few weeks earlier: "The lukewarm beliefs of our grandparents got snuffed out by an arrogant ideal —that men are entirely their own god. No higher power existed than the Russian state and the collective power of its workers. Raised in an environment with no grace, no forgiveness, and no hope for the future, people make selfish choices in vain attempts at self-comfort."

Sergei walked over to the small black-and-white picture on the fireplace mantle. He stared at it and thought about the mother's love he never experienced. Years after someone took the picture, his natural grandmother visited him at the orphanage and told him the sad story of his birth mother who died by the time Sergei learned her name.

A young art student, Sergei's mother acted very immaturely, adrift in an alcohol-induced sea of impulsiveness. She met Sergei's father at a bar in Leningrad. It led to a one-night stand. Weeks after their encounter, Iliana began dealing with morning sickness and contemplated her limited options. She continued drinking and one day led to the next. When the birth neared, a counselor at the local hospital convinced her to give the baby up to a good home. With no job and no home beyond the flophouse where she crashed at night, this seemed to be the only choice, so she agreed. An agency arranged an orderly adoption and Sergei should have gone home with a stable couple from the suburbs.

Unfortunately, Iliana changed her mind when she held her baby for the first-time. Seeing her sincere affection for the infant and hearing her intention to get a job, her parents let her back into their home. They helped her sober up and purchase clothes for work. She even found a job as a cashier at the corner food store. The arrangement worked well for a couple of years.

When the responsibilities of single motherhood got to be too much, Iliana fell back into her old habits. She began staying out late in bars, and soon spent most of her money on alcohol and drugs. When Sergei turned four years old, Iliana became pregnant again. Her boyfriend of the moment quickly ended their relationship. Iliana's parents expressed disgust and insisted she give up Sergei to the state-run children's home.

Sergei didn't cry when his grandmother told him this story. Sadness eluded him; Sergei had no time for it in those days. His daily struggle to stay alive in the sadistic environment of the state-run orphanage took up all his emotional energy.

Growing up, Sergei tried to make the best of his bad situation. His natural leadership abilities attracted others to him, including Alex, who soon became his best friend. They lived like brothers, moving through the orphanage system together. When they got jobs with the same construction company, they seemed to be on the verge of overcoming the past and making something positive of their lives.

Unfortunately, a bar fight landed them in trouble with the authorities in the town of Sochi. Sergei stabbed one of the foreign Olympic athletes. Both Sergei and Alex took part in the fight and were forced to flee Russia for America. To their surprise, the Russian mob waited for them in New Jersey with open arms and immediately hired them to work at a garbage company. In addition to collecting trash, the men got assigned side tasks, doing the bidding of their organized crime overlords. One of the jobs failed, and once again, Sergei and Alex had to flee for their lives.

From that time forward, Sergei felt cursed in every way. He didn't want to do wrong things, but trouble just seemed to follow him everywhere.

The one constant for most of his life remained Alex. The two went everywhere together, eventually settling down near Columbus, Ohio. From the first years in their new town, however, their lives began diverging. There came a spiritual change for Alex; he no longer wanted to troll bars for women. Instead, he began working at a large church and leading the church's homeless ministry. Alex still saw Sergei regularly, but they felt their lives fall more and more out of sync. Alex kept his same first name, but Sergei now went by the name of Sandy. He called it his American name.

As Sandy, Sergei met Caroline, the young American woman who made his life worthwhile. As their relationship grew, she eventually wanted to move in, and Sandy obliged, glad to have the company. They found a little rental farmhouse in the countryside near Grove City, a bedroom community of Columbus.

Due to the pressures of supporting himself and his girlfriend, Sandy's job with a local car racing team brought in less cash than needed to meet all her wants and their needs. Although Caroline worked at a bookstore in the local mall, her small paychecks didn't go far to satisfy her insatiable desire for clothes and make-up. Meals at restaurants, new clothes, and payments on her new car all took a toll on their finances. Sandy did not have valid identification when he fled the Russian mob in New Jersey, so he carried no credit cards and felt afraid to apply for any. Fortunately, a stolen social security number allowed him to work, but he didn't want to draw any more attention to himself by seeking credit. Caroline's checkered financial past prevented her from getting much credit either. This left Sandy vulnerable to overtures from those who would prey on his darker side.

* * *

Rocco didn't call home Tuesday night. All through the wee hours, Marta fretted and paced their condo in Arlington. In the morning, he still didn't answer phone calls from her or Antonio. Marta couldn't sit still another minute. She knew concentrating at work would be impossible. She called her boss at the Department of Energy and explained the situation.

Rocco, where are you! She packed hastily and drove to National Airport, adding an enormous fare on her credit card for the last-minute flight to Columbus. All the while, she continued to dial Rocco's number. "What ifs" popped up all in her mind. Antonio tried to insist that she let him go to Columbus for her, but hearing the determination in her voice, he gave in and simply said, "Keep your receipts; spare no expense. The company will pay for this. And promise me you'll be careful and check in with us frequently."

What if Rocco is sick in his hotel room? What if he died in a traffic accident? What if, what if?

During the flight, she pulled out the small New Testament she kept in her purse. As she thumbed through the pages, Philippians 4:6-7 leapt off the page: "Be anxious for nothing, but in everything by prayer and supplication, with thanksgiving, let your prayers be made known to God; and the peace of God which surpasses all understanding, will guard your hearts and minds though Christ Jesus."

"Oh God," Marta prayed silently. "You know where Rocco is and what has happened to him. Please let me get there in time. Please let me find him and save him from whatever is going on." She felt an odd darkness in response to her prayer, as if the answer lay buried by a thick, black fog. At the same time, Marta felt something strong holding her more securely than ever before—even safer than in the giant arms of her beloved husband.

"Dear, you look so serious," a gray-haired woman in the airplane seat next to Marta said with concern.

"It's my husband," Marta replied. "He's missing, and I'm going to Columbus to look for him."

"Oh my. That is troubling. Tell me a little bit about him."

Marta set down her Bible and thought for a moment. "He's the most admirable man in the world. Tall, strong, beefy build. An Italian through and through. His voice is deep and sexy. When we first met, I thought he sounded a little like Bullwinkle Moose from the old cartoon. Wait, that doesn't sound very sexy does it?"

The older woman laughed and smiled at Marta. "I'm Gwendolyn."

"I'm Marta. I grew up in Brazil and came here to make my fortune and meet a great husband. It took me a long time to find Rocco. He is perfect. He doesn't mind my kinky hair or when I'm too serious. He just holds me and loves me just like I am."

"You look just beautiful. He sounds marvelous. I hope you find him soon. If I lived in Columbus, I would help you look. This is just a connecting flight for me. Can I give you a little piece of advice since you read the Bible and all?"

"Of course," Marta said.

"God always knows best. He loves us unconditionally. Regardless of our behavior, he loves us so much. Hang onto Jesus through your whole life and he will make it an incredible adventure."

"Thanks, Gwendolyn. You made me feel much better."

Just then, the pilot announced their arrival in Columbus airspace. They would be landing shortly. Marta stowed her Bible in her carry-on luggage and prayed one more time. Then, she gazed out the window as the plane descended. The geometric farms, so peaceful-looking and green, smiled up at her.

After arriving at Columbus International Airport, Marta rushed to claim her rental car and, armed with the directions to Rocco's motel, headed straight to the Comfort Inn. Her heart nearly jumped out of her chest as she parked the car and raced into the office. At the registration desk, she showed her identification and asked if her husband checked out of his room yet. A tall woman behind the counter checked the computer screen. When she said no, Marta took a deep breath and asked to be let into his room, fearing that Rocco may be ill ... or worse.

The walk from the front desk to Rocco's room seemed endless. Cars whizzed by on the busy main road. Marta didn't know what to think. *Could Rocco be involved with another woman? Did he have a heart attack and die in his room?* Dreadful thoughts tormented her mind as she followed the hotel employee to room 148. Marta held her breath as the clerk knocked and used a passkey to unlock the door. "Housekeeping, housekeeping," the roundish woman repeated, warning anyone of their entry. She pushed with moderate force on the door and it opened. Sunlight flooded the otherwise dark room. The clerk opened the curtain, allowing light to expose every corner of the room, then walked out.

As Marta looked around, it became apparent that the two queen-size beds lay neat and tidy. She turned on a light near the bathroom and immediately noticed Rocco's shaving kit. She trembled and held the wall to steady herself. She peered into the small inner room, but the bath seemed perfectly in order. Then, Marta checked between the beds. On top of the desk lay part of a Washington Post from two days earlier. The crossword puzzle rested on top, nearly completed in Rocco's sloppy printing. Marta ran her finger over the puzzle as if trying to contact Rocco. *Where are you, my love?*

The trashcan contained only an empty plastic liner, apparently serviced since Rocco last occupied the room. A half-eaten bag of potato chips lay on the counter by the television, secured by a metal paper clip. Marta noticed a folded piece of paper tucked between the cushion and the arm of the room's only comfortable chair. She smoothed the paper on the desk. On it she read the physical address of the RaceRX team headquarters.

In the closet, Marta found Rocco's overnight bag containing only his clothes. One nicer shirt hung alone, probably Rocco's attempt to remove the wrinkles before he wore it on the flight home. But why hadn't he stuffed his hairy torso into that shirt and come home to her?

* * *

Marta's small rental car struggled to accelerate, but she managed to safely merge onto the highway in spite of the car's lack of pep. She headed first to the police station and then to the RaceRX headquarters. The police officer dutifully took her statement and the license plate of Rocco's car, provided by Antonio and Sharon at the law firm. The desk sergeant seemed to perk up when Marta explained that Rocco retired as a police detective.

Just after the interview, Marta e-mailed the police a recent picture of Rocco from her phone. A sympathetic detective named Julie Jung agreed to call Marta if they received any leads on Rocco. Julie tried to reassure Marta that loved ones almost always turn up and are usually just fine. The worried wife in her tried to let that sink into her tired spirit.

Back on the highway, Marta called Sylvia on her lunch break to provide an update, but also for a listening ear—to share her feelings and to receive needed encouragement.

"Hi Sylvia, it's Marta. Is this a good time?"

"You bet, it's my lunch and planning period. How are things going in Ohio?"

"Went by the hotel. His stuff's still there. I take it Antonio hasn't heard from him."

"No, dear," Sylvia said. "He wanted you to know that everyone at the firm is doing all they can to find Rocco. They are having the phone company ping his work phone. Sharon keeps checking his credit card. Nothing so far."

"Well, I've been to the police and they are looking for his rental car too. I will send you a text if I find out anything."

"Thanks. Love you."

"You too, friend."

* * *

Marta arrived at RaceRX headquarters determined to retrace Rocco's steps. Owen Vetter, who met with Rocco, had flown out to the next race, but his secretary got him on the phone. He spoke candidly about Rocco's visit and what they discussed, but he hazarded no guess as to where Rocco went afterward.

Hopping on a plane to Ohio seemed like a good idea at the time, but Marta soon began to doubt herself. She prayed, asking for God's help. Being so far from home multiplied her helplessness and anxiety. With no other leads to go on, she Googled the five largest churches in the Columbus area. Rocco called the place "Six Flags Over Jesus," his lovable vernacular for any mega church. She decided to start with the largest one close to her location. The short drive to The Naz church gave her little time to think.

Marta looked around the large lobby and observed a woman wearing a light blue sweater over her blouse, causing Marta to notice the coolness of the building and shiver. As she approached, Marta saw the sign above her head: INFORMATION DESK. She introduced herself. "Hi, my name is Marta Semones. Do you work here at the front desk all the time? I mean, were you working here the past couple of days?"

The kind woman smiled at Marta, peering over top of paisley reading glasses.

"Yes, dear. I'm here almost every day. How can I help you?"

"My husband may have come by here, probably Monday afternoon or evening. He may have been looking for someone." The woman gave Marta a quizzical look. "Anyway, now Rocco is missing, and the last place he might have gone to is a large church in this area. He is an investigator, and I'm just so worried about him. I have to find him." Tears began to slide down Marta's cheeks.

"Oh, dear. I see. Let me get everyone who is around today, and we will ask them. Here are some tissues. You just sit down over there in the little waiting area. I will be right over."

Several staff members responded to the intercom announcement, including the church's lead pastor. Marta shared her story and even showed them a few pictures of Rocco from her phone. No one said they remembered seeing him.

The pastor suggested they form a circle, which they did. He led them in a prayer that Marta would find Rocco soon. Others joined in and prayed for God to comfort her on her journey and give her tender mercies. Marta shed more tears in the process and accepted hugs before heading back to the parking lot. *The love of other believers fills my heart even in this confusing time.*

As she moved toward her car, Marta stared down at the sidewalk, barely watching what lay ahead. As she neared the fountain in the courtyard, she could feel someone's eyes watching her. The presence moved closer. She jerked her head up to see a blond man walking straight toward her. His striking blue eyes locked onto hers, almost putting her in a trance. She recognized the blond man. *Alex.*

He kidnapped her eight years earlier. Police never caught him or his accomplice. Now, face-to-face with him after all these years, Marta's first instinct told her to run back in the building. *This man drugged me and dragged me from my apartment. Why should I listen to anything he says? I should call the police immediately,* she thought. Instead, she straightened her shoulders and stood her ground. If he possessed any answers about Rocco, she would get to them.

"It's you," he said, with a still-noticeable Russian accent.

"Alex? What are you doing here?" Marta accused, trying to keep the fear out of her voice. It felt wildly disorienting, in the midst of her current crisis, to be confronted with one of the two men that violently abducted her years before. He and his partner held her captive for two nights and even debated killing her. She remembered that Alex argued against offing her, but he was still no choir boy. Fear consumed her, except for a strange curiosity about Alex. She braced herself and held her purse against her chest in a defensive posture. *What brought him to Ohio, of all places?*

"I work here, at this church. This is insane," Alex said. "What are *you* doing here?"

Fear invaded Marta's face again and she tried to walk around him, but he moved sideways and blocked the sidewalk.

"Wait. Sit down for a minute. Give me a chance to talk to you."

Marta paused, reluctant to oblige. Then, she sat down on the stone bench facing the fountain depicting the Bible story of Rachel at the well. "How did you get here to Ohio? Working at a church?"

"Well it is a crazy and long story, but I will give you the short

American version. Sergei and I got in trouble with our Russian friends for botching the job in Washington. Even letting you go—they viewed it as a big mistake. We got paid some money for the job in Virginia and needed to disappear."

Alex's expression softened, suddenly realizing that Marta could report him to the police. "Marta, please don't turn me in. What you told me that day eight years ago about Jesus—it changed my life forever. I could feel my heart change in just those few minutes. Anyway, I asked Sergei to run away from the Russian mob and come here. His reluctance turned to consent when he realized they would probably kill us anyway, if we went back to New Jersey."

"Why Columbus, Ohio? I mean, they have great college football, but you're *Russian*." Marta said it as if no one in Columbus had ever heard of Russia. Her nerves frayed, and she wasn't making much sense. With Rocco missing and this blond mobster in front of her, fear and suspicion danced all over her face.

"It *is* kind of silly, really." Alex put his hands on his knees and chuckled. "I heard that Columbus is where Arnold Schwarzenegger, who is famous even in Russia for his movies, does his big weightlifting competition. I also knew Ohio is a long way from New Jersey." He leaned forward, and his voice took on a more serious tone. "The bottom line is that Jesus Christ filled my heart that day we talked together, and everything changed for me. I now work here at the church; I'm in charge of the homeless ministry. My life is about service to others now. Please believe me—don't turn me in."

Marta's shoulders relaxed a bit as Alex told his story. He seemed sincere, and she sensed that he became a changed man. His once chiseled features looked softer. Overall, he looked almost angelic, with blue eyes and perfectly-sculpted nose. Her fear, though not completely relieved, seemed to morph into mild nervousness. She told him her whole story about marrying Rocco, becoming pregnant, and coming to Columbus to search for him. Alex swore he hadn't seen Rocco, and he assured her that the church people would try very hard to help her look for Rocco. After several minutes, the two of them walked inside the church and Alex made them each a cup of coffee in the lobby. They sat in a quiet corner.

With a coffee in hand, Alex sat down across from Marta. "I have wondered about you and prayed for you so often," Marta said.

"I have done the same," Alex said. "You changed my life."

"This is so unexpected."

"Sergei and I rented a place together at first and tried to look for construction jobs. Lacking the contacts and fearing that the mafia could track us through our American identification, we struggled. Eventually, the money ran out and we came to this big church because they feed the poor and homeless every weekday. I tried to pray and read a little New Testament. With our apartment nearby, I began attending Sunday services. So, one day, while we ate a meal here, I saw the church advertising an opening for the homeless ministry. I'm not proud to say that I lied my way into the job, but what else could I do? After a few years, I got promoted to be the homeless program director. They know all about me now, of course."

"So, how long have you been working at the church?" Marta fidgeted with her purse, still nervous.

"Almost eight years I've been here. Sergei tried to attend church with me for a couple of months. It just didn't work. His heart hasn't changed, at least not like mine. Eventually, he found an automotive mechanic job. Last year, he got a girlfriend too. We have less and less in common. I don't even drink now. We get together on holidays, and occasionally he stops by the church for a few minutes, but I don't see much of him otherwise."

Marta felt a spiritual bond with Alex. Her fear fully dissolved as he talked. They continued catching up for almost an hour. Before she left, Alex begged her one more time not to turn him in for his crimes in the Washington area. Marta promised she would not tell the police about him unless it was necessary to find Rocco. She also promised to think about how the church could help locate her husband—perhaps they could post flyers near the hotel and near RaceRX.

Finally, Marta wanted to leave and get back to her search. The two, former captor and captive, parted company after exchanging phone numbers and even a brief hug. Marta promised to call Alex when she found Rocco. He smiled the most genuine smile at her then disappeared into the church.

Marta returned to her car, then checked in at the police station. No word yet on Rocco and no sightings of his rental car.

Back at the hotel, Marta decided to spend the night, hoping that Rocco would come back. After phone conversations with Antonio and Sylvia, she took a shower, then put on her silk nightshirt and pajama bottoms. Locating a Gideon Bible, she intentionally opened to Psalm 22, the recounting of King David's feelings when his enemies seemed to be defeating him. David thought God slow to help him. Marta could relate. God seemed unfazed by her momentary lack of faith, she thought smiling.

Next, she read the familiar twenty-third Psalm. Marta hated to read the part about the valley of the shadow of death, but she understood God's comfort for King David. God comforted her, too. He would pour out his comfort if it came to that. She hoped it wouldn't come to that. After climbing into bed, she prayed again, urgently and tearfully asking God's help. Exhausted, she fell fast asleep.

Marta slept for about four hours when awakened by a gentle knock at the door. She jumped up and pulled on her robe, but her mind remained groggy and afraid. What if danger lurked on the other side? If the person at the door bore information about Rocco, she didn't want to risk missing it. Gathering her courage, she peered out the peep hole, but saw no one. She moved to the window, pulling back the drape just enough to look outside. Again, no one. Fearful but desperately concerned about Rocco, she unlocked the door and flung it open. Looking to the left and right, she saw nothing. She stared at the parked cars in the almost-empty lot, then looked up at the crescent moon as a plane flew overhead.

A mysterious bank of black fog flowed in and enveloped Marta. As she stepped away from the door, the fog closed behind her. Stepping out from under the walkway covering, she began to float. She slowly rose higher and higher until she could look down on the hotel and even the city of Columbus. She recognized Ohio Stadium where the Buckeyes play football. She called out for Rocco but heard no answer.

Marta came upon an angel, sitting on a bank of clouds. The angel didn't say anything when she asked about Rocco; he just pointed to the east. As Marta continued to float in that direction, it occurred to her that she floated gracefully, far above earth, hovering over several layers of clouds. The black fog gone, the white clouds seemed as airy and holy as heaven itself. A part of her argued that this must be a dream, but she pushed the thought away. Her urgent quest to find Rocco transcended reason.

Next, Marta came upon two little children, a boy and a girl. Their thick brown hair mirrored her own, but their bodies shimmered, adorned in other-worldly light. They smiled at Marta and she could see pure love ... and forgiveness ... in their eyes. Did she know them? If only she could remember. She asked about Rocco, but at first, neither said a word. They just kept staring at her and smiling and looking deep within Marta's eyes. Finally, the little girl said only one word: "Mama." This word cut into Marta's soul. In an instant, she recognized both children as the little ones she aborted so many years ago. She wanted to apologize and cry and beg their forgiveness, but they wouldn't hear of it. Within their eyes churned an ocean of forgiveness. She gathered them in her arms and hugged them securely for what felt like an eternity. After too few minutes, the fog worsened and required her to release the children. As Marta's mind tried to process all this, the fog grew ever thick, and she could barely make out the children hovering only a few feet away. In the fading light, they pointed her even farther to the East.

As Marta continued floating in the direction the children indicated, the clouds below eased and thickened again, finally completely obscuring her view of earth. At that moment, a loud engine almost deafened her as an airplane flew by at an enormous rate of speed. The turbulence upset her flotation, causing her to drift off course ... or at least it felt like going off course. Marta cried out for Jesus, and he appeared beside her, steadying her arm. The two of them floated together to a large, ornate gate, magnificent but surprisingly chained shut. A large, brass lock secured it against intruders. The locked gate made her sad, heart-wrenchingly sad. Her melancholy almost led her to cry, because she could not enter the lush grounds. Then, Jesus put his gentle hands on her head, pointing her eyes to look past the gate and to the right.

There stood Rocco, laughing and talking with Clara Barton under a lush elm tree. Marta recognized the founder of the American Red Cross from an old photo in her seventh-grade history book. Clara must have told a joke. They both laughed hard, as if Clara told the funniest story ever, and Rocco delighted in her wit. For just a moment, Marta wanted to call out to Rocco. She yearned to run over to the locked gate and beckon him to herself. She longed to grasp his big hands one more time. Before she could call to him, Jesus squeezed her arm gently, and she responded by looking back at her Savior. Jesus slowly shook his head. "Not yet. Not until the time." Unexpectedly, Marta felt no disappointment. She knew Jesus was right. He was always right.

CHAPTER NINE

That same night, the multi-colored lights of the huge casino marquee flashed overhead as Emalyn pulled up beneath the pulsating canopy. A distinguished gentleman in a long red coat and black top hat opened her extended cab pick-up truck door and offered his hand. She gladly took it, flashing her large diamond ring in the process. Brushing back the hair from the left side of her face, she slung her rhinestone-studded purse over her right shoulder and headed inside.

Just miles North of Washington, the casino offered a welcome diversion from her prison visits to Sean. With her husband in the hoosegow and her own liberty in the balance, only Emalyn would find this the perfect time for a publicity stunt. So, she painted her face to perfection and shimmied into her favorite cocktail dress. The delicate, diamond tennis bracelet sparkled on her left wrist, balancing the showiness of the ring on her right hand.

In her single days, she frequented casinos and magnanimously accepted contributions from the cowboy poker players along the racing circuit. Now, she just wanted some good press that shouted, "I'm alive! And I'm going to beat this murder rap!"

Quite a few male heads turned as she strutted through the rows of

slot machines in her shiny, white mini-dress and Louis Vuitton Silhouette ankle boots. This persona, that the racing execs wanted her to
embrace, represented only a façade—and not one she usually liked
donning. While she preferred vivacious country girl, she could play a
Las Vegas sexpot if that's what would keep her racing until the end of
the season. She needed the money for her defense and for Sean's.

She flounced her way toward the high rollers' room and was greeted
by the casino manager, Mr. Jaeger. Alerted by his security staff, he
knew what a public relations boon fell in his lap to have stock car
racing's "it" girl gambling in his casino.

"Welcome, Ms. Martin. Thank you so much for coming."

"Enchanted, I'm sure," Emalyn said with mocking formality. She
extended her hand with the over-sized diamond, and Mr. Jaeger kissed
it playfully. His oily, black hair and thin moustache creeped
Emalyn out.

"What are you in the mood for?" Jaeger asked. "Some Baccarat
perhaps?"

"No, Buddy. Show me to the craps table."

"Of course." Jaeger took her arm and led her to the high roller
craps table where four members of the local pro basketball team shot
dice. They all stopped their game and welcomed her enthusiastically.

"Sister racecar driver!" said Raekwon.

"Please join us," another teammate added.

"Would you like credit from the house?" Jaeger tried to be subtle as
he whispered in her ear.

Emalyn shook her head sideways and opened her purse. She withdrew a large stack of hundred-dollar bills, held together by two rubber
bands. She tossed the money in the direction of the pit boss running
the game. The bundle of cash landed with a substantial thud. "This
should get me started."

The basketball players hooted and hollered their approval. "Boys,
let's take the house for everything they've got." Knowing it was
unlikely, her host grimaced while the basketball players yelped and
whooped.

Emalyn knew her way around most of the table games in the
casino. Like most people with more money than sense, she racked up

her share of losses trying to figure out a system that could beat the house. She soon discovered that no one consistently beats the house at their own games. On the other hand, she hoped with a little luck she could beat the odds and take home a tidy payday, just this once. Hadn't the world been rough on her lately? Couldn't lady luck shine her way, just for a night?

More important than winning money, Emalyn searched for the gambler's escape. Like any other addiction, the games offer refuge for a few hours. All she needed to think about was her bets and the numbers that come up on the dice. No dead George Meloncamp. No husband in prison. No federal charges against herself. *Wouldn't it be fun to win enough money to pay for my legal defense?*

Several people recognized Emalyn as she entered the high rollers area, and they began snapping photos on their phones. Jaeger, standing near the wall, grimaced again, this time quite sincerely. While the casino maintained a policy prohibiting pictures, it seemed impossible to control this behavior in a day when everyone walked around with a camera on their phone. Emalyn and the basketball team quickly appeared all over social media.

Raekwon rolled the dice several times, each one a winner for everyone at the table. When he established a point, Emalyn bet heavily inside. He kept rolling good numbers, causing everyone at the table to win money. When the casino changed the game's stick man, the ball player continued, unfazed by the interruption. When a seven brought his roll to an end, Emalyn's winnings mounted to $12,000. "Raekwon, you are quite the shooter," Emalyn said demurely.

"Nothing to it," he said, smiling from ear to ear.

Emalyn bet heavily on her own first roll and added another $5,000 to her easy money. The basketball players laughed and winked at her as she padded their winnings as well.

To her surprise, she found herself ahead by $25,000 at 11:00 p.m. While the basketball players turned conservative and bet almost nothing on the next several rolls of the dice, Emalyn doubled down on all her bets. By midnight, she fell back to even. A few depressive thoughts tried to invade her mind, but she shooed them away. *It's no time to stop when you're even.* By 12:30 a.m., she lost the last of her $10,000 stake and considered getting an advance on her unlimited black card. The basket-ball players decided to call it a night, each one of them still up several thousand dollars. Emalyn sensed the party breaking up, so she asked for Sean's truck to be brought around. As she walked to the big front door of the casino, her emotions completely reversed from when she arrived. Her self-talk became brutal. *How could I give back the whole $25,000? Sean and I have money in the bank, but not enough to hand over $10,000 to a casino.*

The casino's whale watcher offered Emalyn security to escort her home, but she declined. Smith and Wesson served well as her security on the road. When she got in her car, she unlocked the console and removed her revolver. She loaded several bullets and set the gun on the seat next to her. Rolling onto the Baltimore-Washington Parkway, her mood turned even more sour. She turned on the radio and blared music out her open windows hoping it would chase away her blues.

Another losing player, also with attitude, pulled up next to her. She turned the music down to see what he wanted to say, but he began taunting Emalyn. "How fast can that old pick-up truck go?"

"It's a new pick-up truck and it can go faster than that BMW any day of the week," Emalyn shouted.

The BMW engine revved and the young driver glared at Emalyn. As a stock car driver, she knew the penalties if she got caught racing on the highway. In that moment, she didn't care. Her Vuitton boot hit the gas, and Sean's truck skyrocketed ahead.

The BMW couldn't keep up, so she slowed down to gloat. The only thing that could brighten her mood, a little racing put a smile back on Emalyn's face.

The driver pulled up next to her. "So, you want to go on a date, lady?"

Now, it felt like time to get rid of this creep. Emalyn grabbed the pistol next to her and waved it at the BMW driver. He turned ashen and fish-tailed as he accelerated. She laughed. Emalyn decided to let him go, returning the gun to the passenger seat. About a mile down the road, a police car sat with red and blue lights flashing. In front of the cruiser sat the BMW and the very angry young man about to receive a sizable speeding ticket.

As she sped back to her hotel, thinking about the mess she made of her life at the moment, Emalyn decided to call her sister.

"Noelle, are you up?"

"Well, I am now."

"Noelle, do you remember when we were little?"

"Emalyn, it's the middle of the night. Besides, you know I don't remember much from back then."

"Do you remember the Christmas when Mama got us both on the couch with her? She hugged us tight and made us feel so safe. Then, she put that old quilt around us. It felt so warm. How I wish I could go back there and be safe and warm again."

Silence greeted the end of her revisited memory.

After a several seconds, Noelle spoke again. "Well, we can't. We must do the best with the life we have now. Did you drink tonight?"

"Noelle, no. That's not my thing. I guess I'm just a little lonely with Sean in jail."

"Why don't you come home to Tennessee? The boys are always busy with sports and school activities. We would have time to talk, just sister to sister. We can get our hair done and nails done, just hang out like we used to do."

"My life is in shambles. My marriage is crumbling even without the trouble from bumping into George Meloncamp. Sean is in prison, and it is just a matter of time until I join him. Help me. Please, help me." The urgency in her voice would have shaken someone who didn't know Emalyn so well.

"Oh, baby sister. I wish I could help you, but I'm fresh out of magic pills. Money can't solve everything, and I don't have any if it could. You have to buck up and fight. You got everything in your life by fighting for it. Don't give up now. That's what Daddy would say."

"That's it? That's the sage advice I get from big sister?"

"You don't really want my advice, Emalyn. Just go home. Get some rest. Come see me when you can. It will all look better in the morning."

Emalyn hung up the phone and shrieked in frustration. She loved her sister but so seldom got what she needed from her. Fortunately, the call ate up several lonely minutes, and she found herself almost back at the hotel, suddenly exhausted from the night's activities.

The next morning, Antonio became steaming mad when he saw Emalyn's picture on the splash page of Yahoo. The headline read "Racing Bad Girl Undaunted by Murder Charge." The story painted an unflattering picture of Emalyn, a murder suspect, partying away with NBA players at a casino while her husband remained stuck in jail. Antonio dialed Emalyn's number for the third time and again languished in the land of voice mail.

"What could she be thinking?" Antonio asked.

"That is one crazy lady," replied Tasha, his paralegal.

"How do you defend someone who doesn't realize she is in deep trouble?"

Tasha knew better than to respond to the rhetorical question. She smiled, picked up some files, and returned to her cubicle two floors down.

After several hours, Emalyn called back. She meant to remind Antonio that Milos, her team's lead owner, would fly out to Washington to meet with them. "Antonio, I am so dreadfully sorry. Lonely nights do something to me."

"Emalyn, we had this talk before. We are a team. If you don't do your part, the whole affair could end badly for you."

Antonio could feel his headache pulsing at his right temple. He thought he heard her sniffling on the other end of the phone. While the two kept talking, Tasha slipped back into Antonio's office. He tried to wave her off, but Tasha pushed her tablet screen in front of him. The headline of a story on the *Sports!* website announced that the governing body suspended Emalyn indefinitely, pending the outcome of her murder trial. Antonio passed on the information to his client. In an instant, Emalyn went from hangdog sad to fiery mad. Her weepy contrition evaporated, replaced by a desire to fight back. Although several feel away, Tasha could hear Emalyn's rant. She lifted both eyebrows and lifted both hands to shoulder level, imitating a cat about to claw an approaching threat.

Antonio smiled in response to Tasha's attempt at levity, but his ear began to throb as Emalyn hollered into the mouthpiece.

"Those pompous, arrogant suits think they can throw me out of racing when I'm not proved guilty of nothing yet? Sic 'em, Mr. Attorney. Go get them and get them good. Milos is going to hear from me, too. What time is he wanting to meet?"

Antonio hardly knew what to say. Before exiting his office, Tasha scribbled on a legal pad: MILO'S NOT COMING. He passed the bad news to Emalyn, sending her into an even angrier rant.

"I'm going to get all these people. They can't treat me like this. They haven't heard the last of Emalyn Martin."

"Emalyn, these threats helped get you into this situation. Let me suggest you take a breath and rest for a couple of days. We can get back together after." Antonio bid her good-bye and promised Tasha would schedule a meeting soon.

His head swimming from Emalyn's piercing voice, Antonio shut down his computer and pushed his previously rolled up sleeves back down into position. He buttoned his cuffs and walked to the closet to collect his jacket.

Antonio zoomed his new Audi up the parking garage ramp and out onto K street. Relieved to see lighter-than-normal traffic, he nosed over a lane. Since his previous car got totaled, he augmented the insurance money with a few thousand of his own to spring for the newest model. At the entry to the bridge leading to Virginia, he waived the off-the-grid flower guy over to his car. He imagined Rocco doing the same numerous times since he came to work at their law firm.

Without asking the price, Antonio selected two bunches of roses and handed the man a crumpled twenty. The seller nodded his approval and smiled, revealing a gold-plated bicuspid. As Antonio placed the flowers on the seat next to him, the scent of the roses sent a spine-tingling thought through his whole body.

What if something terrible happened to Rocco? What if he and Sylvia and Marta would soon be in a room full of roses? Funeral flowers were the kind of flower arrangements no one wanted to receive. Antonio tried not to accept the thought. Rocco survived all those years as a policeman. He certainly would not die on an investigation for a law firm. Did the thought come from some evil spirit sent to torment him, or could the Holy Spirit be preparing Antonio for some new reality coming? Even after years as a Christian, he wasn't sure, and he intentionally put it out of his mind. One thing became crystal clear: his body was healing quickly from the accident. His once-swollen face returned to normal, and his foot no longer ached when he walked. His ribs seemed the last to heal, still sending occasional bursts of agony to his central nervous system.

Slipping across the Key Bridge, Antonio raced home in ten minutes. The automatic garage door opener cranked open and Antonio pulled in. As Antonio came upstairs, he saw Sylvia light the candles on the dining room table, just above a steaming lasagna, fresh out of the oven. With his schedule, Sylvia learned to prepare meals for him that held well in the oven.

Antonio strode into the kitchen and presented the assorted roses to his wife. The aroma of her tomato sauce, garlic, and cheese almost overwhelmed his senses. Sylvia smiled brightly and gave her man the passionate kiss he eagerly awaited. She cut the ends off the flowers, arranged them in a vase, and placed the bouquet on the dining room table between the candles.

Antonio gazed at her silhouette as she bent slightly to place the flowers in their position of respect. "Where's Marc?" he asked.

Sylvia turned her head toward Antonio, her hair falling to the side of her face, and offered a sly smile. "At Trey's house for dinner and a movie."

"So, he won't be home for a while." Antonio's brain fogged up a bit when Sylvia gave him her come ahead signals. He stated the obvious and froze in his steps, waiting for his brain to recover.

Sylvia sauntered over to her husband, stroked his dark hair, and helped him off with his suit jacket. She sniffed at his collar, no doubt smelling the fragrance she bought him as a Christmas gift. Her scent sent shivers up his spine. Dinner would have to wait. Their passion would take away all their worries, temporarily.

CHAPTER TEN

A loud knock rattled the window of Marta's hotel room. She jumped out of bed. The dream seemed so real, but not as real as this knock at the door. After another fruitless day of searching for Rocco, she slept like the dead. Marta rushed to the closet and threw on her bathrobe. Just before she opened the hotel-room door, a plane roared overhead, vibrating the windows of the hotel room.

Marta unchained the lock, hoping Rocco waited at the door. Without looking through the peephole, she flung open the oft-repainted door. A young, uniformed female officer stood with Detective Julie Jung. Knowing what they came to say, Marta gestured them both inside. Her stomach began to ache, and her head throbbed. Absentmindedly, she backed up and sat on the side of the bed. Like a child, she looked up expectantly at the mature police detective. Though Jung's weathered face appeared full of kindness, Marta wanted her to hurry up and spit out the news she came to deliver. In those incalculably long seconds, Marta's blood pressure zoomed higher and higher. She thought she might pass out before hearing what happened to her beloved Rocco.

"We are so sorry to tell you this. It appears that we have located the body of your husband, Rocco Semones." Detective Jung spoke the words without emotion. "I know this is hard to hear."

Marta didn't cry, and she didn't pass out. She struggled to comprehend. Body meant dead body. Body meant Rocco equaled dead. She leaned forward, almost folding her body in half, trying desperately to unhear the words she so badly wanted spoken just moments ago. In the company of two strangers, she felt completely alone in the room.

How Marta wished one of the women would touch her or find some way to bridge the tremendous gulf between herself and the rest of humanity. The severing of her one-flesh union, swift and excruciating, set her adrift. She felt like tissue from her organs and sinew from her bones extracted instantly, without anesthetic. Some evil-spirit surgeon operated on her insides without permission. He removed her sense of well-being, her hope for the future, and even her ability to breathe.

Detective Jung moved closer and placed a hand on her back. "We know this is hard to accept. Take as long as you need. Is there someone you want us to call to be with you?"

Tears fell down. Marta couldn't have been more alone in Columbus. The only person she knew was a man who kidnapped her eight years earlier. Marta would call Antonio and Sylvia in the morning, but not right now. How could she tell Antonio that his brother died? *Oh Rocco!*

"Do you know for sure it is Rocco?" Hope's last glimmer faded fast, but it couldn't help but spark once more.

"Yes. We are certain, but we need you to come with us to officially identify the body."

Marta nodded in agreement. The police women waited while she slipped into the bathroom and changed into her blouse and pants from earlier in the day. Her chest felt strange. She wondered if the rumbling in her chest could be a heart attack. She took an aspirin from her purse and downed it with a few sips of tap water. She sat on the toilet for a moment and sobbed into her hands then washed her face and combed her hair. She put on Rocco's favorite shade of lipstick. Her beloved, or at least his remains, waited for her. She must go to him with the right lipstick on.

* * *

Several days later, Antonio stood by Marta at the funeral home. She swayed slightly in front of Rocco's casket, seeing his embalmed body for the first time. Antonio watched the interaction between his sister-in-law and the body of his brother. Rocco's sweet face looked so peaceful. Those cute, chubby cheeks rouged up for the occasion. He looked handsome in his black suit. The boutonniere—Sylvia's idea—was intended to remind Marta of a long-ago high school dance back in Brazil. Antonio wished Marta and Rocco had met years earlier. She seemed good for him. Antonio held Marta's arm in his, standing as tall and sturdy as he could muster. She needed a real man beside her in these worst moments of her life. It was the least he could do for his brother and for his wife's best friend.

The first guests began to arrive for the visitation. Sylvia stood at Marta's other side, speaking familiar Portuguese words of comfort in her ear.

"Why didn't we stay in Brazil?" Marta whispered to Sylvia, also in Portuguese.

Sylvia kept her hand on Marta's back for support as the first visitors —members of Rocco's intramural basketball league—filed by. The sight of the tall men entering the funeral home as a group comforted Antonio. He recognized several of them from basketball teams on which he and Rocco played. Many offered kind words for Marta about her husband. She smiled back through tearful eyes. Grace held her up when her spirit wanted to fall to the floor and sob.

Antonio shook each hand firmly. He didn't cry; he didn't know why. His emotions felt completely disconnected from this reality. Truth be told, the whole issue of Rocco dying had failed to register in his brain. It represented a horror uncontemplated. Even as the visitation happened, Antonio felt nothing amiss at all. The timing for Rocco's death happened all wrong, years too early. Rocco looked too healthy, too invincible. Antonio's subconscious mind would suppress any feelings until such time as Rocco's death made sense. For now, it just didn't compute.

While he was a uniformed police officer, other men died in the line of duty, but Rocco always made it home alive. In life's grand production, Rocco always played the pall bearer, not the deceased.

Next in the receiving line, several lawyers from Morgan and Montgomery came by with their spouses. While most of them didn't know Rocco well, his death while investigating for the firm made the visitation and funeral a near-mandatory corporate event. Several ostentatious flower arrangements arrived from the various partners, lawyers, and administrative personnel from the firm. Antonio looked around the room, smiling at the forty or so flower arrangements.

When a young man dies, there are many mourners and much attention paid to the widow, Antonio recalled his mother saying once. The outpouring of love and affection for Rocco poured like a salve on Antonio's soul, though one of marginal effectiveness. The family's heartache could not be fully relieved, even with this large crowd of mourners.

Marta's hairdresser squeezed her in a hug. "Oh, sweetie, I'm so sorry," the hairdresser said, bussing Marta on the cheek.

"Thanks for coming, we appreciate it," Marta said, sniffling.

Police officers wearing their dress uniforms poured into the room like a sea of navy blue. Several of Rocco's former co-workers from the precinct made their way through the line. Marta graciously listened to their offers of help and accepted an envelope stuffed with cash, a collection taken up by Rocco's police and firefighter friends. At Marta's request, Antonio put the money in his suit jacket for safe-keeping. Marta explained three times to three different officers that she and Rocco lived in a condo and she wouldn't need anyone to mow her lawn.

After ninety minutes of visitation, Marta couldn't have been more exhausted. Her feet ached, her back hurt, and her emotions felt permanently frazzled. Finally, two women from Marta's tennis league became the last mourners to pass in front of the casket. They hugged Marta and offered any help they could provide.

When the wake completed, Marta sat down wearily on the front row and stared at the casket. "Honey, what happened to you? I so wish you could have made it home to me. I miss you so much. You won't ever see your baby." Sobbing deeply, her whole body convulsed. Antonio comforted her by just sitting there at her side. When Sylvia returned from the ladies' room, she embraced Marta. They cried together.

"I'm so sorry," Sylvia said. "I'm so, so sorry."

"How could this happen to me?" Marta bent over almost convulsing with each word.

Antonio walked to the back of the visitation parlor. The raw pain touched some inner part of his heart. He stared out the window at the beautiful summer evening. Like his mother always said, it should be raining when someone dies. The sun is for living and happiness. Rain is for hanging out and being sad.

A single gunshot to the back of the head ended Rocco's life. He sat in his rental car in Columbus, Ohio at the time. He experienced no struggle, no pain, no terror. The bullet travelled downward, sparing his face. All the terror belonged not to Rocco but to his family.

He looked good lying there in his casket, Antonio thought—better from this distance of thirty feet away. His only brother joined their mother and father in heaven. Rocco's death tipped the scales for Antonio—more of his loved ones resided in heaven than on Earth. While the two brothers had consoled each other just a few years prior when their dad died unexpectedly of a heart attack, it became Sylvia's turn to comfort him, as well as Marta and Marc. Sylvia excelled at being a great comforter.

The four left the funeral home. In the car, no one spoke at first. Finally, Antonio broke the silence. "Do you want to spend the night in our guest room?"

Marta thought for a minute, saying nothing at first. "Yes, but I need to stop by the condo and get a few things. Sylvia, will you go up with me?"

Antonio stayed with the car, parked outside Marta's condo building. The two women said nothing in the elevator and looked relieved when it stopped on Marta's floor. As she reached to put her key in the lock, the door pushed open. "Did I forget to lock the door?" Marta asked. As the door opened more completely, Marta gasped.

"Someone could still be in the apartment," Sylvia whispered. Marta rushed into the modern-looking condo. Her eyes studied the room carefully as she panted with excitement. Quickly, she raced around behind the sofa, then peered behind the counter in the kitchen. Down the hall, she looked in the apartment-sized bathroom. No one there. With ferocity, she tore open the door to the bedroom and then the master bathroom. Breathing heavily, she looked in the second bath as well. Whoever did this must have escaped. *Good thing for them,* Marta thought.

* * *

"I'm thinking of going to the gym this morning. Do you think that's all right?" Antonio tilted his head to the right and looked for Sylvia's reaction on her face.

"Sure. Take Marc with you if you like. He is probably tired of sitting around here, too. Be back by 10:30 so you and Marc will have time to get dressed. We don't want to make Marta nervous about being late. I may drive her to her apartment to help her get ready. If I do, I'll text you. Is your foot well enough to work out?"

"It's better from the physical therapy. I'll probably just ride the exercise bike for cardio. Are you nervous about the break-in at Marta's condo?"

"No," Sylvia said. "I feel terrible for Marta to have to go through that, too. You read about these burglaries all the time. Some thief sees the announcement in the paper and comes when they suspect everyone will be at the wake or the funeral."

"You're right. Just so much going on. My first thought: it could be related to Rocco's death somehow. That's probably a stretch though. We will be back shortly from the gym."

"Okay, husband. See you soon."

Antonio hugged Sylvia tightly but let go when a twinge of survivor's guilt invaded. He wished Rocco had married young like he and Sylvia. Just now pushing 40, their twentieth anniversary was just two years away.

As soon as Marc finished lacing his basketball shoes, father and son took off like caged animals seeking freedom. After they left, Marta emerged from her room. Her hair shot out in all directions, frizzy and mussed from her fitful hours in bed. Sylvia gave Marta a long, assuring hug. The new widow felt some of her anxiety and pain melt away.

"Did you sleep at all?"

"Not much."

"Do you feel like telling me what happened in Columbus, besides having to identify Rocco's body?"

Marta sat down on the couch and gratefully accepted a cup of coffee. "It seems like a dream now. I retraced Rocco's steps as much as possible. RaceRX seemed to be a dead end. Since he was traveling on business, the boss of that team talked to me by phone. He seemed very nice and didn't seem to be hiding anything, but he offered no answers either. Next, I followed a lead I found in Rocco's room. It led me to a big church where Rocco may have gone, but no one recalled seeing him. The people there shared their kindness and prayed with me. It felt like God preparing me." Marta started to shed a few tears.

"It's okay, honey, if you don't want to do this now," Sylvia said while draping an arm around Marta. Remembering the omelet on the stove, Sylvia walked back over to the kitchen area.

"There won't ever be an easy time or a good time," Marta said. "Something strange happened as I got ready to leave the church. I ran into one of the guys who kidnapped me several years ago."

Sylvia stopped tending the omelet and turned to face Marta. "You have got to be kidding me!"

"No joke. Do you remember my telling you about Alex, the one I thought may have accepted Christ while he held me hostage?"

Sylvia nodded as she lifted the bottom side of the omelet with a spatula, checking it. The toaster popped up and Sylvia transferred the large, whole grain slices onto their plates. "Yes, I remember."

Marta told Sylvia everything of note about her trip, including Alex's plea that she tells no one his whereabouts.

"Do you suspect Alex may have had something to do with Rocco's death?" Sylvia asked in a way that made Marta feel naïve. "He committed a kidnapping and maybe even a murder. Then Rocco ends up dead? Do you know how that sounds?"

"I know. I suppose it crossed my mind, but I really don't think he played a part in Rocco's murder. He seems to be a changed man. He has worked at the church for several years, running their homeless ministry. I can't believe Alex had anything to do with Rocco's murder. A voice inside my head witnessed to me as Alex recounted his story. I felt like God wanted me to believe Alex."

"Okay, let's suppose Alex knows nothing and did nothing to cause Rocco's death. Didn't he have a partner, some other Russian guy? Is he still a criminal?"

Marta hadn't thought much about Sergei until Sylvia asked the question. *How could I have been so stupid? Alex may be a Christian and living the life of a believer, but perhaps his Russian mob friend killed Rocco.*

"His name is Sergei. While Alex is a changed man, I don't know much about Sergei. Alex said they have drifted apart. The other Russian guy acted more violent and meaner, even before Alex's conversion. What if Rocco stumbled onto Alex, then Alex told Sergei, who in turn killed Rocco to try to keep their new lives secret? This could have nothing to do with stock car racing or Emalyn."

Sylvia flipped the omelet onto a plate, already adorned with sliced tomatoes and the cinnamon toast. She handed Marta the plate, giving her a sideways hug as she did.

* * *

When Antonio and Marc arrived at the gym, they found Trey playing basketball on the upper floor with a couple of older guys and a friend from the high school team. Despite his foot pain, Antonio joined Marc and Trey, playing three-on-three for almost an hour.

Antonio felt his body unwinding from all the grief and torture of the past week. Although it hurt to play basketball on his still-healing foot, the physical exertion cleared his mind. After a couple of games, Antonio begged off and decided to hit the showers. The boys could play a few more minutes before they would have to leave for home.

The locker room, stinky as always, made Antonio feel close to his brother as he changed out of his drenched t-shirt and shorts. As soon as he felt the water flowing out of the shower head, Antonio began to weep. His body shook as he tried to process the reality of never again speaking to Rocco. The individual shower stall gave him some privacy, though his feet, ankles, and crown of his head remained visible below and above the heavy, plastic curtain.

After shedding his tears, Antonio lifted his hands and silently praised God. He didn't feel thankful for his brother's death, but he felt joy in knowing for sure where Rocco would spend eternity. The sting of death removed, at least for a few moments, as Antonio envisioned his big, hulking brother hugging Jesus and walking on golden streets. Suddenly, Antonio realized how weird he probably looked, standing in the shower with his hands raised. He turned off the water and dried off.

After collecting Trey and Marc, Antonio returned home to find Sylvia reading her Bible and listening to Christian music. While Marc jumped into the shower, Antonio stretched out on the sofa, and Sylvia lifted her Bible so he could place his head in her lap. She stroked his hair with her long fingers. He cried again.

Antonio and Sylvia got dressed mindlessly. Sylvia vetoed the tie Rocco gave Antonio for Christmas, saying the sport's team logo on it looked too informal for a funeral.

The Audi traveled the few blocks to Marta's condo. As promised, the Arlington police stationed men outside the building and at the door to her unit. Marta emerged from the building looking like a rock star with a black, tight-fitting dress and aviator shades. She fiddled with her wedding ring out of nervousness but tried to act brave by smiling at the officers standing near the circular drive.

After picking up Marta, the foursome made their way to the funeral home several miles away. Unlike the previous day, no formal visitation preceded the funeral. Some visitors passed by the casket on their own then came to greet Marta, Sylvia, and Antonio in their seats. Marc hung out in the lobby, waiting for Trey and two other teammates to arrive. He greeted Emalyn and her sister, who arrived just before the service began with Millard and Jesse Estes in tow.

Antonio and Sylvia went back to the row where Emalyn and her entourage sat quietly.

"Thank you all for coming," Antonio said.

"Oh sweetie, we are so sorry for your loss," Emalyn said while hugging Antonio and kissing him on the cheek. Her sister, Noelle did the same, though it represented her first time meeting Antonio. She smelled of heavy perfume and bore only a small resemblance to Emalyn, with brown hair teased up to the moon. Then she and Emalyn moved on to comfort Sylvia in similar fashion.

"This is a tough one," Millard said, shaking Antonio's hand.

"Sorry for your loss," Jesse said while glancing around the room. "Not a fan of funerals."

"Me neither, particularly my own brother's," Antonio said.

Antonio surmised that Jesse fell into the category of those who fear death and all its trappings. Both Jesse and Millard Estes looked awkward wearing suits—definitely out of their stock car racing element. Millard's light-gray two-piece had to be at least two sizes too small. His massive gut stuck out over his belt and beige socks looked odd being matched with black loafers. Jesse's three-piece had equal and opposite problems, cuffs hanging down over his hands and pant legs dragging the floor. Unfortunately, the long pants did not completely cover his black tennis shoes.

The music began promptly at eleven A.M. One of Rocco's favorite contemporary Christian songs played during a montage of pictures projected on a screen above the casket. The snapshots captured various stages of Rocco's life and memories with relatives and friends. Marc gathered the pictures into a PowerPoint presentation timed to worship music. Antonio smiled at Rocco's round face on his first day of kindergarten, his awkward smile at a junior high school dance, his triumphant look graduating from high school. Rocco looked so young when he graduated from basic training in the Army Reserve. Proud and tall in his first police uniform, he towered over his supervisors on graduating from the police academy, and later, accepting his rank of detective. Finally, the wedding shots clicked by, causing murmurs and quite a few tears among those in the audience. Marta's smile in the final picture haunted several guests for days to come.

Antonio presented a poignant eulogy, needlessly apologizing at the beginning if he failed to complete it. God helped Antonio deliver the words with eloquence. His re-telling of boyhood pranks and humorous moments before Rocco's wedding helped to lighten the mood a little.

The pastor preached a brief and focused sermon about heaven and how to get there. The funeral gave Marta joy beneath the pain when two young men made professions of faith at the end of the preacher's message. Maybe something good came of what the devil meant for harm.

After the eulogy, Antonio noticed Marta suffering a moment of panic as she probably realized the service rolled inevitably toward its conclusion. Common to many mourners who have lost someone dear, the sudden realization must have rushed in. *After this service is over, we bury the love of my life. Can't we keep it going a little longer?*

The guests filed out, again shaking hands or hugging Marta, Antonio, and Sylvia. The attendant closed the casket and secured it shut. None of them would see Rocco's face again in this life. At the cemetery, Marta broke down again as the honor guard handed her an American flag, folded with precision. She clutched it to her chest and sobbed inconsolably. Although stoic throughout the service, Marc cried as well upon seeing his Aunt Marta's pain. Antonio put his arm around his boy.

Finally, at the conclusion of the service, Rocco's temporal body was lowered into the earth. The hopes and dreams for a long marriage faded. All descended out of sight to be covered over by dirt and time.

CHAPTER ELEVEN

Escorted by a deputy, Antonio walked through the lower level of the federal jail across from the courthouse. His escort stopped and unlocked the door of Meeting Room B. Antonio took a seat at the metal table and waited. He wasted hours in this room numerous times before, waiting for other prisoners to be brought in for meetings. He stared at the stark white walls and counted the number of hard, asbestos tiles on the floor between the door and the table where he sat. Time dragged.

God, why did You let my brother die? I know You are good all the time, but it doesn't feel like it now. While You allow many terrible things to occur for reasons I cannot fathom, this has to be one of the worst. Rocco did not even get to hold his baby. He was a great man and a super brother—and a solid Christian. How can this world be better off without him?

After sitting alone for twenty-five minutes, the door finally opened. A bored-looking guard ushered in Sean Martin and removed his handcuffs. Before Antonio could greet Sean, another man joined them. Antonio rose and shook hands with both of them.

"Bates. Nathaniel Bates. I am Sean's attorney."

"Antonio Semones, attorney for Emalyn Martin. Glad to meet you. How are you, Sean?"

"I'm dying in here." His face reflected his stress, though he looked less puffy from his weeks of involuntary sobriety. Crow's feet surrounded his eyes, much more noticeable than when they'd first met. "My mind can't take the constant pressure. There are some very bad dudes in this place. What if I don't make it out alive?"

Antonio expressed regret at the situation and passed along Emalyn's hope that Sean would be out of jail and home very soon. In agreement with Bates's terms for the meeting, each of Antonio's questions would be answered only after Bates agreed that Sean could reply without incriminating himself. After several warm up questions about Sean's actions before the race at Pocono, Antonio got into the heart of the matter.

"What was in the envelope that you passed to the member of the RaceRX team?"

"I'm sorry, Antonio," Bates said. "He can't answer that."

Antonio shot Bates a look. *What good is this meeting if Sean can't answer my questions?* He tried again. "Why did you speak with a member of the RaceRX team?"

Sean looked at Bates who nodded that he could answer. "That mechanic for RaceRX helped with and observed some changes made to Emalyn's car. He assisted someone from our team in tweaking Emalyn's car after inspection to make it run faster. The modifications fell outside the rules of the racing governing body. He could have reported us. I made an executive decision to give him some money to ensure his confidentiality."

"Did these changes have anything to do with the explosion involving George Meloncamp's car?"

Bates nodded again. "No way. The alterations increased the performance of Emalyn's car by a few miles per hour at most. It could not have played a part in the explosion of another team's car."

Antonio surmised that the hush money situation came as a result of blackmail, which the prosecution could just as easily say related to George Meloncamp's death. Antonio didn't want to know too much more about the pay-off.

"Did Emalyn know about the rules infraction or the money?"

Sean answered before Bates signaled his approval. "I didn't tell her.

To my knowledge, she didn't know. This scheme came from me. It's a win-at-any-cost world. No wins equal no endorsements, which means no money."

"How would you describe your relationship with Emalyn?"

"We have a marriage. There are good days and bad. She is an independent woman, very determined. At times, she is also kind and loving. We argue, but I need her more now than ever. She is my whole world, the only thing that matters to me."

Antonio kept the questions coming for a half hour. Mostly he asked about the race team, their finances, and who else may have wanted George Meloncamp dead. Eventually, their time ran out.

As they said their good-byes and the guard re-handcuffed Sean, Bates asked for a reciprocal meeting to question Emalyn. Antonio agreed to set it up for the following Monday or Tuesday.

Back in his office, Antonio clicked on his television to see how the sports news channels covered Emalyn's suspension. Fortunately, the only mention of the suspension rolled on the crawl at the bottom of the television screen. He would have to check back in the early evening. Antonio couldn't help feeling he missed something about the whole situation. But what?

Antonio spoke into the speaker phone on his desk. "Tasha, could you come up to my office?"

Tasha arrived within a few minutes. "What's up?" she asked.

"Let's go over what we know so far. I need someone to brainstorm this." Moments later, she hurried back into his office, iPad tucked under her arm, carrying two cups of coffee from the pantry.

"Emalyn is a big rival of George Meloncamp," Tasha began. "She bumps him and his car explodes, killing him. Police suspect murder. Residue of a bomb is found. A video surfaces of Sean Martin paying off a rival team's mechanic. Police believe that Sean, and probably Emalyn, cooked up a conspiracy to kill Meloncamp. They arrest Sean Martin. Your brother noses around Ohio and someone kills him while Sean sits in jail. So, we know it wasn't Sean."

After sipping his coffee, Antonio picked up the dialogue. "Their narrative is based on Emalyn's motive to win at any cost. But wouldn't she know that she would never get away with killing her main rival?

The timing ... why would she make all those threats right before she planned to kill him?"

"Maybe her dislike for George Meloncamp overwhelmed her good judgment?"

"Yeah, and then her overwhelming dislike carried her through the process of building a bomb and secretly planting it in Meloncamp's car? No, too much planning and preparation went into this for it to be seen as a rash decision. Who else possessed adequate motive?" Antonio asked.

Tasha responded with more questions. "Any other team that trailed him in the points race? Someone from Meloncamp's team who wanted him out of the way? Someone who took advantage of Emalyn's threats to blame it on her?"

"Maybe. We need some more investigative work. Let's get the firm's other investigator to this week's stock car race in Ohio. Have him talk to me before he goes. Basically, we want him to find out who else would benefit from Meloncamp's death and report back anything at all suspicious."

"Should I call BF directly?" Tasha asked.

Antonio nodded, wincing at the sound of the man's name and something Freudian in the way he referred to the guy as "our other investigator." He didn't like using BF, but he really could see no other choice.

Benjamin Franklin Honecker, or BF as he liked to be called, reeked of old-school private eye. Though also an investigator for the firm, he bore no resemblance to Rocco. Where Antonio's brother could be described as kind, paternal, and caring, BF spit out words like they cost him $1,000 each. He didn't care at all what people thought of him or his actions. Rocco epitomized a police background; BF's experience was ex-Army intelligence. Rocco struck most people as charming and polite; BF maintained only a thin veneer of professionalism, but he could also be downright rude, even manipulative. Some called him the firm's fixer; when the firm faced a mess, BF would fix it. He lacked Antonio's Christian ethic and Rocco's respect for the law. His only moral code bestowed loyalty onto whoever paid him—and to himself.

* * *

When BF touched down in Columbus, he immediately drove to the
police station. Detective Julie Jung introduced herself then ushered
him into a meeting room, closed the door, and invited him to have a
seat.

"Thanks for seeing me," BF began. "What do you know about the
Semones killing?"

Detective Jung leaned back in her chair. She took a healthy drink
of black coffee, rolling her eyes over BF's desire to get right down to
business. "Here's what I know. Rocco Semones nosed around out at
the RaceRX complex. His meeting with a guy named Owen Vetter
was uneventful but must have triggered a lead of some sort. We
traced the pings from his phone and learned he didn't leave the
complex right away. Afterward, he went to a church. I wrote down
the name and address for you here. He then went to a farmhouse in
the country. Here is the address of that house. We went by but
haven't found anyone at home." With resources running thin, Detective Jung stated no objection to BF staking out the farmhouse
for her.

"Thank you for those two leads. Where did Rocco proceed from
there?"

"His phone pinged near the Ohio State West Campus in a remote
parking lot. They found him slumped over the steering wheel of his
car. The coroner fixed time of death twenty-four to forty-eight hours
prior to when the campus police found him, so it looks like he died on
a weekday evening when the parking lot would have been crowded
with students' cars. The campus police found his body later, after many
of the cars cleared out. A single gunshot to the back of the head
proved fatal."

"Any idea about why he went to the campus?" BF asked.

"Not sure. I can't let you take this, but you can look at it and make
notes if you want. These are his phone records during his time in our
area. Two calls to Tennessee, two to the Washington, D.C. area, and
one to RaceRX here in Columbus. Do you know why he may have
called Tennessee?"

"Our client and her team live in Tennessee. I'll check with her and get back to you."

The meeting, a mere exchange of information both parties already knew, went on another twenty minutes. BF felt undaunted, but he realized he faced a lot of difficult work. Outside the police station, he folded himself back into the rental Camaro. His habit of requesting a sporty car yielded this red Camaro, his least favorite model. Not grossly overweight, just big and beefy, his long legs balked getting in and out of the car. He felt cramped and uncomfortable. To make matters worse, trying to see out the small rear window gave him fits, which worried him whenever he backed up. As he drove out of his parking space at the police station, a Prius honked at him. BF stopped and let the glorified golf cart pass.

Out on the highway, he called the two Tennessee numbers that Rocco contacted in his final twenty-four hours. The first call went to Emalyn. BF pretended he called to ask some follow-up questions. She answered the queries quickly, and they both hung up. Millard Estes picked up after BF dialed the second number he'd written down.

"This is Millard, can I help you?"

"My name is BF Honecker. I work with Emalyn's defense team. I'm re-tracing Rocco Semones's steps for his time here in Ohio. I guess he called you the Monday before he died?"

"Yes."

"Can you tell me what he asked about? It is important."

"Oh certainly. He asked about the RaceRX Racing Team. He asked me what I knew about the mechanics on that team. Unfortunately, I couldn't offer much help. I know some of the other crew chiefs, but unless a mechanic is a big pain or has done something stupid, I probably wouldn't have heard of them. I talked to my son, Jesse, about it, but he didn't know their guys either."

"Do you remember anything else about the conversation?"

"He asked about someone named Sandy. I hadn't heard of him. You probably can figure it out through RaceRX, if he is one of their guys."

After hanging up, BF got off at the exit closest to RaceRX. His visit fell after hours by thirty minutes or so. Not fully night yet, the sun disappeared beyond the horizon but still offered minimal lighting.

After pulling into the parking lot, he walked to the front doors, knocked, and then tried opening one of them. It didn't budge, locked up tight. The only light inside emanated from a six-by-five-foot display case, featuring several stock car racing trophies and topped with the RaceRX logo.

BF walked down an exterior, concrete staircase to the back side of the building, rounding the corner near the first of five large glass garage doors. He peered through the glass but saw no one inside. He continued walking past four more garage doors until coming to a sturdy conventional door. BF knocked, but no one answered. The place looked deserted except for a few vehicles parked near the door where he stood: two RaceRX company pick-up trucks and a long, enclosed trailer with no exterior markings. He reasoned that those vehicles belonged to the company, probably not representing any people currently inside.

BF decided to pick the lock. As soon as he entered, an alarm box beeped on the wall near the door. Knowing he only had a few seconds to enter the correct code, he strode to the control box and entered the numerical street address of the building. The alarm beeped once more then turned itself off. The small colored light changed from red to green. Although his mind held a plan B, it never ceased to amaze him how many homes and businesses used their own address as the alarm shut-off code.

There seemed to be little else on the ground floor other than the service bays and the office where he stood. BF rifled through the desk and found nothing of interest. Then he opened the unlocked file cabinets. Looking through the cabinet, financial documents representing purchases of parts for the team's cars took up most of the space. After pawing through three of the four drawers, he eventually found performance appraisals of the mechanics. He extracted the one for Sandy Macon. He found it interesting that Sandy earned the label "good worker and competent mechanic." BF's eyebrows raised when he read that Sandy "needed to control his temper." Taken in total, the document was only marginally interesting—not what BF hoped to find. He needed Sandy's address and social security number to find out more about him—especially something he might wish to hide. Could he be illegal? Have a criminal record?

Exhausting all the files, BF returned to the desk drawers and combed through their contents until he found the emergency contact roster. Sandy's home address and phone number popped out at him. He entered the information in his phone. Assuming the address was current, he closed the cabinet and prepared to leave. After a quick look in the remaining desk drawers, he decided the office held nothing more of value to him.

As he moved toward the exit, BF heard a faint metal clinking sound in the shop area. He turned off the office light and crouched under the window facing the shop. While the window was covered by venetian blinds, he craned his neck and peered out between two of the slats. The shop looked dark, and he saw nothing out of the ordinary. After a few moments, some of the shadows moved about, but BF couldn't tell whether someone lurked out there or his imagination played tricks on him. Pistol drawn, he slowly opened the shop door. A low growl grew into angry barking. Two German shepherds lunged at BF, one of them rearing up on its hind legs, bearing an impressive set of fangs. The other dog nipped BF's gun hand.

BF slammed the door shut and panted for several seconds. When he calmed down, he noticed a trickle of blood emanating from his right hand. Teeth imprints served as a noticeable reminder, but the blood looked minimal. BF hurried out the same door he'd entered. The disturbance with the dogs caused him to forget to re-set the alarm. He moved quickly past the five glass garage doors, aware of the dogs barking and snarling from inside. He ran up the steps, looking around furtively to see if anyone noticed his actions. With all still appearing calm at the front of the race team headquarters, BF returned to the relative safety of his rental Camaro by the front entrance.

After again loading himself into the car, BF used a KFC napkin to clean up his hand. *Who says eating fried chicken is bad for your health?* he thought, amusing himself. He headed for Sandy's house, guided by his GPS. Only then did he notice that the address mirrored the one given him by Detective Jung. He literally retraced Rocco's steps—or at least his tire tracks. As evening approached, the darkened sky did little to help him find his way. When he came near the farmhouse, BF pulled off the road, *perhaps parking in the same spot where Rocco parked days earlier.* Hidden between two rows of corn, the car would not be visible to anyone who pulled into the driveway of Sandy's house. As BF hiked back to the house, he was serenaded by crickets and other creatures of the night.

The farmhouse looked dark, and he saw no car in the driveway. His feet crunched loudly walking along the gravel driveway. A large street-light mounted to a telephone pole near the house illuminated the side of the house and the outbuildings beyond.

Arriving at the back door, BF studied his reflection in the glass panes and tried to peer inside. His dark, closely cropped hair framed dark eyes and a hefty nose, broken several times in various altercations. Through the window in the upper half of the door he could see an old-fashioned farm kitchen. The wood table in the center of the room, half covered with newspapers and assorted junk, seemed sturdy enough. His flashlight lit up the only ornamentation adorning the kitchen: a banal-looking ceramic hen on the kitchen counter.

With ease, BF picked the lock on the back door and let himself in. Dishes sat unwashed in the sink, and small bugs milled about the crumbs on the counter. The landline phone rang, which would have startled a less-experienced investigator. BF ignored the ringing phone and wandered through the small dining area to the adjoining living room. Scant furniture, just a couch, an uncomfortable-looking Windsor knock-off chair, and a coffee table, failed to fill up the modest living room. A relatively new HD television sat on a decrepit library table. On the living room wall hung a Russian flag from the post-cold-war era. *Enemy territory for sure*, BF thought.

Walking through the living room into what once merited the title of parlor, BF spotted a motor scooter parked just inside the front door. Sandy apparently didn't trust leaving his scooter in the unlocked, unattached garage. The parlor contained no other furniture except for a coat tree with five or six men's jackets and a white coat. The latter garment looked obviously smaller than the jackets, and BF surmised it belonged to Sandy's girlfriend.

A single bedroom and a small bathroom made up the rest of the house. BF looked through the medicine cabinet, finding nothing more than toothpaste, a razor, shave cream, an over-the-counter pain medicine, a generic stomach tonic, and two prescriptions. One prescription in Sandy's name read "as needed for anxiety," and he did not recognize the other medication for the girlfriend.

Obviously remodeled in the 1970s, the wallpaper in the bedroom sported a black-and-white checkered pattern. The unmade bed included dark brown sheets and pillows tossed around casually. On the nightstand sat a checkbook atop a box of checks. Looking at the check register, the bank balance surprised BF: more than $7,000. *Most mechanics don't have large bank balances*, BF thought. Only a modest number of checks appeared missing from the checkbook. The majority of entries mentioned rent and utilities, living expenses. Until a few weeks earlier, the balance in the account never exceeded $1,000. The windfall came recently.

As BF exited the bedroom, headlights shone through the front windows of the house. Someone had come home. The driveway ended near the back door where BF entered. There seemed no way to retrace his steps without being seen. He rushed to the bedroom window, which faced the opposite side of the house from the driveway. Unlocking it, he yanked upward with all his might. Keys jingled outside the backdoor and the handle squeaked, responding to someone's firm hand. The window in the bedroom remained hopelessly stuck, repainted many times and probably not opened in the past twenty years. BF tugged furiously, but it wouldn't budge.

Someone entered the kitchen and turned on the overhead lighting, tossing keys on the table. He or she must have walked to the refrigerator, grabbing a canned beverage and opening it. Whoever it was headed into the living room to watch television.

The television hummed as it warmed up, and a man hummed a song BF recognized from the radio. A Russian-language television station came on, and BF heard two voices yammering back and forth. He remained stuck in the bedroom, peeking out from behind the armoire. He saw two soccer teams dancing up and down the pitch on the screen in the living room.

After several minutes, BF crept out from the hiding place, trying not to make any of the floorboards squeak beneath his black loafers. By the time Sandy noticed a strange reflection on the television, he heard a gun cocking behind his head.

"Don't move, Sergei," BF ordered.

"I wouldn't dream of it, but you can call me Sandy. That is my American name now." Sandy's gravelly voice reflected his days as a hood in Russia. BF's gun didn't cause panic as it might have years before.

"Alias, you mean."

"Are you from New Jersey?"

BF realized that Sandy must have wondered why he remained alive. They both knew that real-life hit men don't toy with their prey—every second an adversary stayed alive was a dangerous one. Pull the trigger and exit quickly. That's how you do it when your job is to kill for a living.

"Who sent you?" Sandy asked.

"It isn't who you think. I'm here about the murder of George Meloncamp. Who hired you to rig his car with explosives?"

Sandy said nothing at first. "You have the wrong idea. I didn't touch Meloncamp's car."

"I saw the videotape of you taking hush money from Sean Martin," BF said. "Why else would he give a mechanic from another team so much money?"

"You have it all wrong. I helped Sean's team with some needed alterations to their car. He merely paid me for mechanic work."

"Tell me this. Were you involved in a kidnapping and murder in Virginia eight years ago?"

Just then, BF heard a loud, metallic crunching sound. His vision blurred and his knees buckled. A second blow rendered him unconscious. He collapsed on the wooden floor.

* * *

Antonio shuffled into the old Methodist church with stunning stained-glass windows and fancy woodwork. Antonio didn't connect with this type of worship facility, but his purpose didn't involve his wants and needs. Marta called and asked him to meet her there.

Marta sat in the second row from the front, praying in whispers. The two of them were nearly alone in the large chapel except for a homeless man dozing in the back row. Antonio walked up the center aisle and sat down next to Marta. He looked at the beautiful architecture and simple symbolism of the cross, altar, and pulpit at the front of the auditorium. Neither said anything for a few minutes.

Finally, Marta turned to him and whispered, "I don't know if I believe in God anymore."

Antonio waited for a moment before responding. "Marta, that is a normal feeling after a tragedy like this. These things shake everyone's faith. I don't feel as safe as I did before. It increased my concern for Sylvia and Marc immeasurably." Although he talked a good game, Antonio was fighting his own battle with doubt. Like many Christians, he assumed safety from tragedy came included with faith: no extra charge.

Marta shifted uncomfortably on the wooden pew. "It isn't about my safety or even the baby. I used to think if I followed Jesus and listened to God's Word everything would turn out okay. My understanding included blessings in this lifetime and eternity in heaven. At a minimum, I thought long life came included in the deal. Look at Rocco. He didn't drink or chew or hang with women who do. Now, Rocco's dead and everything seems shattered beyond repair."

Antonio stared at his sister-in-law with great empathy. What could he say that would spark her faith again? "Marta, God didn't stop loving us. He didn't let my brother die for no reason. He orchestrates our lives for our eternal best. That may amount to some pain and confusion at times. We are so small compared to the vastness of this world, and yet God and his plan is even bigger."

Marta went on to recount details about her doubts and fears since Rocco's death. Although she felt like God held her during the events around the funeral itself, now she felt numbingly alone. She missed Rocco terribly.

"How could God make me wait so long to find the man I love and then snatch him from me so quickly? We only enjoyed eight years together." she asked.

Antonio felt inadequate to answer her questions. How could he defend God when he himself wondered many of the same things? "This I know. God doesn't do evil. The person who did this to Rocco did a very evil thing. A life has been taken, and it isn't fair. God knows all these feelings we are having, and he wants us to trust him even in the face of all our questions. That eight years of joy gives you a starting place. Maybe you can't thank God for taking Rocco so young, but you can thank him for eight great years with the Roc."

Marta seemed comforted in part by Antonio's words. She smiled a little, and her tears stopped. They both sat in silence for a few more minutes. Someone began playing organ music softly in the background. Parishioners began arriving for a noon-time service of some sort. Antonio laid his left hand on Marta's shoulder and prayed over her for five minutes or so.

Afterward, Antonio stood up. "I have to get back to the office. Did you take the Metro? May I drop you off somewhere?"

Marta nodded, and the two retraced their steps down the long center aisle and through the wooden doors. As they approached Antonio's car, a bullet whizzed past them, hitting the gas tank of the car ahead of them. Gas began leaking out. "You have got to be kidding me," Antonio said.

Antonio and Marta jumped in the Audi and sped away, zigzagging through downtown Washington traffic. As they passed the U.S. Capitol, the blue Mustang approached again and the sound of another shot rang out. Antonio held the wheel steady and tried to joke with Marta about New Jersey tourists in town. He saw no smile cross her lips. She reflected neither humor nor fear; Marta's face contorted with rage.

"Let me out of this car!" Marta shouted. "I want to get my hands on this guy! I want to kill him with my bare hands."

"No can do, expectant mother. There are some Capitol police right over there. I just want to lead him over that way." Antonio pointed the Audi to a small guard shack on Constitution Avenue. Two armed officers stood nearby. By the time the Audi pulled up next to the shack the Mustang had galloped away.

CHAPTER TWELVE

BF roused as the morning sunlight streamed through the basement window. He tried to move his hands but realized they'd been taped firmly behind his back. With his legs similarly duct-taped and secured to the metal desk chair, BF had little mobility. His head ached, but his vision slowly cleared. When he tried to turn his head to look around the room dizziness reminded him, he still felt a little nauseous. Fortunately, his captors didn't tape his mouth shut. This thought brought waves of gratitude, and it overwhelmed him for a moment. Claustrophobia would have engulfed him.

Sitting very still for a moment, he listened, but heard nothing upstairs. He couldn't yet assume Sandy and his friend left the house, but it could be a possibility. After several minutes, he rocked his chair to see if he could get up on his feet. He looked around the dingy basement to find it only sparsely furnished. Two small, mud-splotched hopper windows provided the only natural light. His foggy brain tried to interpret the pools of darkness and the shafts of light.

An old metal desk, probably a mate to the chair he found himself bound to, stood against one wall. Dusty boxes sat abandoned in one corner of the basement. Cobwebs reflected a few beams of light, giving him the creeps as he considered the spiders that might share his temporary home. An older model woman's bicycle leaned on the far wall, looking like it hadn't been ridden in forty years. Layers of dust covered the bike seat and tired-looking streamers hung from the handlebars. Wooden stairs led up to the main floor of the house. BF could see no other exit.

After looking around, he rocked his chair again to see if he could stand. With difficulty, he made it to his feet and managed to hop a little with the chair still taped firmly to his ankles. His new mobility allowed him to see what had been behind him. Spotting an old tool bench containing a few dusty relics, he hop-walked to the bench, looking for something to free himself. The effort increased his headache, and a new wave of nausea swept over him.

BF wondered if his hands could reach the top of the workbench. He couldn't see anything on the strong, wooden structure to cut the tape, anyway. He knew he must hurry in case Sandy returned. Perhaps his freedom rested with a metal vise, mounted atop the bench. If he could lift his hands high enough to scrape the duct tape on the vise, perhaps he could rip it. Turning his back to the heavy, mounted tool, he tried, in vain, to lift his hands enough to reach its edge. After several frustrating minutes, he gave up on that idea and sat back down on the chair to rest.

Next, he hop-walked to one of the basement windows and tried to look outside. As he got close to the window, his eyes caught a miraculous sight—an old, rusty nail protruding from the cinderblock wall. A little lower than he would have preferred, but it would work. He felt sure of it.

With the chair tilted to one side, BF scraped the nail on the duct tape until it split, freeing his hands. BF breathed a sigh of relief. Removing the tape from his feet took only a few moments.

Free from his restraints, BF crept up the creaky stairs, listening again for his captors. Hearing nothing, he turned the knob and tried the door. It opened with ease—no lock. BF peeked in the bedroom and saw that most of the dresser drawers stood open and empty. The bureau also sat open and picked clean. BF reasoned that Sandy packed quickly and fled with whomever deserved responsibility for the bump on the back of his head.

* * *

The next morning in Antonio's office, BF recounted his meeting with RaceRX mechanic Sandy and his overnight imprisonment.

"That's probably the same Russian guy who kidnapped Rocco's wife many years ago," Antonio said.

"Tell me more," BF said.

"I suspect Rocco nosed around RaceRX, recognized the man, and followed him home. But why didn't Sandy kill you if he proved willing to kill Rocco?"

"Good question. Perhaps he realized more and more people would come investigating. It made more sense to clock me on the head and run for it."

Antonio and BF thought about the hypothesis. "The police put out a bulletin," BF began. "Sandy and his accomplice won't get far in his current vehicle unless they took the accomplice's car. The police are trying to determine who hit me and what car they may be driving."

"Did you learn anything from Sandy's house, his belongings ..." Antonio's voice trailed off.

"He denied being involved in the death of Meloncamp. His bank account appeared to reflect the large payment from Sean. Sandy's story seemed convincing. He claimed that he got paid because of some enhancements to Emalyn's car, not to place explosives on Meloncamp's car. Oh, and he has a girlfriend. The police ran a BOLO on her too. Caroline something, I got the name from her prescription in the bathroom."

Antonio rested his chin on his hands, releasing a long sigh. This matched the story Sean Martin told Antonio during their jail visit.

"Money could definitely be the motive," BF said. "His house looked barely furnished. He lived simply and may have been hard up for dollars, but for some reason I believe what he said about Meloncamp. It also corroborates what Sean told you."

"So now we have a witness in the wind who perhaps could help our case but whom we can't locate. Even if this former mobster told you the truth, it leaves us back at square one with Rocco's murder. It also doesn't help us find out who killed George Meloncamp and why."

"I will keep checking into this Sandy/Sergei guy and see what else I can learn. Is it okay for me to talk to Marta?"

"She is a strong lady and she definitely wants Rocco's killer to be found, but call ahead and ask her if she's up to it. And please, BF, go easy on her, okay?" BF gave him a noncommittal look, and Antonio continued. "Let me write down her cell number for you. She's been at our house about half the time since the murder. She and Sylvia are very close."

BF accepted the paper with Marta's number and stuffed it in his chest pocket. He nodded to Antonio and left without a goodbye.

Antonio looked out the window, watching people on the sidewalk below. Each one seemed to be shuffling along, jockeying for position, not unlike Emalyn's stock car races. Did these ants realize the relative unimportance of getting to wherever they headed thirty seconds slower? That reminded him that Emalyn planned to come to his house for dinner at seven o'clock. He phoned Sylvia to see if he should pick something up for supper.

"Honey, can you talk?" he asked, always hesitant to call her at the school where she worked.

"Yes. You aren't interrupting anything."

Sylvia's voice made Antonio feel warm and safe, particularly with the new life growing inside of her. "Just wanted to know if I should pick something up for dinner tonight. You remember that Emalyn is coming over?"

"Of course, I remember. I'm pregnant, not facing dementia." Sylvia chuckled. "That sounds great. Marc wants to invite Trey over also, but I told him that I would have to ask you. What's the plan after dinner? Are you two strategizing on her case or what?"

"Quite the opposite. I'm hoping you and I can just relax and talk to her. She needs to get her mind off the trial and her suspension. We need to keep her out of trouble. BF is on to something, and I want to give her some hope."

"Perfect," Sylvia replied. "I'll tell Marc that Trey can come over, but they will need to make themselves scarce after dessert. Oh no, I just remembered there is a teacher's union meeting after school. I hope it doesn't go too long. You may have to stall a few minutes, but I can get the dessert. Do you plan to get the food at Tara Thai? Maybe get an assortment of dishes, and we can serve it family-style. Hopefully, everyone will find something they like. I'll get a strawberry-lemon cake from the bakery down on Washington Boulevard, near the school."

When she hung up, Antonio smiled at his phone. Somehow, he felt sure that Sylvia would carry this child to term. He wondered if he still had his baby skills—It had been so long since Marc needed changing.

***

The doorbell chimed loudly, and soon Antonio answered it. "Hey, welcome," Antonio said.

"Here I come with my hair teased up to the moon, a souvenir from my visit with Noelle back in Tennessee."

"You look great as always," Sylvia said from behind Antonio. "I love those earrings."

Emalyn paired the high hair with dangly black diamond earrings. "I only wear these on special occasions."

Antonio figured Emalyn's white blouse and white pants served as a desired departure from the sleek, black outfits she usually wore. Maybe she decided this night should show her feminine side.

Sylvia showed Emalyn into the great room, which opened to the large, modern kitchen. Antonio followed. He invited her to sit down and rest before dinner, but she indicated that she would rather stand for a few minutes. Sylvia handed an iced tea to Emalyn, who accepted politely. Antonio finished putting water glasses around the dining room table.

"Emalyn, thanks for joining us," Sylvia said, welcoming their guest. "We are glad to have you in our home. I didn't have time to cook after work, so Antonio brought home Thai food. Will that be okay?"

"Sure will, Sylvia. No need to apologize. I don't cook either."

Antonio could just imagine the look on Sylvia's face, but he didn't look up from his table-setting duties. Not only did Sylvia cook, she was pretty good at it. Besides, he knew cooking remained one of her major love languages.

Emalyn looked around the family room and complimented the

décor, particularly the furniture, a blend of Craftsman and Shaker. She walked up to a digital picture frame on the mantel. As the pictures flashed by, Antonio caught her smiling when she saw photos of herself and her crew with members of the Semones family and Trey. Then, something out on the patio must have caught Emalyn's eye, and she wandered to the French doors.

Antonio loved the small backyard fountain glistening in the garden, pouring down over carefully arranged rocks and feeding into a small koi pond. He could barely hear the sound of the running water from the dining area, but he figured Emalyn was listening to it.

Walking back over to where Antonio had just placed the last napkin, Emalyn said, "The sound brings back memories of the creek near my childhood home in Tennessee. The water, the house ... even Sylvia all exude the peacefulness and calm that seemed to have slipped away from my life, if I ever knew it."

"Come on and sit down for dinner," Sylvia said to Emalyn. She hollered for the boys to come to the table as well.

Everyone converged on the table. The boys came from the basement, fresh off a foosball mini-tournament. Antonio seated Emalyn at the place of honor, and the rest took their usual seats, except Trey, who moved next to Marc to make room for Emalyn.

"Boys, it's so good to see you all again," Emalyn said smiling.

"It is so cool that you came to our house," Marc said. "You are a legend." Emalyn blushed a bit and smiled in return.

"Nice to see you again, ma'am," Trey added.

After a short blessing by Antonio, everyone passed dark blue serving bowls and platters loaded food, including a couple of dishes that Emalyn didn't recognize. She took a good serving of the pad Thai but tried a small amount of the other two main dishes. Everyone listened intently as the boys told stories about their summer basketball league, each one trying to sound more heroic than the other. Sylvia added a story about the school where she taught, which recently received national recognition for a new reading program.

Fifty minutes passed quickly as everyone ate until full and laughed in all the right places. Emalyn seemed quieter than usual to Antonio. He suspected she felt out of place, so he suggested they all eat their strawberry-lemon cake in the living room. After setting their dinner plates in the farm sink, the crew filed into the living room. Antonio carried in the tray of desserts, serving Emalyn and the boys first. He placed two pieces near where he and Sylvia would sit after Sylvia served coffee. The boys ate their dessert in about three bites, then hurried off to do homework as Sylvia had instructed.

"We would probably never use this room if we didn't have dessert in here once in a while," Antonio said as he poured Emalyn a second cup of coffee.

Sylvia signaled that she wanted more coffee also.

"If possible, this dessert is even better than the rest of the meal," Emalyn gushed. "Thank you so much, Sylvia."

"It is from the cutest little bakery near my school. It is so easy to gain weight from the food there. One of the faculty or staff has a birthday or other occasion weekly. I wanted to cook for you, but the school made other plans for me this afternoon." Sylvia then changed the subject. "Tell me what you like about stock car racing."

"Well, many things. The excitement of coming to the track and knowing that a whole team of people is depending on me to represent them well. The sponsors, mechanics, pit crew—everyone has worked hard just to get us out on the track. When the engines start for the first time on race day, that still sends a shiver up my spine. Truth be told, racing is a lot like life. It includes hard work and a lot of luck. Pit a lap too early, and you might lose the race when a caution flag comes out. Catch a fender, and you watch the end of the race from the garage or the hospital. Attention to detail by the team and me matters, but sometimes it just comes down to good old fate. Fortuna, the Italians call it."

Antonio smiled at the reference to Italians. Being Italian, he knew a bit about Italian literature and the subject of Fortuna. Sylvia tried to steer the conversation in the direction of faith and Jesus, but Emalyn wouldn't take the bait. Eventually, Sylvia tried a more direct approach. "Emalyn, what do you believe about Jesus?" Antonio almost spit out his coffee, not expecting such a blunt question.

Emalyn stayed silent for a minute. A lump welled up in her throat and she began to tear up. Sylvia touched her hand, and Emalyn responded by pulling her hand away.

"I felt a little lost after Daddy died. Sean came along and swept me off my feet about a year later. All the time we dated, I kept wondering if Daddy would like him. Lately, I wonder if I made a mistake marrying Sean. His addictions and character defects don't fit well with mine."

"Every marriage hits tough places," Sylvia said, looking self-conscious about trying to take Emalyn's hand. She crossed her arms over her chest and leaned back a little on the couch.

"Oh, I know. We have always argued. Momma tried to raise me right and take me to church. I quit going. Put my foot down. Since then, I just take care of things on my own. Of course, there *is* a God. I know that. He doesn't bother me, and I don't bother him."

"But God loves you," Sylvia said. "He wants to help you with your life."

Antonio prayed silently.

Emalyn stared at Sylvia a minute, as if deciding how much she wanted to say. "Well then, hopefully He knows that I want out of this trouble. Just let me drive my races. That's all I'm asking. When I'm on the track, I know I'm doing exactly what God created me to do. I wish Mama could have seen it."

"When did your mother pass away?" Sylvia asked.

"Too long ago," Emalyn said. "Daddy remarried eventually. Fortunately, he waited until us kids left home. His second wife, Denise, hates me. She felt jealous about all the time and attention Daddy spent on me, not to mention the money for racing."

"That explains the grave in Ohio that Rocco photographed for you," Antonio said. "He sent me a copy, too. I guess he thought it might be relevant to your case."

"Yes. The rift between Denise and the rest of the family is not small. It's all been bad blood since Daddy died a few years ago. She never had a lot of money, but Daddy came along and took care of her. She expected that when he died, she would get his share of the racing company that employs me."

"I take it that didn't happen," Antonio said.

"No way. He left that to Noelle and me, knowing that I would buy out Noelle. I did, and that's one reason I don't have as much cash in the bank as the magazines say that I do."

"Where does Milos fit in?" Antonio asked, wondering how he could threaten to fire Emalyn if she partially owned the race team.

"He's the majority stock holder. I only own twenty percent. Milos owns fifty-one percent."

Changing the subject, Antonio tried to move the conversation along. "Did Sylvia tell you that your lawyer and his wife are expecting a child?"

"No, she didn't," Emalyn said with her old enthusiasm. "That is about the best news I've heard lately. Rocco's widow is also pregnant, as I recall. That must make you happy to be pregnant at the same time."

"We think seventeen years between our children is just about the right interval for us." Sylvia flashed Antonio a grin as she spoke.

"One at a time—that way we can play a zone defense. We only have to play man-to-man until Marc finishes high school," Antonio said, laughing.

Emalyn laughed too and kept smiling as they went through the few known details: female, four months along. Marc will be heading to college when their daughter turns about eighteen months old.

"How do you do it? Stay so positive about everything? Your brother just passed away."

Antonio didn't take offense at her blunt statement. He expected it from Emalyn, and he sensed an opening. "When we first married, Sylvia and I determined that we wanted our love to be the long-term kind. We define love as level of commitment, not just romantic feelings. The funny thing is, I still have all those romantic feelings about Sylvia, too. She is my honey baby for life."

"I thought that's what Sean and I used to be, but ..." Emalyn said, lowering her chin a little.

An awkward silence descended on the room, as everyone considered her words. No easy answers came to mind. Antonio continued to pray.

"But?" Sylvia asked.

"But we have hurt each other so many times. One of us did something, and the other did something back to get even. Before long, our marriage seemed more like a war than a romance. We can't un-say all that has been said or undo all the mistakes. Truthfully, we've stayed together because of the business. Without it, I'm not sure why I should stay married to him. His words are abusive."

"God can heal marriages, too," Sylvia began. "Where are you with your faith?"

Emalyn looked back, with a blank look on her face. Here was *that* subject again.

"Do you believe in Jesus?

"Honestly, no. I heard all about Jesus as a child, from a Sunday school teacher who made fun of me all the time and a minister that ran off with another man's wife. Christianity never rang true for me. Too many hypocrites. My god is me and the good fortune of life. Maybe the real reason I don't believe is that a long time ago, something bad happened to me at church. I never told anyone, except Mama, and she didn't believe me."

Emalyn kept quiet for a moment, staring at her hands. Just as Antonio thought she determined not to say anymore, Emalyn spoke up. "This older boy from our youth group forced himself on me. My dad hadn't retired yet, so he couldn't be around, stationed somewhere in Germany at the time. Mama thought I made the whole thing up. She thought everyone at church lived like a saint. The things this boy did weren't the worst things that have ever happened to a girl, but his advances traumatized me. Rather than argue with Mama, I just stopped going to church. The molestation came about the same time I started getting interested in cars. Mom and my sister still went to the church, but I hung out with a neighbor and worked on engines instead."

"Wow," Sylvia began, breaking the silence. "I'm so sorry all that happened to you. People are all too human sometimes, but it doesn't invalidate God's love for us or his plan for our lives. He loves you, Emalyn."

"Well, all that's water under the bridge now. Pray for me if you want, but I think we should just leave it there. I'm happy where I am, at a truce with a God."

Emalyn stood up as if to signal there would be no more discussion.

"Then let's leave it there," Antonio interjected. "You know that Sylvia and I are always available to talk to you about anything. You are more than a client; you are a friend. We care about you and Sean."

"Thank you very much, Antonio. And you too, Sylvia. Thanks for the great meal. Your home is lovely. It is getting late, and I'd better head back to my hotel."

With that, everyone stood up, exchanging good-byes at the door.

CHAPTER THIRTEEN

B F Honecker and Marta sat quietly at her kitchen table. Holding the phone in one hand and Alex's business card in the other, she dialed. Her heart sank when he answered.

"Alex, it's Marta."

"Oh, Marta. I'm glad to hear from you. Are you all right? I've thought about you often since we met that day."

Marta recounted Rocco's funeral, BF's run-in with Sergei, and the desperate hunt for Sergei. "I ... I'm okay. It's hard. There are so many questions still, about how Rocco died. Why did he have to die? Who killed him? We have to find Sergei. He has valuable information."

"Are you asking me what I think you are asking?" Alex said, sounding crestfallen to the point of despair.

"You have to help us find Sergei. If not, an innocent man may go to jail for the rest of his life. What's more, I may never know who killed my husband. That is too much for me to bear."

"Marta, you don't know what you're asking. Sergei is my number one, lifelong friend. Since early childhood, we have been on life's journey. How can I betray my blood brother? For years, he looked out for me at every turn. Without Sergei, life would have eaten me alive and spit me out."

"Alex, you have to understand. It's either do the right thing and help the police catch Sergei or abandon everything you've built and go into hiding with him. I have to find my husband's killer. For all I know, you are harboring the man who shot Rocco."

"It isn't Sergei. I know it isn't. He is a different man, too. He has a girlfriend. Love is changing him." After pausing, Alex continued, "Besides, I asked Sergei, right after I ran into you. I know when he is lying. He told me the truth. He may have been involved in tweaking up Emalyn's car, but he was not involved in blowing up that George guy. No way."

"If that's the case, he won't mind telling the police the same thing," Marta said.

"He is facing serious charges back in Virginia. How can he trust you? How can he trust the police? He might spend the rest of his life in prison."

"We might be able to get him some kind of immunity deal," Marta said. "Either way, he must do the right thing. I am giving you thirty minutes to get in touch with him. If not, we call the police and tell them that you can help find Sergei."

Their call ended. Marta pushed the red button on her phone several times to make sure the line disconnected.

BF stared at her for several seconds. "You did good," he said.

Marta went into the kitchen to make coffee. The minutes seemed to crawl as neither spoke. She poured the coffee into two cups, placing flavored creamer and packets of sweetener on a tray. She then added two slices of coffee cake, forks, and napkins and carried the tray to the table. The minutes dragged by while BF drank his coffee, saying nothing.

* * *

The Ford pick-up ran up fast on a Ford Prius.

"Why do they drive in the left-hand lane," Sandy exclaimed. "You know no Prius is going fast enough to be in the left lane, ever!"

"Just calm it down," Caroline responded. "We don't want to attract attention. Leave the little Prius alone."

"They just drive me crazy. I wish I could pull them over and punch their face in."

"I'm hungry," Caroline said, hoping to change the subject. Perhaps Sandy would take his anti-anxiety meds if they just stopped for dinner.

Dutifully, he pulled off Interstate 70 at the Champaign exit. Sandy wanted a good meal, not knowing how long he and Caroline might be on the run. The flat terrain of Illinois made for monotonous driving, but he wanted to keep heading West. The more states he could put between them and Ohio the better. After scanning the usual fast food fare by the highway exit, he decided to drive farther into town, closer to the University of Illinois campus. Caroline spied a prime rib joint on the right side of the road. "Look, there's a bunch of cars. I bet that one's good."

Inside, traditional décor mixed with numerous pictures of University of Illinois heroes to give the place a homey, collegiate feeling. Although they preferred a booth, only tables were available. Sergei thought it best to eat quickly and get on down the highway. After scanning the menu for just a couple of minutes, he motioned the waiter to come take their order. He and Caroline both selected prime rib meals, with Sandy getting the largest cut of beef, baked potato, and a beer. Caroline ordered a smaller cut and a glass of red wine.

While they waited for the food to arrive, Sandy slipped out to the back-parking area to exchange license plates with one of the locals. He found another truck owner and relieved them of their tag. Although it took an extra five minutes, he did it a second time to another truck, thinking the double switch might ensure that the police would have a tougher time tracing the stolen tags back to him. By the time the first owner reported his tags stolen, hopefully he and Caroline would be well down the road. Sandy figured it would take longer for the police to track down the second set of tags.

Back in the restaurant, Sergei stopped in the men's room to wash his hands, which were covered in dirt and grime from the license plate hokey pokey. It took a few minutes to get his hands clean.

By the time he returned to his seat in the restaurant, Caroline exuded nervous energy.

"What took you so long?"

"I will explain later. Everything is fine, just play it cool."

"Don't do that to me again," Caroline said, eyebrows furrowed. "I don't want to be left alone out here in the middle of nowhere. Two guys in suits sashayed by, and I nearly had a heart attack."

Just then, the meals arrived, and the prime rib looked just grand. The smell of mushrooms and onions and freshly-cooked meat filled up their senses and piqued their anticipation. Melted butter streamed from their baked potatoes and sizzled a bit on the hot, metal plate.

Suddenly, Federal Agents pounced. "Put your hands up!" screamed a gun-toting Agent standing behind Sandy. Caroline instantly responded by doing as commanded, dropping her fork onto her glass plate with a loud *clink*. A second agent circled around behind and handcuffed her. She gave Sandy a frightened look.

All Sandy could think about was his magnificent prime rib wasted. Why couldn't the Feds have given him five more minutes, at least, to taste the fabulous meal?

* * *

Two days later, Antonio and Emalyn sat on uncomfortable wooden chairs, facing Judge Norris. The judge buried her face in legal documents, reading as fast as possible while the three of them fidgeted and waited for the District Attorney. Reams of paper sat in neat stacks on every surface in Judge Norris's small office. In the ten minutes Antonio and Emalyn waited, a paralegal entered and exited three times, usually removing folders from a stack on the judge's desk or adding one to the in-box. On one of the trips, she just filed a document in the top folder near Antonio. She wore her long brown hair back in a ponytail, and Antonio thought her black-rimmed glasses must have been three times larger than needed for a face that small.

At the clerk's third appearance, Judge Norris looked up with slanted eyes and pursed lips. Somehow, the paralegal understood her unspoken question and responded, "The district attorney said he will be here in two minutes. That happened about five minutes ago. Do you want me to call again?" A slight shake of the head meant no and the paralegal removed another bulky file from the large stack.

Finally, the district attorney and his assistant arrived, apologizing as they entered the office. The assistant district attorney handed a manila, legal-size folder to the judge and a similar one to Antonio. Emalyn fidgeted in her seat. Antonio noticed clicking as she picked at her finger nails. He smiled at her, but Emalyn looked away out the window.

"Judge Norris, Mr. Semones, I am sorry for the delay. We had to finalize this paperwork. Based on some new information, we are dropping all charges against Ms. Martin and her husband," Solomon Levy announced flatly.

"Enlighten me," Judge Norris said. Her voice held a modicum of annoyance and condescension.

"A new witness has come to light. The man we previously suspected of planting the bomb has been apprehended. He has a different story as to why he took money from Sean Martin. His account is consistent with Mr. Martin's and very specific about what he did for the payment. Apparently, he took the money to doctor Ms. Martin's car to make it run faster. While outside the rules of stock car racing, it is not a crime, and we don't think this issue significantly contributed to Mr. Meloncamp's death."

"If you drop the charges, do you understand that I will be reluctant to allow you to reinstate them?" the judge asked.

"We understand. The witness passed a polygraph. He is cooperating with law enforcement on another serious matter, and we believe him to have credible information about crimes committed eight years ago in the Commonwealth of Virginia. He is being turned over to the FBI for a larger investigation into organized crime in New Jersey. It is likely he will end up in the Witness Protection Program."

Antonio's mind whirred as Levy spoke. Get to the point, he thought. Antonio sat forward in his chair as if he intended to say something, but the judge cut him off before the first words came out.

"In light of this new information and the recommendation of the District Attorney's office, I'm going to drop all charges against Emalyn and Sean Martin," Judge Norris said. "Case dimissed."

"Hot dog!" Emalyn shouted. "Hubby is getting out of jail."

In light of the new information, Judge Norris ordered the charges be dropped against Emalyn and Sean, and that Sean be freed from custody.

Hours later, Antonio, Emalyn, and Sean's lawyer met Sean as he walked out of the lock-up. The couple hugged a long time. Then, Sean shook hands with the two attorneys. A new season dawned for Sean and Emalyn, but Antonio could only think of the huge price Rocco paid for Sean's freedom. His brother died, and Antonio wouldn't see him again in this life. Sadness would be Antonio's frequent companion until he joined Rocco in heaven.

Back at the office, Antonio called Sylvia, now on break from her teaching position. "Honey, it's me. What are you doing?"

"Marta and I are sitting here having coffee," Sylvia said.

"I have some good news. They dropped the charges against Emalyn and Sean. Tell Marta that her detective work with BF paid off."

"That is good news. I will tell her. How are you doing?"

"I'm feeling happy for Emalyn but a little down about Rocco. We still don't know who killed him or why."

"Antonio, keep the faith. God will let us know everything if we just keep believing. Love you."

Pushing the end call button, she turned to Marta and relayed Antonio's news. Then, she suggested they pray for Antonio.

"Dear God and Father, you know everything. We don't understand the big picture, but you sure do. For some reason, Marta's sweet husband and Antonio's brother died way too young for our human hearts and minds. It would bring comfort to your precious children if you would show us who killed Rocco and why. Please reveal this to us and help us to act correctly upon the information."

Marta continued the prayer, "God, I don't know how to be a widow. It isn't something I ever wanted to be. Please show me your purpose for the rest of my life. One day at a time and one step at a time, guide my steps and help me find my way. Help me to be the best possible mother to the little life that is growing inside of me. Please help Sylvia to carry her child to term also and let them become friends, pointing each other to you. Please show us who ended Rocco's life and bring accountability for this serious offense. We forgive him or her, but we want your accountability to be required of him."

After praying, the two fell silent.

"Marta, do you have any intuitive feeling about who may have killed Rocco?"

Marta thought for a minute. "I don't know. When I think about the people close to Emalyn, Sean comes to mind. Maybe they owed a lot of money or something. His actions may have been about money. Marc and Trey heard Sean and Emalyn fighting, but Sean passed the lie detector about not planting the explosives or having anything to do with it. Also, Sandy passed the lie detector. Who else stood to gain anything significant from George Meloncamp being out of the way?"

"Good question. Hey. What if the target wasn't George, but Emalyn?" Sylvia blurted out something she had been pondering. "Perhaps we've been looking at this wrong all along."

"What makes you say that?" Marta asked, gazing into Sylvia's eyes.

"Well, the thought's been going through my mind. She definitely makes enemies with that mouth of hers. Who would benefit from having her and George—or just her—out of the way?"

"Sylvia, any one of the other teams could have been after Emalyn. Even that back-up driver of hers ... Millard's son, Jesse."

"We should check him out more thoroughly."

"Hold it. I will get Antonio to have the law firm's investigator do it. We've all been through enough excitement for a lifetime."

Marta squeezed Sylvia's hand, but the determined look on her face said that she didn't plan to entrust solving her husband's murder to anyone else.

CHAPTER FOURTEEN

Emalyn sat in the driver's seat of her Chevrolet stock car. Though her space-age helmet provided excellent views of the track, she was glad that her visor hid the tears trickling down her face. For some reason, she usually cried out of only one eye. "Probably should get that checked out by a doctor," she once told Antonio, knowing she wouldn't find the time. Emalyn may have doubted she would ever race again, yet here she sat at Dover Raceway, ready for her qualification run. The smell of gasoline, leather, and sweat surrounded her. She could even smell the undesirable odor of the driver who occupied her seat in her absence. *Jesse may be a nice boy, but he smells worse than five-day old fish. The crew is going to be doing some scrubbing tonight*, she said to herself.

She revved the engine, then began her warm-up laps. The raw power and speed fed a place in her soul. Like a barren woman suddenly able to conceive, Emalyn felt reborn and thankful for it all. The voice of her familiar crew chief echoed from her ear piece. Millard shouted, "It's show time!"

Emalyn knew this type of car like an old friend. The Chevy responded as she begged it for more speed in the straightaway, and it handled well through the turns. The rest of her ride seemed a blur, but she remembered hearing the voice in her ear indicate that she qualified for the race the next day. She didn't care what row she qualified in, pole position or back of the pack. Emalyn knew she landed back into the game. *That's all that matters.*

* * *

Antonio and his family also sped along the New Jersey Tollway, heading to Dover, Delaware. This time, Marta served as the fourth passenger. Unlike their previous trip to the race in the Poconos, the mood remained solemn all the way to Dover Raceway. Surprised that Marta wanted to come along for the race, Antonio knew from Sylvia's smile that it would be best to include Marta. He would later learn that Marta operated within a larger agenda than staving off loneliness. She made up her mind to find out who killed Rocco and why. Her prayers went up to heaven throughout the trip.

After checking into the hotel near the raceway, the foursome ate at Restaurant 55. A bit early, only two other parties dined in the restaurant. The burgers and fries initiated a tranquilizing effect on Antonio and most of the family, but Marta seemed strangely energized.

"Marta, are you okay?" Sylvia asked.

"Yes. Just thinking about something. Isn't that Emalyn's crew chief over there?" Millard and Jesse sat tucked in a corner booth, devouring their bacon cheeseburgers.

"That's correct," Antonio said with a smile. "You met them at the funeral. They look deeply involved with their food. This bodes poorly for Emalyn tomorrow. I can't see myself moving very fast after this meal. Hope they recover quickly."

After exchanging pleasantries with their waitress, the Semones family exited the restaurant and headed for the Audi. A large pick-up truck parked next to Antonio's car. It bore a decal with Emalyn's car number, making it obvious that the truck belonged to either Millard or Jesse. Something in the back seat of the extended cab truck caught Marta's eye, but she said nothing.

When they got back to the hotel, Marc and Sylvia wanted to go swimming. Once alone for a moment, Marta turned to her brother-in-law. "Antonio, I know this car is your baby, but would you mind if I borrow it to pick up a couple of things from the drug store?"

Her request struck Antonio as odd, but he would do anything for his sister-in-law. "Do you want me to take you?" he asked.

"No. I need a little space."

Antonio understood her need to breathe ... or at least he thought he did. In no time, Marta familiarized herself with the Audi and slipped out of the hotel parking lot onto the main road. Returning to the parking lot of Restaurant 55, she pulled in next to the pick-up truck. Before she could get out of the car for a good look into the truck's back seat, Millard and Jesse came out of the restaurant. Marta slouched down, acting involved with her phone.

The white pickup left the parking lot, traveling just a few blocks to the Holiday Inn. Marta followed close behind. As the men exited the truck and walked into the hotel, Marta parked and jumped out of the Audi. She crept to the truck, trying not to draw any suspicion. She peered into the side window then used her phone to take several pictures through the window. She couldn't make out the name on the papers in the back seat, but Marta thought she knew the logo from an invoice she'd seen before. She walked around to the other side and took a couple of additional snapshots.

Marta glanced back nervously at the hotel entrance several times, then peered again into the backseat. She recognized the holster clip lying next to the papers on the seat. Rocco used a similar one to carry his weapon. While it wasn't Rocco's clip, the owner of the truck obviously carried a gun.

As Marta glanced back at the hotel, her eye caught movement on the fourth floor. A man pulled back the drapes and stared down at her. The reflection of the light prevented her from making out whether it looked like Millard, Jesse, or just some random male, but she knew for sure that the man looked in her direction. Rushing to turn around, she almost tripped over the bumper of a blue Mustang parked next to the truck. She jumped into Antonio's Audi and peeled out of the parking lot.

Back at their hotel, Marta found Antonio at the pool and quietly returned his keys. She sat down next to Sylvia and watched Marc doing laps in the water. "I'm going to turn in early," she said. "I want to read a bit before the news comes on. What time will we go to the track tomorrow?"

Antonio looked to his wife. Sylvia thought for a moment, then said, "The race starts at one o'clock. Why don't we meet for breakfast at ten and head over afterwards?"

"Sounds good."

Marc completed his swim, and then they all headed back to their rooms. Everyone turned in and slept soundly, not knowing that a killer lurked just outside their hotel pondering his next move.

* * *

Antonio peered through binoculars as the cars rounded the turn on the far side of the track. Emalyn zoomed along in twelfth place. He followed her car down the back straightaway and into the turn nearest them. Ironically, it seemed to be about the same place in the stands where they sat at the Pocono raceway.

"Is it my imagination, or can I see Emalyn's smile from up here?" Sylvia asked from beneath her floppy hat.

"I know what you mean. Even inside the car and with her helmet on, she is giving off this glad-to-be-alive and happy-to-be-back vibe," Antonio replied. "Where's Marta?"

"She probably just went for a coffee or something," Marc said, unconcerned. She sat near the end of their row, next to Marc. She must have slipped away, but Antonio couldn't remember when or if she'd offered an explanation.

Twenty minutes passed, and the race continued under the green flag. Emalyn worked her way up to eighth. Antonio continued to study the action through his binoculars. His gaze followed Emalyn as she pulled into pit row. He wondered again why Marta hadn't returned.

Millard observed as the crew fueled Emalyn's car and added two fresh tires. Then, Antonio saw something that engulfed him in terror. The pit crew member nearest the right rear tire paused near the fender, then jumped away as the car pulled out of the pit. Did he see something unusual? *Oh, no. How could I have missed this?* Antonio jumped up and pushed past Sylvia and Marc. "Stay here!" he told them. He raced up the stairs, stumbling slightly on the top step. Still regaining his balance, he made his way onto the main concourse that ran around the grandstand. He bumped into a man carrying four beers, causing significant sloshing and earning him some ripe language. "I'm sorry!" Antonio said, not looking back.

Antonio ran as fast as he could toward the garage area, searching faces as he went. Guards stopped him at the gate to the garages. He pleaded his case and eventually convinced the sergeant in charge of security to walk him back to the garage used by Emalyn's team.

"I have to walk you back there," Sergeant Brickman said. "No civilians just walking around this area. It would be a security breach."

Antonio tried to get Sergeant Brickman to walk faster, but the shorter man ambled along.

"This could be quite urgent," Antonio said.

"Understood." Although his response indicated concurrence, Sergeant Brickman didn't increase his pace at all.

When they finally arrived, the large bay door rested in the down position. "Looks all locked up tight," Sergeant Brickman said. "Nothing to see here." Brickman started to turn around and head back to the gate.

Ignoring him, Antonio pounded his fist on the adjoining office door, but it brought no response. The tall lawyer pleaded his case with an intense expression and aggressive posturing of his tall frame. Without saying anything more, Brickman pulled out his pass key. He led the way inside as Antonio followed. They could hear a muffled voice coming from the two large service bays as they approached.

Suddenly, multiple gunshots rang out, and Sergeant Brickman fell to the ground. Raising his hands in surrender, Antonio stared down at the fallen officer in disbelief. The sergeant's neck wound bled profusely. As he flopped over, Antonio could see darker blood flowing from his side.

Jesse Estes held a .9 mm in his right hand. A few feet behind him and to his left stood Marta, unharmed for the moment.

"Isn't this party getting a little crowded?" Jesse's breath was heavy as he spoke.

"Are you crazy? We have to get this man medical attention now!" Antonio blurted out, still in shock from how fast everything was happening. He trembled with fear, then knelt down and tried to apply direct pressure to Brickman's neck.

"Maybe I *am* feeling a little crazy. You all ruined a perfect plan to finally get me behind the wheel of a stock car ... permanently. It almost worked, but *this* one's husband felt compelled to come nosing around. It's all because Emalyn's money bought her an expensive defense attorney."

Marta stared at the back of Jesse Estes's head. Her human side wanted to put a bullet in his skull. Her follower-of-Christ side wanted to forgive him and then see him face accountability, justice for his crimes.

"You killed George Meloncamp just to improve your chances of being a stock car racer? Why?" This astonished Antonio.

"Why do you think? I gave up a normal childhood, everything you took for granted. I gave up my mom to follow Dad around everywhere. I gave up high school friends. I gave up everything for racing. That driver slot should have been mine. Then, the owners decided it would be cool to have the only woman driver—Emalyn, with her phony southern accent. She doesn't even know how to drive. I knew she would bump into him eventually and boom!" Jesse's voice echoed in the garage.

Antonio looked down at the Sergeant dying beneath him. He prayed and tried to think of a way to signal for help. "You have to know it's over," Antonio said.

"Why does it have to be over? Everyone knows there is a psychotic killer still on the loose. Couldn't it be you or even the lovely lady here?"

"You have gone mad," Antonio replied "Emalyn is the team's driver, and she will be for a long time. You have to see that."

"Maybe. Or maybe her days are numbered."

Jesse looked down at Antonio's shoes, then back at Marta, who stood a few feet behind him.

"Tell me the truth!" she screamed. "Why did you kill Rocco?"

"It seemed just a matter of time until he figured out what happened. His snooping around in Ohio became a fortunate accident.

He got on the trail of the wrong guy and called my dad to get his opinion. Do you know how much I paid to get a last-minute flight to Columbus even after I claimed I needed a bereavement fare? The airline made me pay a fortune and run to make my connection in Atlanta. Catching up with Rocco took a lot of effort. The easy part involved luring your husband out to the OSU campus; said I was student with information he needed. I came up beside his car in that parking lot. He never saw it coming. Bam! How convenient that another suspect lived right in that same town. Then, this little lady messed that one up, too."

As Jesse spoke, Marta crept back, trying to get just out of Jesse's peripheral vision. She'd brought a gift for him and decided it was time to give it to him.

Focused squarely on Antonio, Jesse raised his gun and aimed for his chest. Marta, having the confirmation she wanted, slowly slid her hand into the pocket of her sundress. With great care to not be seen or heard by Jesse, she drew her weapon. Antonio kept Jesse talking long enough for Marta to carefully aim. As instructed by her concealed carry training, she silently disengaged the safety. She made sure Antonio stood clear of her line of fire.

"Please don't do this. Turn to God before it's too late," Antonio pleaded. "Jesus can forgive anything. You just have to believe in him."

"It's already too late. I've made my choice. Now say your prayers because the next bullet is coming your way." Jesse's finger reached for the trigger.

Two shots rang out. Marta pumped the bullets into Rocco's killer and watched Jesse crumple to the floor. It felt surprisingly good, satisfying even. Like Rocco, Jesse didn't see it coming. He lay dead moments later. Marta pierced Jesse's heart, much the way he pierced hers. She ran over to his body and kicked his gun away. Then, she kicked him in the ribs a couple of time, just for good measure.

Antonio's eyes widened and his jaw dropped as he watched events unfold. For a few seconds, he felt paralyzed, staring at Marta. Then he knelt back down to Sergeant Brickman and attempted to apply direct pressure to his neck wound. From the feel of the body, he knew the law enforcement hero had departed for the afterlife.

"We have to hurry. I found this in the garage." Marta held up a package which used to contain plastic explosives.

"Jesse must have intended to blow up Emalyn," Antonio said. "In his twisted mind he thought Emalyn was the last obstacle between him and getting back behind the wheel of the team's car."

Marta and Antonio ran out of the garage and into the center of the driveway. Antonio started shouting, which attracted the attention of the security guards at the entry gate. One of them came running his way. He quickly explained the situation and asked that the guard use his walkie-talkie to get the race stopped. From the tone of the conversation between the guard and whoever spoke on the other end, Antonio could tell that the race wouldn't be stopped so close to the end without more extreme measures.

"Stay here and explain what happened," Antonio told Marta as he ran back toward the raceway. "I have to try to save Emalyn."

Antonio raced past the one remaining security guard, running as fast as he could around the interior of the grandstand. The deafening sound of cars whizzing around the track failed to drown out the track announcer. "Emalyn is going around Jackson. She is now secure in second place. Look at Martin go!"

No, Emalyn! Antonio ran faster and pushed through the crowd as he neared the elevators to the tower where the announcer and race officials sat. With no time to explain the whole story to the guard standing near the elevator, Antonio grabbed the identification lanyard from the neck of an older lady waiting in line for the elevator. Flabbergasted, she couldn't speak at first. As she recovered, Antonio barged into the last spot in the departing elevator. Once inside, he flashed an innocent smile at a young woman who shot him a suspicious look.

When the elevator doors opened, Antonio rushed by an usher and followed an arrow pointing to the race officials. Fortunately, he found the third door clearly marked, and a wild-eyed Antonio burst in. "You *must* stop the race. Emalyn and the other drivers are in extreme danger."

The Race Director Gerry Garrard and other officials glanced over at Antonio, but they did not move from their perches overlooking the race. Their actions communicated they intended to ignore the intruder until the race ended.

"Do you hear me? A bomb is planted on her car, and she doesn't know it."

Finally, the oldest-looking man stood up and walked toward Antonio. "Look, young man. The race will be over in three laps. We can't stop it now. She has survived all the way through the race. She'll make it this last little way without a problem. Trust me, these cars are safe."

"Other racers and the crowd are in danger. You have got to believe me." Antonio increased the intensity of his speech to full-on ranting now. His red face was covered in sweat, his body bent over with emotion and breathlessness. His hand was still red from Sergeant Brickman's blood; how could he make these boneheads understand?

Another official murmured into his walkie-talkie. Antonio realized the man called security to remove him, a disturbed individual in their eyes. He had to make them get it. Emalyn's life was in danger! He prayed for divine guidance. At last, Gerrard turned to Antonio. "Young man. I can't just stop a race without a reason. You don't have any proof. Why should we believe you? How can we believe you?"

"There are two bodies in the garage area right now. Call security and ask them. Jesse Estes, Millard Estes' son, placed plastic explosives under Emalyn's car. If she bumps Jackson or anyone else, her car will blow up, taking her with it and who knows how many others. You are going to have another Pocono on your hands. Do you want to take that chance, knowing you could have prevented it?"

Gerrard thought about Antonio's words for a few seconds. Up until this point, Antonio's story seemed far-fetched, the rantings of someone mentally ill. Now, it became clear the man knew at least something about Emalyn and her team. On the track, Emalyn's car charged around the third turn, making every effort to pass the race leader's Toyota.

Garrard spoke to the flagman through his walkie-talkie. "Pull it out!" The flagman knew this abbreviated instruction to pull out the yellow caution flag, slowing the racecars.

As Emalyn careened around the last turn before heading to the straightaway, she edged into the lead, her bumper drawing ever nearer the lead car. Fortunately for her, his Toyota exhibited just a little more acceleration than her Chevy. She missed him. As he pulled back in front of her by a car length, they both saw the caution flag come out. In less than two minutes, she pulled into her pit stall.

Antonio, Garrard, and another racing official stormed into Emalyn's pit, coming up behind Millard.

"What's going on here?" Millard barked with surprise.

"We need to check Emalyn's car," Garrard explained.

He and the other official grabbed the mirror used by the pit crew and checked under her car. Everything must have looked like it belonged, then Antonio saw Garrard drop down to the pavement.

"Get everyone out of here! Call the bomb squad!" Garrard hollered loudly. Millard grabbed Emalyn's helmet from her and tossed it behind him. He helped her climb out of the car through the window, and they both ran together to safety.

CHAPTER FIFTEEN

The spacious beach house sat on a dramatic hillside overlooking the Pacific Ocean. Antonio, Sylvia, Marta, and Marc stood outside the large, glass and mahogany front door. Emalyn bounced into view in the hallway, throwing open the mammoth door.

"Hey, you all made it!" Emalyn gushed. "Thanks so much for coming. I have been so excited about seeing you again!"

"How could we miss a chance to visit your Malibu beach house and be with you and Sean? How many months has it been, three?" Antonio asked. "Thanks for your kind invitation."

"They told me this place would be hard to find, but you guys followed the breadcrumbs and found me. Can the paparazzi be far behind?"

Everyone smiled at her humor and stepped across the threshold. "Thank you for having us," Sylvia replied as she walked in. "We so appreciate your hospitality."

Everyone followed Emalyn down marble stairs to the spacious rec room. A large leather sectional and two mid-century modern chairs provided an especially cozy perch for looking out over the million-dollar view of the Pacific. An all-white, quartz fireplace crackled in one corner of the room. Outside the thick windows, waves rolled toward the shore. The picturesque backdrop framed Emalyn as she sat in a large, purple chair facing them.

"Sean is sorry he isn't here to greet you. I'm probably not supposed to tell you that he's at an AA meeting. He plans to meet us at the restaurant later."

"So, he stopped drinking?" Antonio queried. "That is great news."

"One day at time, that's what they say. It is a miracle though really, an answer to prayer. I couldn't believe it when he told me his love affair with booze was over—I couldn't imagine Sean without alcohol. It seemed like Santa without his reindeer or Gladys Knight without her Pips." She looked at Marc, "Don't ever get started on the drinking, young man."

Marc smiled and said, "No ma'am."

Emalyn then gazed at Sylvia and Marta. "Ladies, are you both coming right along with those babies inside?"

"Yes," Sylvia said. "God has been so good to us through the whole thing. Three more months for me and two more for Marta."

"Hard to believe we are all out here in California," Marta said.

Antonio filled Emalyn in on everything that happened since they last spoke. Marta didn't say much, as it brought up the whole ordeal of taking a life.

"Marta, how are you getting along?" Emalyn readjusted a tasteful pillow as she listened for the response.

"Shooting Jesse exacted a toll on me. Larger than I could have imagined. Even though he probably would have killed Antonio and me, over time I came to wish the police would have handled it instead."

"That is understandable. We've had some changes, too. I needed to let Millard go; it was hard to do. He's been a great crew chief, but I just couldn't feel safe with him anymore. Even with no sign he knew Jesse's intentions or actions, I still couldn't put one hundred percent trust in him."

"I get that," Sylvia said. "It looks like his son acted alone, both in planting the bombs and in shooting Rocco. Still, it would be difficult to have Millard on the other end of your ear piece while you are buzzing around the track at those speeds."

"One reason I wanted to have you all out here is to tell Marta how very sorry I am about Rocco and the way things turned out. Rocco will always remain my hero. Without his work, you and Antonio may not have solved the crime in time to save me. Or ... who knows ... I might be rotting in a jail somewhere."

Marta didn't say anything. She smiled, trying to hold back tears. Pointing to the baby growing inside of her, she composed herself. "Rocco died doing what he loved. I don't know why evil seemed to win this time, but I trust God that someday I will know the reason."

Emalyn picked up an oblong piece of paper. "This is for you," she said. "I want you to have this check to establish a college fund for you and Rocco's baby."

Tears began to stream down Marta's face. She didn't think much about money or particularly worry about it, but the gesture of concern and love overwhelmed Marta. As Emalyn stood and stepped in her direction, Marta stood up as well and hugged Emalyn and Sylvia.

After a long silence, Emalyn walked to the French doors. "How about a walk on the ocean?" She led them all down steps made of rail-road ties to the beach. The visitors walked along quietly, looking out over the ocean. The sun just starting to set exploded in colors, forming an amazing tableau. A few waves rolled onto the shore, but the group still found plenty of room to walk on the gravelly sand without getting their pant legs wet. Marc snapped pictures with his phone, including an Instagram-worthy shot of Emalyn admiring the sunset, wearing her sporty sunglasses.

Antonio thought about his brother and the love they shared. It was hard for him to believe that chapter of his life closed so abruptly. He would have to wait until heaven to see Rocco again. He wouldn't forget his beloved brother's face or his large, bear-like frame. He would need to go on without Rocco's physical protection and his spiritual encouragement. Without his brother, Antonio felt more vulnerable, less invincible.

Marta listened intently to the waves. In the distance, it sounded like Rocco calling her name. The deep voice boomed, reminding all of them of specific times when Rocco lived, loved, and laughed with them. The sun began to set and the reds, yellows, and oranges painted the western horizon in brilliant light.

"We should be heading back," Emalyn said after everyone drank fully of the ocean's charms. "Sean will be at the restaurant any minute now. I don't want to get a speeding ticket racing over there."

Everyone laughed again. Antonio looked out over the horizon and wondered what Rocco might be up to in heaven.

EPILOGUE

Rocco's View

Rocco looked around the hotel room. The early evening sun still filled the small space, and he sure didn't feel like going to bed yet. He turned on the television, more for noise than entertainment. A game show played in the background as Rocco searched through the style section of the Washington Post. He munched on potato chips until guilt overrode any semblance of hunger. It happened every time he went out of town. Why couldn't he stop eating? Closing the package, he got up and placed it on the desk several feet away. Maybe the distance would ease the temptation to wolf down the whole bag.

After finding the crossword puzzle in the Post, he set the rest of the paper on the desk and sat back down in the comfy chair. Pulling a pen out of his pocket, he began to fill in the blanks, one by one. One of the clues about the Olsen twins from an old television show made him smile. This sent Rocco's thoughts into daydreams of finally having his own child. Maybe it would be a cute little girl with pigtails and freckles.

All his adult life, Rocco had wanted to be a father. As a cop and a bachelor, the risk seemed too great that he might father a child and then not be there to take care of it. Now a more mature Christian, Rocco prayed and turned his fears over to God. Even if he couldn't be there, Rocco trusted that God would always watch over Marta and his child.

Rocco tried to imagine taking a son fishing or a daughter to an amusement park, but there appeared a strange void as he prayed. It felt like a blank wall. This experience felt new for him, though he seldom prayed into future events. He spent most of his prayers on gratitude or healing for some friend or relative. Why couldn't he see a picture of himself and his baby enjoying a playground or walking to church together. *God, are you hiding something from me?*

The phone in the hotel room rang, interrupting his thoughts. The volume must have been turned all the way up. Startled a little, Rocco walked over to answer it. "Rocco Semones," he answered.

"This is someone with information about the death of George Meloncamp," said the voice on the other end.

"Okay, I'm listening."

"Can you meet me over at Ohio State? I have a class on West Campus and could meet you afterward at 9:30 p.m."

"Why can't you just tell me over the phone?"

"I'm afraid. The guys that planted the bomb might come after me."

"You are going to have to at least tell me something to get me to drive all the way over there at night."

"My information is about one of the race teams. They wanted George Meloncamp dead. I have evidence, proof to give you: a surveillance tape." After stating the exact location for the meeting, the man on the other end hung up.

Rocco set the room phone back in its cradle without giving a definitive answer about whether or not he would come to the meet-up. His curiosity soon sent him to the closet to retrieve the shirt he'd worn all day. He buttoned it over top of his undershirt. Picking up his keys and large wristwatch, he turned off the lights and headed to his car.

The night drive to the large campus went quick and easy. Rocco used his GPS to get to the correct parking lot at Ohio State's West Campus. In the first minutes he sat there, three or four people trickled out of the modern building's closest exit. Rocco got out of his car and stood next to it so any would-be informant could see him. Then, a mini-rush of thirty or more students poured out of two other exits near the other end of the building. Most of them boarded an inter-campus bus, probably to return to their dorms on the main campus. The warm, early September air smelled fresh and relaxed Rocco.

As the time neared 9:45, no one else had exited from the building for several minutes. Rocco felt all alone in the parking lot, waiting in a sea of cars with his parking lights on—another signal to his potential informant. He climbed back in his car, pretty sure the trip had been a waste of time. Pulling his phone out of his shirt pocket, he contemplated calling Marta but decided to wait until his meeting either happened or not.

After a loud pop, Rocco had a most disorienting experience. Two beings clothed in white took him by the arms and instantly started flying straight up and at a high rate of speed.

Please enjoy this excerpt from another Brimstone Fiction title.

PROLOGUE

B ecause of their wickedness, Adonai deposed the elves from the throne of Alrujah and again established humans as rulers of the land. He appointed King Solous to bear the weight of the crown. Through his bloodline shall Alrujah find salvation.

—The Book of the Ancients

King Solous set every pair of free hands in Alrujah scrubbing the blood from the streets. His general, Galdarin Korodeth, already had his troops remove the bodies of the men and the elves. Entire families, moving in from outlying areas, spent hours on hands and knees with buckets of soapy water and stiff-bristled cleaning brushes. The cobblestone streets would be stained red for years to come.

King Solous walked among the people, touching shoulders, whispering words of encouragement and thanks. Often, he'd find masses of children huddled together as they scrubbed, their parents looking on from down the way.

His heart broke. The children should be playing, should not have to see such grotesquerie. He knelt beside a group of young ones, took a brush from their bucket, and scrubbed the streets alongside them.

Their conversation lulled, so he told jokes to lighten the mood. Uneasy laughter was better than no laughter at all. They'd lost enough of their childhood to the War of the Suns. Now, in victory, was the time to be jovial and lighthearted. This is why they'd fought in the first place—for freedom from the oppressive hands of the elves, for the right to rule themselves, for the right to enjoy life.

He'd earned the respect of the people in battle; now he sought to earn their respect in peace.

Behind him, the clang of armor brought Solous to his feet fast. But the soldiers had not engaged an enemy. Instead, they'd snapped to attention at the approach of General Korodeth.

Solous smiled. "Old friend. Have you come to help clean?"

"I wish I might, but matters of state demand our attention. The angels have again assembled in the throne room."

Solous touched the shoulders of the children nearest him. "Your work will be rewarded in the prosperity of Alrujah." As they walked toward the castle, Solous put his arm around Korodeth. "Did you ever imagine we'd be here? We used to dream of great battles, of commanding armies, but those were the dreams of oppressed children, born into the hand of slavery."

"We were fishermen," Korodeth said with a grim smile. "I'd hoped only to captain a boat."

"How old were we then?"

"Fourteen," Korodeth said.

"And now, the entire kingdom looks to us. Angels heed our call and follow our commands."

"Adonai has called us, old friend," Korodeth said. "He promised us the keys to the kingdom."

"I know, but I didn't anticipate this. Children scrubbing blood from the streets?"

"Not all streets are so stained. There are places where blood does not run," Korodeth said. He nodded toward the gates of the castle gardens. The silver-clad guards posted there snapped to attention, straightened their backs and pressed fists to hearts.

Within the castle garden, no blood stained the leaves of the trees, the grassy knolls, the crocuses and callas, or the violets and vincasor.

Solous had taken great care to ensure no blood be shed within the castle walls. He could do little about the elven soldiers outside the walls, but Pacha el Nai, angel of Adonai, had personally walked Solous to the throne of Alrujah and negotiated the transfer of the throne from elves to men. That done, the men turned their attention to rebuilding.

"You've posted sentries?" Solous asked.

"At each entrance, both secret and public. Our most trusted soldiers guard your quarters and the throne room."

"Your talents stretch far beyond the battlefield, Galdarin."

"Thank you, my lord."

Solous stopped him just shy of the throne room doors. He lowered his voice to keep it from echoing down the stone halls. "Without you, we could not have won, even with the seven angels."

"Thank you, Solous. But Adonai's calling rests on your shoulders. Even without me, He would have enabled your victory."

Solous clasped the man's shoulder. "He sent you to me. Even before we were soldiers, even before we commanded armies. We fished beside each other. The miracle He's worked in my life is only matched by those He's worked in yours."

Korodeth smiled. "Come now. You must take the throne and act the king."

Solous nodded, then opened the doors to the white marble throne room. He passed the massive columns supporting the roof to the front where seven massive beings stood before him. He and Korodeth fell to their knees, pressed their foreheads to the marble floor. "You honor us with your presence, servants of Adonai."

Pacha el Nai, a massive angel three and a half spans tall with white wings stretching near to fifteen spans, led six other angels, all equally colossal. Still wearing his burnished steel armor from the final battle the day before, he slipped his helmet off and tucked it under his arm. A sword hung at each hip, one beside each leg. Even sheathed, they hummed with power. "Rise," Pacha el Nai said in the voice of two men. "Adonai alone is worthy of your honor."

Solous and Korodeth stood, ascended the dais to the golden, purpleupholstered throne. Solous sat, but Korodeth stood beside him. "You honor me by heeding my petition for an audience," Solous said.

Behind Pacha el Nai, Belphegor stepped forward. His head sprouted two horns a hand's length each. Armored in silver and gold, his legs bent at awkward angles. Unlike Pacha's white wings, his sprouted tawny feathers tipped with gold. While Pacha looked human, Belphegor had a faunish look. "Adonai wishes us to speak with you. But first, speak what you will. Why did you summon us?"

Solous gestured toward his old friend standing beside him. "Before your assembly, I wish to honor Galdarin Korodeth. Under the watchful eye of Adonai's servants, and with his blessing, I bestow upon him the title of Archduke of Alrujah. His honor exceeds that of all other men. Indeed, if I did not wear the crown, he would. Let it be known among those esteemed angels assembled today, and in the presence of almighty Adonai, that if ever my bloodline were severed, Korodeth, being chosen among men by Adonai as being noble and true, shall ascend the throne."

Korodeth immediately knelt, a paragon of humility and honor. He spoke with a reverence and formality worthy of a loyal subject. "May it never be, my king. Adonai preserve you and your line. May the calling of the line of Korodeth be to stand beside that of Solous from now until eternity."

Pacha el Nai said, "Adonai has heard your decision and honors your wish. May it be as you say."

Korodeth stood, his head still inclined to Solous. "I am unworthy of this honor, my lord."

"If you are unworthy, Korodeth, none in Alrujah will ever be esteemed worthy." Solous turned to the angels, put a fist over his heart. "Esteemed servants of Adonai. Give us his words."

Pacha el Nai spoke again. "Adonai blesses you, Solous, King of Men, and you as well, honored Archduke Korodeth, who leads both men and angels into battle."

"Adonai has been faithful," Tiamat said. "He has returned the throne of Alrujah to men. Rule under his name. Establish a kingdom marked by peace and prosperity." While not as tall as the other angels, he had the largest wingspan by far. His blue and gold feathered wings glimmered as if scaled. He wore no armor on his chest or back, but both arms were sleeved in a scaled blue metal embedded with rubies. His eyes burned cobalt, and lightning danced from feather to feather. He commanded weather, used strong spells to counter those used by the elves. Seldom did a blade come close enough to strike him.

Abaddon stepped forward. "Good king, Adonai has entrusted our service to your wisdom." He spoke with a buzz and a rattle. His obsidian armor matched his black wings. Broad in shoulder and chest, Abaddon wielded a two-handed sword with awesome ferocity and cowed the armies of the elves.

King Solous motioned to the guards posted near the entrance. "Bring stools for our guests to sit. This may take some time."

The guards vanished through the spotless white marble doors. Solous appreciated his decision to keep bloodshed from within the castle walls. His was a heart committed to peace, though the same could not be said for all the angels assembled before him.

Legion wore full plate armor fashioned entirely from bronze. His white wings reflected its light and glowed gold. In one hand, he wielded an enormous spiked mace. It'd take five men to heft its weight. In the war, what magic the elves used against him dissipated across his shield and armor. Few could stand before his might, and the angel reveled in his strength, relished his charge to overthrow the armies of the elves. He was a being created for battle and war.

Solous cleared his throat. "Your services?"

"The corruption of the elves began with Shedoah's hand. Adonai has thrown him beneath the deep of the Alrujahn Sea," Moloch said. He also had black wings. His cloak shimmered like onyx but flowed like fabric stitched with lightning. Thin in body and limb, he wielded the very power of life. To him alone, Adonai had entrusted this awesome authority. Solous's troops had taken to calling him the Angel of Death, a term which instilled fear on both sides of the war. He spoke little, but his mere presence unnerved monarchs and warriors alike.

Maewen, the only woman of the group, let her long golden hair spill over a circlet of bismuth. On her chest, she wore golden mail, and her legs were sheathed in scales of jasper. Emerald tipped both ends of her barbed spear. While smaller than the other angels, her battle prowess made her one of the most feared of the seven. "Seven seals bar his return." She spoke with the voice of a crackling fire, and her lips shone red.

The guards returned with the stools. Tiamat furled his wings and sat on the ornate red-upholstered stool. Back straight, his voice carried the weight and force of a tornado. "We have recorded our power in a book of magic."

Galdarin Korodeth said, "This book is already penned?"

"Aye," Maewen said, her voice an angry furnace. "Indeed, the very ink is imbued with our powers."

Archduke Korodeth folded his arms. "The book must be sealed, lest man or elf or dwarf find it and usurp it. Power like that could rend the world."

Of course. The wisdom of Korodeth became plain again. Mankind could not be trusted with such a force. Short of Adonai, only Solous had the ability to seal the book and the magic contained within it. He stood, moved to the glass case on which the tome was displayed. He whispered a few words over it, and the glass vanished. He took the book, felt the power surging through him. For a minute, he considered holding it, keeping it for himself. A book like this would virtually ensure immortality. Imagine what he could achieve if he reigned for centuries. What good might he accomplish?

But if he ever lost it? Man was not meant to live for hundreds of years. Forgive my selfishness, my lust for power, Adonai, he thought. He pressed his hand to the leather cover, tapped into the power entrusted to him by almighty Adonai, and bound the magic in enchantments stronger than Alrujah had ever seen. "There is no power within Alrujah that may shatter these bonds."

Moloch spoke, his voice a dusty buzz. "The elves practice strange magic, as do humans and dwarves. Today, there may be no power to break your bonds, but the power of the people grows. The book will not be safe here."

"It must be hidden," Abaddon said.

"Indeed," Solous said. Turning to Korodeth, he said, "You must hide the book. Tell no one of its location, even me. The secret must die with you."

Korodeth whispered in deference. "Your Graciousness, a matter so important cannot be trusted to hands other than your own. I urge you, good king, hide the book yourself. Indeed, is anyone else in the kingdom worthy of such a responsibility?"

"Such a task requires time. I have a kingdom to rebuild, trust between races to establish, and skirmishes to settle. Within the kingdom, there are no hands I trust more than yours, no mind so noble and able, no heart more humble, no wisdom more discerning. You alone are worthy to undertake such a task."

"If there were another, Your Graciousness. Perhaps one of the assembled angels?"

"This is a matter of men," Pacha el Nai said. "Adonai has entrusted the book to Solous. It is his to entrust to you."

Korodeth stood, put fist to heart, and said, "Very well. It will be as you say. With your leave, I will prepare myself for the journey ahead."

Solous nodded, and Korodeth made his way out the back of the throne room. King Solous turned to the assembled angels, still seated patiently. "Adonai wishes me to use your talents in the establishment of my kingdom?"

"He trusts your will. We are at your disposal," Maewen said.

Solous pressed his folded hands to his chin. He'd not considered how to use the angels after the war had been won. He'd assumed they'd return to the heavens and not return again until needed. How then, to use battle-scarred angels? How might they help reestablish the kingdom?

They must bring the people to trust in Adonai. A kingdom unified in faith would not fall. Korodeth would say the same thing. "Far be it from me to disagree with Adonai, though I am humbled by such an honor. His Hand has established my kingdom and will hold it fast in his grip. Be His fingers, then, and establish His church among my people. Watch over them. Defend them from the corruptive power of Shedoah."

"So be it," Tiamat thundered. "Where shall the churches be established?"

Solous sat, contemplated the map of Alrujah. Much of it would need redrawing, but the land itself, the cities, remained. What was destroyed would be rebuilt. He had only to discern which people would best respond to each angel.

Rising again, his finger on a map, he said, "Maewen. I've moved the elves to the island city of Harael. They are devastated from the war, and many still resist the rule of Adonai. They are a stubborn people, but your beauty and graciousness give you the best opportunity to gain their respect. Yesterday, they were our enemies. Today, they are our people; they are Alrujahns. You've shown your love for the people, and I pray you do so again.

"Moloch, you have gained the trust of the peoples of the Callbred mountains and forests. Their towns and villages have been ravaged by war. Use your powers to bring them life again.

"Abaddon, your battle prowess has impressed the swamp dwellers of Pellbred. They are a stiff-necked people, but loyal. Guide them in the practice of the worship of Adonai, and the swamp will again flourish.

"Tiamat, the coast of Alrujah will be safe under your watchful eyes. Your powers will protect our sailors and ensure the prosperity of our kingdom. The people of Sylvonya are thirsty for direction. Your strong hand will provide for their needs.

"Belphegor, you led the dwarves, who took up arms with humans to march against the elves. Your leadership helped us secure Dalova. I charge you now, protect the people whose hearts you've won, within the bellies of the mountains and hills, to establish the church of Adonai and lead them in the ways of our God.

"Legion, your troops overcame the elven stronghold in Yeval Forest. The people have come to call it the Bleeding Grounds, and they live in fear. Establish a strong presence as we rebuild what the elves accomplished. In Orensdale, you will build the church of Adonai and lead the people in peace as you led them in war.

"And finally, Pacha el Nai. To you, I entrust the very heart of Alrujah. By your hand, you overcame the fist of the elves in Alrujah. With your strength, you oversaw the transfer of the throne. Among all the angels, you shed the least blood but won the most victories. Your wisdom and love of peace must establish the church of Adonai here in Alrujah and Varuth, in Harland and Weileighn. The four cities compose the heart our very economic and military strength. Keep us from corruption and greed."

The angels nodded in agreement and vanished with a flourish and shimmer. Solous dismissed his guards and again sat the throne of Alrujah, again felt the weight of the crown. He thought of the children and women and men scrubbing the cobblestone streets of Alrujah.

Adonai, he prayed, accomplish Your will. Protect the book, that Alrujah may never again know war as it has known these long years.

* * *

In the centuries after King Solous's reign, Alrujah's fortunes waned. The kingdom had fallen far from the prosperity and peace the fabled king worked so hard to achieve. The problems facing the kingdom weighted Archduke Pentavus Korodeth's heart.

He knelt on the white marble floor of the throne room of Alrujah. As Captain of the King's Watch, he was expected to give his report to his king and friend.

Ribillius was the twelfth king in the line of Solous. Korodeth wished the monarch had enough sense to realize what a gratuitous expense it was to sit on a throne fashioned entirely from gold. Ribillius hadn't fashioned the throne, but he refused to sell it, though the money would feed thousands. Far be it from Korodeth to mention this to his king. Ribillius would rebuff his suggestion as an offense to Adonai. The throne, the monarch was fond of saying, had been established by Adonai himself.

Ribillius stood and waved his guards away. The marble doors closed after them, and the king sat on the steps of the dais. He motioned for Korodeth to sit beside him. "You don't bring good news anymore," he said.

"There is little good to report," Korodeth said carefully.

"I find it hard to believe that in a kingdom the size of Alrujah, your spies can't find anything positive."

"Forgive me, my lord. I have entrusted my soldiers with finding potential threats to the well-being of your throne."

"There are always threats to my throne," he said.

"Never as many as now, my lord."

Ribillius crossed his arms over his heavy belly and sighed. "What news, then, Captain?"

"Orensdale has given itself to the worship of Legion. Sylvonya proclaims itself for Tiamat. Both cities have ceased trade with Alrujah, Varuth, Harland, Weileighn, and Dalova."

"And our people starve," Ribillius said, the heavy gold crown slipping down his forehead.

"Droughtworm has made its way within our walls as well, my lord. Each morning, my soldiers drag the dead to the sea. There are more each sunrise."

Ribillius stood, paced the throne room, ran his hands over the smooth marble columns. "Do you remember when we were children, Pentavus? The most we worried about was whether or not we'd be caught stealing pies from the kitchen. Now, there aren't enough pies to feed our people." Korodeth stood, clasped his hands behind his back. "There is a way to heal the land," he said tentatively. Ribillius shook his head. "Do not dishonor this throne room with your talk of Shedoah again. He is the reason we're in this mess. It is his touch that poisons the land, that breeds distrust among our people, that fuels the diseases that cripple our cities."

"You misunderstand, my lord. It is his hand that can heal us. I understand your devotion to Adonai, but your faith is misplaced. The prophecies say—"

Ribillius spun. "Prophecies? You mean lies. Shedoah is the deceiver of old. You've read The Book of the Ancients. You've read The Book of Things to Come. You understand what true prophecy is, and yet you cling to half-truths and lies? What of our fathers and their fathers? As long as men have sat the throne of Alrujah, we have dedicated our kingdom to Adonai. His power established our throne, and the suffering we face will not cause us to turn our backs on Him now."

"Our fathers were deceived. Their faith was strong, but misplaced. As is yours, my lord."

Ribillius's face flushed red. "If you were any other man, I would kill you where you stand. We've been friends since birth, but that alone will not stay my hand if you blaspheme again. Adonai's name will not be defamed."

"Then send me away, my lord. I will not turn from my faith, and you will not turn from yours."

"King Solous established your line to the throne. I cannot send you away. Even if I could, I would not. You are as close as a brother to me, Pentavus. You are a loyal and trusted friend, misguided as you are."

Korodeth's heart fisted. What could he say to convince his friend of the truth of Shedoah? He'd tried countless times, and each time, was dismissed. "How do you explain the suffering? If Shedoah is chained in the deeps, if his power is sealed with seven seals, as you say, how may he touch the land? How may his influence or corruption conjure droughtworm, cause cities to renounce Adonai?"

Ribillius righted the crown on his head. "The seals must be weakening. The Book of Sealed Magic must have been found. Rumors of the Mage Lord must be true."

"They are rumors only, my lord. I've seen no evidence of a Mage Lord at work."

"You've told me the signs with your mouth. The droughtworm, the poverty, the distrust, the fall of faith. What more evidence do you need? We must find him, must restore the seals. Have your soldiers keep a close eye on Orensdale and Sylvonya. No—their faith has already fallen. He'll turn to cities closer to Alrujah, try to garner strength closer to the seat of our faith. Watch Dalova. Viceroy Gerald is a good man. We cannot afford to be without him."

"My lord," Korodeth said. He used a practiced deference and kept accusation far from his voice. "These commands have the feel of desperation, not of logic."

"How would you proceed were you in my place, Pentavus? Continue to let our people fall to starvation and plague? Wait until your precious Shedoah breaks his seals and turns us all to slaves, turns us all to corpses?

"No, my lord. As always, you speak with wisdom." Korodeth put a fist over his heart and inclined his head.

Ribillius nodded. "I'm sorry, my friend. I didn't mean to snap."

"No apologies necessary, my lord."

The king returned to the dais steps and sat. "I have court in an hour. Leave me, my friend. Bring me news as it comes. And please, try to find something positive to report."

"As you will, so it shall be done." Korodeth exited through the back door, navigating his way through the dank stone hallways to his office overlooking the city square. The smell of death soured the scent of lilacs and lavender. He sat at his desk and pulled an ancient scrap of parchment from within. As he whispered over it, the paper shriveled with age.

Though his door never opened, Korodeth detected a presence within his office. A moment of concentration identified the man as Argus Berand, brother of the traitor Trieli. As far as his Chameleon Soldiers went, Argus was one of the best. He'd proven his dedication and loyalty, not only to Alrujah, but to Shedoah himself. "You have news from Yeval Forest?"

The man removed his hood, exposing his face. The rest of him was armored in enchanted mirror-mail, making him invisible to the eyes, but not to Korodeth's keen perception. "We made it as far as Orensdale."

Korodeth did not turn his attention from the well of ink, over which he cast a simple enchantment. "What news?"

"They've burned the Yeval monastery and erected a church of Legion."

"Good," Korodeth said. The Shedoahn Prophecies continued to be filled. Before long, Shedoah would discontinue his willful submission to the false deity Adonai. He would rise and crush Adonai and again restore order and peace and prosperity to Alrujah.

But that could not be done as long as Ribillius sat the throne. "News of Varuth?"

"Firmly devoted to Alrujah and Adonai."

"And Dalova?"

"The same."

The time to act drew near. Korodeth scrawled on the parchment: "He who controls the daughter controls the king." He rolled the parchment, tied it carefully with black twine, and whispered a last enchant-ment over it. Only Ribillius would be able to read these words. A simple trick of twisting spells, but it would speak to his ability as a mage—something even Ribillius didn't know about. He handed the parchment to Argus. "Leave this where the king will find it. Do not be detected."

Argus replaced his hood. "As you will, so it shall be done."

CHAPTER 1

And four shall rise. And they shall be in the world, but they will not be of the world. They will be in it, but will not belong to it. And one from Alrujah shall come alongside the four, and they shall act as one, and they shall free the land from oppression with a mighty triumph, and they will be called the Hand of Adonai.

—The Book of Things to Come

In the late afternoon, Oliver found Lauren in her pajamas, ankle deep in the snow, a foot away from the edge of the steep cliff overlooking North Chester, Minnesota. The wind circled around her feet and pulled the bottoms of her pink pants near up to her knees. Ice crusted the tops of her slippers. She stared out over the valley. No footprints; she'd been there a while. The snow reddened her ankles, and he wondered why she hadn't worn socks.

He came up behind her quietly and slowly. "You okay?" he asked.

Lauren didn't move. "We're on the mountain."

"I know."

"Not this mountain. In Alrujah. Vesper's Mountain."

Oliver took a few more steps and stood next to her. Of course she'd be thinking about the video game they'd created together. She always was. Then again, he was, too. Still, her fascination with it, her fantasies about leaving earth and being magically transported into a digital world, concerned him. She was too eager to leave the real world, and that would only make it harder for her to live in it. "Are you sure you're okay? Your mom is worried."

The dampness of her cheeks had crystallized into ice diamonds. Had she been crying or just been cold? "I'm surprised she realized I was gone," she said.

He took his jacket off and put it around her shoulders. "I'm worried, too."

She turned back to the valley. Snow slipped from the slate sky. It covered the buildings below. The gray clouds obscured the sunlight, made it feel much later than four in the afternoon. Already, the shops and homes below had their lights on. All of North Chester did, for that matter.

Lauren standing this close to the cliff made Oliver nervous, made him wonder what exactly she had in mind. "Can we go inside?" He folded his arms over his chest and shivered.

Lauren put her head on his shoulder. He liked the gentle weight of it, how he had to bend a little to his right so she wouldn't have to stand on her tiptoes. "Don't you ever want to go? To get away from here?" Her voice wavered, either from sorrow or from her chattering teeth.

"Of course I do. Wouldn't spend all my free time running code if I didn't."

"I mean really go. No more school, no more bullies, no more embarrassment or harassment. In Alrujah, I'm a princess. Here, I'm a fat loser nobody."

"Come on," he said and shivered again. "It's not that bad."

She pulled her cell phone out of the pocket of her pink flannel pajama bottoms. She punched a few buttons and handed it to Oliver. Sarah the Skeleton, the "hot" girl from chemistry, had sent her a message. *If I wuz as fat as u Id kill myself.*

Oliver sighed and put his arm around her shoulder. "First of all, you're not fat. Second of all, she's retarded. You have to know that."

"She's not retarded," Lauren said. "And she's not the only one who thinks that. Maybe she's right."

Oliver thought of the cliff, how close she stood to it. "Let's go inside and talk, okay? Sarah's dumb. She thinks anyone over fifty pounds is fat. It's not your fault you're not a skeleton like her."

Lauren faced him. She held her arms out to her sides, palms facing him. "Look at me, Oliver. Tell me I'm not fat."

She sounded like a wife asking her husband, "Does this dress make my butt look big?" No answer would suffice. Still, he had to say something. He thought for a minute of how to say what he wanted to say but didn't act fast enough.

The red on Lauren's cheeks deepened, embarrassment adding to the crimson chill. "See, you can't say it."

He crossed his arms, tucked his hands into his armpits and shivered. "Other people may think you're fat. But I don't. Neither does your mom. It's not your fault. The doctor said once he finds the right medication, you'll start to slim down some."

Lauren wiped at the iced line of tears trailing down her cheeks. "Stupid thyroid," she mumbled. "Bailey Renee calls me fat, too."

"She's your little sister. She's supposed to call you fat." He gritted his teeth to keep them from chattering and pulled her head to his chest. Remarkably, the chill of her ears pushed through his sweater and shirt, froze his chest above his heart. She'd been out here far too long. Hypothermia long. He had to find a way to get her inside, but she'd have none of that talk until he'd soothed her self-loathing.

He put his arms around her and held her tight. He could warm her a bit while he tried to talk her away from the edge. She shivered. He said, "You may not have a magazine-type body right now, but you are beautiful. You have a face that inspires poetry."

She laughed. "Wow, what a line. You should save it for Erica."

Erica. He thought of her dark eyes and her black, black hair. "Somehow, I don't think Erica would appreciate it the way you do." Snow melted on his blue sweater. A minute later, the flakes froze to the cotton and made it stiff with an icy crust. Ice streaked her wavy blonde hair. "We're going to freeze out here. Let's go in."

"I'm tired of being a nobody."

Lauren wasn't a nobody. She was his best friend, and God loved her very deeply. Still, he'd told her all that before, and she shrugged it off. She didn't like hearing how valuable, how loved she was, how much God loved her, how she was a child of God. She wanted only what she couldn't have—the approval of shallow teenagers. Instead of basing her self-worth on what God thought of her, she depended on the opinions of too-skinny students. He wanted to tell her again, but it'd do no good. She'd only argue with him and refuse to go in until he'd agreed how worthless she was. So, instead of repeating the old debate, he simply held her tighter. "Let's talk inside. It's cold."

She laughed. "I can't feel my feet. I can't walk."

He took her laughter as a good sign, though he failed to see the humor of numb feet. Sighing, he turned around and knelt in the snow.

"What are you doing?"

"Piggyback ride. Come on."

She laughed again, a high staccato sound like the chirping of a bird. "I'll crush you, Oliver."

"No chance. I'm as strong as a bull."

"You're a toothpick is what you are. Put you and Sarah the Skeleton together and you might weigh a hundred pounds."

"I'm Vicmorn, the mystic monk, m'lady, and I'll carry you with the power of Adonai to your castle in Alrujah."

She put her hands on his shoulders, wrapped her legs around his sides. With her chin on his head, she mumbled, "Whatever, crazy monk. Now, giddyup, horsey."

Oliver complied. He stood up, careful not to lose his balance or grunt. She'd take either as a condemnation of her weight. Instead, on his back, she felt the way he saw her—a thin girl, a heavy heart. His legs, now numb with cold, pushed forward. Each step pressed his ankles further into the snow. He wouldn't wobble, wouldn't even breathe heavy. He wanted her to feel weightless. It would only be a matter of time before the doctors found a balance of medication that would slim her down to the weight she should be, her real weight. Maybe she'd be happy when she was thin again. Had her happiness simply gone into hibernation, or had it quietly died for good?

When they got to her porch, Oliver wiped his feet. He set her down, took her slippers off, now wet and hard with ice, and set them next to the door. She leaned her forehead on his shoulder and said, "I don't want to go back to school tomorrow."

"You and about ninety percent of the school population." He hugged her. Not a romantic hug—a comforting embrace, one that told her that—even though they loved other people, and even though those people didn't love them back—they at least had each other. "Including me."

* * *

As always, dinner started quietly. Oliver sat next to Lauren, which had become the norm over the last few weeks. Lauren was thankful he stuck around more. It made her family a little more tolerable.

Lauren hardly touched her chicken and stuffing. She stared more than ate, using her fork to pick the chicken apart. Good as it smelled, she wasn't hungry. Anything she put in her mouth would end up on her hips anyway. Safer not to eat.

"Excellent dinner, Ms. Knowles," Oliver said. He shoveled the last bit of stuffing into his gaping maw, wiped his mouth, and sat up straight. He folded his hands in his lap like some kind of reform school student. Sometimes, she really hated how perfectly polite he was, how kindly he treated her family. Maybe because they treated him so nicely in return. At times, she believed her mother would trade her for Oliver, no questions asked. What parent wouldn't want a thin, well-mannered, straight-A genius?

Her mom's bangs slipped from behind her ear and swished across her face. She readjusted them. Smiling, she said, "Thank you, Oliver." Then, without the smile, "Eat your food, Lauren."

"Not hungry."

Her mother, shoulders slumped and eyes heavy, sat at the head of the table, the place their father used to sit. Instead of the stiff-backed oak chairs everyone else sat in, she sat in a black leather computer chair. She'd hardly taken off her gray suit jacket before she served dinner from the crock pot. "Don't make me go through all this again, please, Lauren. Hungry or not, you have to eat."

Bailey Renee, in all her perfectly slim beauty, sat at the foot of the table, opposite their mother. Oliver talked a lot about God, but Lauren couldn't understand why God would make Bailey Renee so beautiful and Lauren so ugly. Talk about unfair. Bailey ate twice as much as Lauren and stayed twig thin. She played varsity basketball for North Chester High and maintained a 4.28 GPA. Academically, she could give Oliver a run for his money. She'd pulled her light brown hair into a ponytail. Wisps of bangs tugged themselves free and framed her face like a portrait. Nose deep in a calculus book, she went out of her way to ignore Lauren.

Beautiful, smart, athletic, loved. Perfect. The exact opposite of Lauren. It's like they didn't even share a gene pool. And it all came so easily to Bailey. She hardly had to work at any of it.

Freshmen weren't even allowed in calculus, but the counselors made an exception for Bailey Renee. Didn't everyone? Wasn't she the standout exception to humanity? Nothing could be more irritating than having a sister who excelled at absolutely everything.

The only thing Lauren could do that Bailey Renee couldn't was drive. And even when Lauren picked her up from practice after school, the other girls on the team looked at Lauren funny. They'd stare at Bailey Renee, then at Lauren, as if to say, "You're related to that?"

"How was your day, sweetie?" her mother asked Bailey Renee. Bailey was "sweetie." Lauren was "Lauren."

"Good," Bailey said.

Lauren pushed her stuffing around. Her fork scraped the ceramic plate.

Her mom sighed and dropped her fork. The steel rattled as it bounced off the table. "You know what? I give up. I don't even know what to do with you, Lauren."

Oliver fidgeted in his chair. The fingers of his folded hands tightened as he stared at his plate.

"What?" Lauren asked, as if she didn't know which lecture was coming next.

"Every day it's the same thing. I have to scream at you just to get you to eat. I have to threaten to take away your stupid video games to get you to do your homework. I have to put passwords on every computer in this house so you don't waste all your time on that dumb game. Your grades are slipping, and you don't even care."

"I have a 4.2, mom. My grades aren't slipping."

"You had a 4.4 last year."

"I can't believe you're even saying this right now."

Her mom pressed on. "And you don't eat, either, no matter how many times I tell you to. Honestly, do we need to put you in counseling? Seriously?"

Bailey Renee glanced up from her book. She grinned at Lauren.

Lauren dry swallowed. Her words came out as a whisper. "Are you saying I'm crazy?"

"That's not what I'm saying at all. I'm just worried, and I'm tired, and I can't do this anymore. I work hard to make sure I can put food on our plates, and you don't even touch it. Do you know how frustrating that is?"

"Maybe you should quit," Lauren muttered.

"Excuse me, young lady?"

Bailey Renee said, "Settle down, Lauren. You're such a drama queen."

Oliver could help. Why didn't he defend her? Instead, he stared at his hands in his lap, then pushed himself from the table. "I should go."

"No, you can totally stay," Bailey Renee said. She stared at him with a wide grin. "You can show me that scripting language and physics engine you designed."

"Sit down, Oliver," Lauren's mom said. She pushed her hair behind her ear and wiped her mouth with a paper napkin.

Embarrassment and outrage heated Lauren's throat, burned the back of her eyes. She wanted to throw the plate at her mother; she wanted to kick the chair. It was bad enough being the ugly duckling, and now her mom thought she was crazy? She took a deep breath, dug deep in the pit of her stomach, and found the worst thing she could say. She pointed a finger at her mother, poking the air in front of her. "No wonder Dad left you."

"Lauren," Oliver said quickly.

"Whoa," Bailey Renee whispered. "Harsh."

Too late. Her mother's face turned from irritation to absolute despair. She opened her mouth to say something, but didn't. Her jaw hung half-open like an unhinged door.

Lauren stood up fast, dropped her fork, and stormed out of the room.

* * *

The last time Oliver had knocked on Lauren's door, they were in third grade. At some point in their friendship, which stretched back to kindergarten, knocking had become superfluous. But he knocked now, a gentle knock, a modest supplication for permission, not just to enter, but to speak.

"Go away," she said.

"It's just me."

"I know."

He opened the door anyway. She sat on her bed, legs crossed, Xbox on. The shelves lining her walls—something her father had installed for her before he left the family ten years ago—had once been filled with stuffed animals. They'd long since been replaced by books. She may not get straight A's, but few people on the planet read more than her. And, impossibly, she'd somehow filled as many journals as books she'd read. Most had to do with Alrujah—the world that formed in her mind, that took its roots in her journals, in her sketchbooks. It'd taken Oliver the better part of a year to compile all her notes, all her sketches, into the master file for the game. But he hadn't minded. She'd conceptualized a real, breathing world.

The 32-inch LCD TV on her desk provided the only light in her room. He'd grown accustomed to her sulking in the dark. And, as always, she took her anger out on her Xbox. She played some button-mashing brawler, though she'd beaten it several times. She wasn't in the mood for a challenge now. She wanted to use the avatar she'd designed, some ridiculous female ninja, to slice through competitors with graceful ease. Right now, she wanted to see something bleed. "So how long am I grounded?"

"You're not," Oliver said. He sat on her chair and rolled back over the wood flooring so he could better see the television, then put his feet up on her bed.

"How long do I have before she wants me to move out? Do I get to pack my things first?"

Oliver tried to suppress his frustration with Lauren. She hadn't always played the victim like this. But in middle school, when other students started shedding baby fat, hers clung to her bones relentlessly. Sure, she'd lost friends over it, the plight of the unpopular, but he'd lost just as many, maybe more, just for sticking by her side. How often had she thanked him for that?

He understood how hard it was to be unpopular. Truth be told, he was every bit as physically unattractive as her. What with his loppy arms and too-thin waist, his patchy beard and uncontrollable hair. But he didn't care, didn't let others get him down.

Maybe, he thought, it stemmed from her father leaving. It must. Oliver, at least, had two parents at home who reminded him how much they loved him. They sacrificed for him, supported him. Poor Ms. Knowles just seemed too tired to be as supportive as she wanted to be.

But Lauren didn't have the patience to see that. She'd been hurt enough by words to know how to use them as a weapon. And so she erected her vocabulary as a defense strategy. She'd hurt those who hurt her. He sighed. "You made her cry. Did you know that? She left the room right after you, but I heard her crying through her door."

Lauren paused the game. She set the controller on her pillow and lay down. "She called me fat and crazy. What was I supposed to do? I'm tired of being fat and stupid and unlovable. For once, it would be nice for someone to look at me without cringing. You have no idea what it's like." Her voice got softer as she spoke.

But he did have an idea, a very good one, in fact. He'd tried to tell her that on several occasions, but she'd have none of it. No room for Oliver in Lauren's pity party. So he pushed on, determined to be the strong one, determined to be the encourager. Isn't that what God had called Christians to do? To love and encourage?

He stood up and stretched his legs, tired of the constant battle he fought to combat the damage done by insecure, selfish teenagers. He'd done what he could with Lauren. Tonight, whatever seeds of love and encouragement he tried to sow would end up in the gravel beside the road. Crows would snatch them up, eat them before they had a chance to put roots in Lauren's hard heart.

His phone beeped, and he checked it. *Coming home soon? It's a school night.* "Mom wants me home. But before I go, I want to say a couple things. I want you to listen, okay?" He spoke with the gentleness he'd learned from his father, spoke with patience and perseverance. "First of all, you're not fat. I'll say that every time you say you are. Secondly, you need to apologize to your mother. I don't think you understand how deeply you hurt her tonight."

"Serves her right," Lauren whispered.

"Please, Lauren. You really have to stop. I know your mom hurt you, but she at least meant well. What you said—" he paused. "It was mean and vengeful. That kind of attitude is only going to make you feel worse." He pulled his jacket on and fixed the sleeves of his sweater. "Good news, though. We're close to a Beta. I'll have one ready by the end of the week. Two days, if I can get some time to focus on it."

Lauren sat up. "Really?"

"Really."

"Playable? Really really?"

"Really really playable."

She grinned. "Well, go home and get to work." She pulled her journal from under her pillow. The worn leather torn near the front corners, the binding creased and worn. She tossed it to him. "I came up with more stuff if you can work it in."

He went to catch it but fumbled it instead. It collapsed to the floor and pages spilled out. Ah, awkward adolescence. He had no idea how athletes kept their feet straight. He could hammer out thousands of lines of code in a couple hours, so why should simple hand-eye coordination give him such grief? "I'll get right on it, Princess."

She laughed like the caw of birds. "Good. Now get going, you crazy monk."

* * *

When Oliver got home, he stayed in his car. He turned the engine off and pulled his phone from the center console. Snow collected on the edges of the windshield. He waited for a few minutes, letting the warmth from the heater dissipate until the air inside the car took on a chill. He composed a new text message to Erica, as he did nearly every night. This time, though, he decided to actually send it. *What r u doing Tues after school?*

The air cooled rapidly. His finger felt stiff, almost numb. He swallowed his unease like a pill. His breath came out in tendrils of mist. He put his jacket on. His phone beeped. *Who is this?*

He should have known better. He wasn't even supposed to have her number. A week ago, as he walked down the science hall of North Chester High School, he'd overheard her giving it to a friend, and he memorized it.

He should have introduced himself, maybe said something witty, something funny and memorable. But Oliver wasn't known for his wit. He put the phone in his pocket, buried his hands in the folds of his jacket, and closed his eyes. He started the car and let the engine heat up again. His parents would hear him. His '82 Honda was neither a classic nor quiet. But he couldn't go inside until he'd said his piece. If he went inside, his parents would want to talk. They'd want the full run-down of his day, and he'd give it to them. Then, he'd lock himself in his room and get lost in the coding of Alrujah. He wouldn't text Erica until two AM, likely. Too many distractions within the walls of his house. His car was quiet, peaceful, cold. Here, he could concentrate on not making a fool of himself.

Of course, he hadn't done too good of a job so far. But he was tired of loving and never daring to say anything about it. If Lauren wasn't brave enough to talk to Aiden, the North Chester High School football all-star, then Oliver would be the brave one. He pulled the phone out again and texted, *Oliver from Bio*. He put his hands in front of the heater.

How did u get my ###?

He knew she would ask this eventually, and he'd devised an answer. On Facebook. He had, the day he heard Erica give her number to the friend. Wanted to double check to make sure it was legit. Plus, Facebook seemed much less stalkerish than the full truth.

A beep. *Whats up Tues?*

The snow melted away when it hit the pewter gray hood, still warm from the drive from Lauren's. *Want 2 show u something in the comp lab. A game I made.*

Talk 2 me 2moro

Oliver grinned and closed his phone.

OTHER BOOKS BY DAVID L. WINTERS

Driver Confessional (2017)

Five Christmas Plays: With Joy Inside (2017)

Sabbatical of the Mind: The Journey from Anxiety to Peace (2016)

Co-Authored

The Accidental Missionary (2019) with David Bredeman

Taking God to Work: The Keys to Ultimate Success (2018) with Steve Reynolds

AUTHOR BIOGRAPHY

David L. Winters is an author, speaker and humorist who lives in the suburbs of Washington, D.C., fighting traffic, dodging partisan political attacks, eating out and trying to keep his weight under 275 pounds. Since his award-winning book Sabbatical of the Mind broke in 2016, he continues to push the envelope producing fiction and non-fiction with a supernatural element. If you meet him at a conference or book-signing, remember that he thinks he's quite funny and means no harm. Under no circumstances feed him nachos with jalapeno peppers.